Tallowed Ground

Valona Jones

*For Annmarie,
Happy Reading!
Valona Jones*

for Charmain,
Happy Reading!
Jdean Jane

Tallowed Ground

A MAGIC CANDLE SHOP MYSTERY

Valona Jones

This is a work of fiction. Names, characters, places, and incidents are a product of the author's imagination, or are used fictitiously, and any resemblance to actual persons living or dead, business establishments, events, and locales is entirely coincidental.

Tallowed Ground
A Magic Candle Shop Mystery
Book 3 of 5

ISBN Trade Paperback 978-0-9997054-8-3
COPYRIGHT © 2024 by Maggie Toussaint

All rights reserved. No part of this book may be used or reproduced in any manner without the written permission of the author or Muddle House Publishing, except in the case of brief quotations embodied in critical articles or reviews.

Contact information: maggietoussaint@darientel.net
Cover art by Martha Whidden

Muddle House Publishing
1146 Tolomato Drive SE
Darien, GA 31305

Published in the United States of America

Dedication

This book is dedicated to the authors of Booklover's Bench. Nancy J. Cohen, Terry Ambrose, Debra H. Goldstein, Cheryl Hollon, Diane A.S. Stuckart, and Lois Winston are hardworking authors who are unfailingly generous with their time and talents.

Acknowledgments

Critique partners Polly Iyer, Marion Deland, Gayle Nastazi, and Carolyn Rowland helped sharpen this manuscript. Thanks also go to my editor, Jaden Terrell, who helped with the final shaping. Thanks always go to Craig for his unflagging support and encouragement. Couldn't have done it without you. Any mistakes in the book are my own.

Chapter One

Valentine's Day marks the anniversary of Grandmother and Grandfather's deaths, a day our entire family embraces the Southern tradition of calling upon our deceased family members. In previous years there'd been other families similarly visiting throughout Bonaventure Cemetery. This year it was only the three in our group as far as I could see.

"Here, Tabby. Take this." Sage shoved her picnic basket my way and bent down to scooch out of her strappy sandals. Relief radiated from her face. The ruffles on her filmy dress and her curtain of shiny dark hair fluttered in the light breeze of an unseasonably warm winter day. "The sand gets in my shoes every time. It's annoying."

I eyed my fraternal twin sister with suspicion. Due to centuries of changing sea levels, all of the Georgia coast and north to the fall line running across the state from Columbus to Augusta was a succession of sand dunes and prehistoric ocean floor. In high traffic areas like the cemetery, sand predominated the narrow ruts of unpaved lanes. "It's always sandy here. You prefer going barefooted in the graveyard. Why can't you own it?"

"I admit nothing," Sage shot back, darting away before I could hand off the basket.

As if I could make her wear shoes. She preferred going shoeless year round while I had opted for hiking boots to make sure in an absent-minded moment I didn't twist my ankle again. I hefted my double load and followed her, thankful for the ponytail holder keeping my blonde hair out of my face.

My boyfriend, Dr. Octavian "Quig" Quigsly, gazed my way, his brown eyes masked by dark glasses, his arms bulged from carrying the large cooler of pie and drinks. There'd been a time when I compared his physique to that of Clark Kent. Now that I knew him in all senses of the word, I accepted him as a full-on Superman. He brightened my world and accepted my quirks without asking too many questions.

And I did have some quirks.

Quig also carried three collapsible canvas chairs on his back. We'd parked in a distant lot because Sage insisted we needed the exercise. "Are we there yet?" he asked.

"Follow me," Sage said, forging ahead on the sandy lane. Overhead, Spanish moss draped over oak branches in ghostly swags, framed by a vibrant blue sky. The thick limbs gleamed with the Kelly green resurrection fern fully hydrated from yesterday's shower. Beside us, six-foot-high azaleas and camelias screened many of the graves, with buds prominently displayed on the camelias. Soon this place would be camelia blossom central.

The cemetery was roughly three miles from our Bristol Street home in downtown Savannah, though that was too far to walk lugging all this stuff. Thank goodness Quig insisted on driving. Usually I felt peace when I entered the cemetery, but today my skin felt prickly, as if someone walked over my grave. Then my thighs and shins chilled in a most irritating way.

I shrieked and dropped the picnic basket and the blankets

I held, feeling foolish about the outburst even as the icy sensation subsided. I gathered everything and stomped after my sister. "Dadgummit. Ghost dog mugged me again. Why can't he leave me alone?"

"He luuuuvs you," Sage teased as she spun in a circle. "Good thing he's drawn to you because I'd retaliate if he pounced on me every time we visited."

"There's a ghost dog?" Quig asked.

"The cemetery boards claim Savannah cemeteries aren't haunted," I hedged, not wanting to get into why a ghost dog liked my energy.

"But you felt something?"

"Oh, yes, though the chilling sensation is gone already. Sage never gets ghost-hugged. Just me, the ghost dog magnet of the family."

"You're special that way," Quig said.

"Perhaps." I hated keeping certain secrets from him, but I had no choice. It was the Winslow way.

I rested the picnic basket on the Johnny Mercer memorial bench, named for Savannah's renowned songwriter, who penned the lyrics for Henry Mancini's "Moon River," "Jeepers Creepers," "I'm an Old Cowhand" and more, to shift my blankets to the other side and move the basket to a different hand.

Our family kept shrinking in number, but Sage and I continued keeping the family tradition of running The Book and Candle Shop with Gerard Smith and his cousin Eve as our clerks. Without their help, we'd be in a world of hurt.

"Where is everybody?" Sage asked, tiptoeing along one of the block borders as if it were a balance beam. "Usually this place is crawling with people. It's unnaturally quiet. Might be a swarm of zombies around the next bend."

So far we had encountered no one in our hike from the parking area. Guess people were keeping away from the area due to two recent homicides near the historic cemetery. We'd considered the wisdom of staying home for about five seconds. Tradition mattered more to us. Besides, Sage and I could take care of ourselves.

I drew in a breath of fresh air, that perfect blend of right-off-the-river freshness and pungent evergreen scents. "No thanks on the zombies. I look forward to a peaceful lunch. But you're right. Even the birds are silent today."

"Zombies," Sage said over her shoulder as she hopped into the lane again. "Just sayin'."

"Cut it out." I warily scanned the headstones and monuments surrounding us. Zombies weren't here, and I wanted the day to be perfect for Quig. "Show respect for the departed. And the quiet could stem from the recent murders in this area."

Sage pointed to the sky. "Look."

I looked. Six vultures circled above us, their piercing gazes stone cold. "Must be roadkill nearby."

"Or something." Sage halted, her voice drifting off.

I caught up with her in four quick strides and set the picnic basket in front of her. "What?"

"Looks like someone else got here first."

I followed her gaze to the Wayfare block where my grandparents were interred. Unlike the other graves in the same plot, Dwayne and Rosemary Waltz's twin slabs looked immaculate. Not one oak leaf remained, no bits of moss clung to the headstone either. "Huh. Wonder who cleaned their gravesite?"

"Who cares? It's one less thing on our to-do list today. Probably a taphophile anyway."

"A what-o-phile?" Quig asked.

"My sister is showing off, that's what," I said. "See the inscription underneath their dates?"

Quig read it aloud. "Felled by an assassin."

"People who are drawn to the rituals of death, taphophiles, often make rubbings or take photos of this headstone because it's unusual."

His confusion radiated in erratic energy pulses. "People do that?"

I sent out a cancelling wave, and Quig's aura calmed immediately. He didn't know anything about my extra energetic gears, and out of necessity I kept it that way. He still gazed expectantly at me. I realized I'd forgotten to answer his question. "Some people plan their vacations around visiting historic cemeteries to take rubbings or photographs of the inscriptions."

"This is news to me. Guess I spend too much time at the morgue and not enough at cemeteries. Nobody considers that hobby unusual?"

"Don't know about that, but it's usual to the people that do rubbings. There's even an association for this group. We looked it up after Sage discovered that two-dollar word."

"An assassin killed your grandparents?" Quig asked after reading the headstone. "Why?"

I shrugged. "We never knew. Mom said she'd tell us one day, but one day never came. Sage found their obituary in the newspaper archives, but the scant information didn't clarify matters. We don't know our ancestry beyond this point."

"That's quite a mystery," Quig said. "With your interest in puzzle solving, I'm surprised you didn't dig into it further. What about your aunt? Did you ask her?"

"Repeatedly. She was no help at all. Auntie O said if Mom wanted us to know she would've told us."

He chuckled in disbelief. "The two of you couldn't hound it out of her?"

"Let's just say stubbornness is a family trait," Sage said from the next lot over where she'd been murmuring to the plants.

She does that a lot because plants are her thing like candlemaking is mine.

"I'm the third wheel here, and I don't want to overstep,

but I don't understand the need for secrecy within a family," Quig said.

I shrugged in answer though I appreciated his diplomacy. "Let's set up our chairs outside of the block outline. Last year the new grounds guy chased us out of the main plot. Just as soon not have to move once we get settled in for our visit."

Quig lowered the cooler and placed our chairs. Sage dug inside the basket for the tin of Mom's ashes, which she placed on the headstone. My gaze lingered on the small bronze plate with her name, Marjoram Waltz Winslow. Maybe one day we'd agree on where Mom should be buried. Until then, we'd keep her with us in the tin.

I knelt beside my twin as she said the honorary words in a reverent voice. "In the name of the heavens and earth and all the directions, we share our love for Rosemary and Dwayne and Marjoram. May their ways of spreading peace and joy be reflected in us as we make our spiritual journeys. Grant them a sacred rest, peace, and radiance until the new day dawns. So be it."

After the ancestors' prayer, Sage poured water from a small chalice in each ordinal direction. When she finished, we held hands and touched the ground with our other hands for a moment, sealing the prayer by grounding our shared energy.

Then she lit a small cemetery-sized tea light candle in my Savannah Sunshine scent and placed a glass globe around it so that it wouldn't blow out or be inadvertently knocked over on the stone. The candle created an atmosphere of energetic support and heaven knows, we needed that.

Candle burning connected the physical world with the spiritual world, as we'd always been taught. However, every visit here had been calming and meditative, and I hoped that would be the case today. I focused on the inviting glow and the flame's aura until it grew and grew. As I inhaled the sweet scent of my creation, I sent out my good intentions for family past and present.

When our ritual ended, Quig gave me a hand up and then offered one to Sage. "Ready to eat?" he asked.

I grinned at him. "Oh yeah."

We unwrapped subs from Southern Tea on Bristol Street and then raised our canned sodas in a toast to our relatives. The coconut and salt air fragrance of my golden candle perfumed the air. Pride swelled in my chest that I'd created this scent, this sacred connection linking us to our heritage.

Quig ate methodically and fast. Sage, as usual, picked at hers. I inhaled my spicy meatballs. Didn't know where the huge appetite came from, but I had my sights on Sage's leftovers until I remembered the pecan pie in the basket. My mouth watered at the mere thought of that decadent treat. Definitely needed to save room for pie.

"You're quiet today," I said to Quig.

"Busy at work. Everyone wants answers to the new homicide cases. I don't have any."

"I see." Even though I'd promised Quig I wouldn't get involved with any cases that didn't involve my family and friends, these new cases tugged at me in the worst way. As the Medical Examiner, Quig had inside information, but so far he'd been mum about the investigations. "Can you share any details?"

"Ongoing investigations," he said. "The cops are withholding key facts from the media about both murders, and that's the part I can't discuss with you."

"Because you need to keep your job."

"Yes."

Though I admired Quig's integrity, I dearly wanted the inside scoop in this case. My extra skill set had nothing to do with mind reading, but my sister had become adept at getting though locked doors in the guise of sleuthing. We could get into the morgue and its records if we wanted. However doing so might point back to Quig, and I wouldn't risk his career.

Right on cue, a cemetery security person arrived and asked what we were doing. I explained that we were the Winslows, the granddaughters of Dwayne and Rosemary Waltz, and this was our annual family tradition to visit with them.

The guy called it in, and then he nodded to us. "Sorry to have disturbed you. You're cleared to stay as long as you like. Wish more families honored the old traditions."

After he pulled away, Sage said, "If worker bees didn't change so frequently, the staff here would recognize us. I'm glad their boss remembers our names."

"Me too." I glanced over at her plate. "Not hungry?"

"Appetite has been squirrely lately." My sister paused to take in my rounded eyes. "And it's not *that* either."

By *that*, she meant our aunt's unrelenting campaign for us to reproduce before our family line died out. Right now there were exactly three of us: Sage, Auntie O, and me. "Funny. My appetite is greater these days. My mouth's watering for that pie."

Quig smiled but didn't comment about appetites or reproduction.

Smart man.

"Each slice of pecan pie is loaded with more calories than we should consume in a meal," Sage continued. "I'll pass. You can have my slice."

I studied her with my other vision. She'd insisted on bringing pecan pie this year, her fav, and now she didn't want to eat it? Something felt off about that. Though we were fraternal twins and originated from different eggs, our energy manipulation abilities were more similar than I'd initially believed.

Each family member descended from Rosemary Waltz inherited the talent to manipulate energy. Sage and I saw auras and could give and take energy at will. Sage hated to run at less than a full tank, so she topped off by asking for energy from me or by taking it from whoever passed into her orbit. I recharged naturally every night so I never stole energy from anyone.

Sage's dark aura pulsed erratically, alerting me something was amiss. "You never pass on this pie. What gives?"

She stabbed her fingers through her hair. "Something's up with my weight. I've lost a few pounds, but my clothes fit the same."

"That is weird." No point suggesting my sister visit a doctor. We'd never been sick a day in our lives. Whatever might be happening with Sage, we'd figure it out sooner or later.

"I must've eaten something that disagreed with me. You wouldn't believe the things Brindle fixes for us to eat. I've had more natural, raw, and fresh everything in the last few months than I've eaten in my entire life. He's trying to convert me to a healthy lifestyle. I will not go into that darkness willingly."

Sage and her live-in boyfriend hit a rough patch when he got spelled, thought another woman was Sage, and got caught in a state of undress with said interloper. It took heavy duty persuading for Sage to forgive him, but she'd accepted him back in her life and home.

The candle on the headstone flickered wildly. "Look!" Sage knelt before the candle.

I joined her. "This has never happened on a calm day. The spirits are telling us something."

"Surprise!" rang out from behind our chairs. Quig rose to his feet instantly and then pulled me up from my graveside perch. Much to my delight, Auntie O and her male companion Frankie stood there with grins on their faces. Auntie O looked polished and stylish as usual. Frankie looked a bit grim, and his skin seemed pale. What was up with that?

I hugged Auntie O, the men shook hands. "Is it safe for you two to come out of hiding?" I asked Auntie O as I hugged her. Our energy fields overlapped and intermingled, and I didn't want to let her go.

"Not yet, but we had to join you for the visitation. It's tradition." Auntie O broke free of my hug to embrace Sage. "My it's so good to see you gals. Looks like running the shop agrees with you. Everyone is the picture of health. Any news on the baby front?"

Sage and I shared a knowing glance at the instant plunge into Auntie O's favorite topic. Even though I'd known Quig since elementary school, we'd only been a couple for four months, and we were still figuring things out.

I cleared my throat. "Neither of us is in the family way."

"Too bad." Auntie O's glance took in Quig and the flickering candle. "I thought you wanted a family."

"Yes, ma'am. I do."

She glared at Quig. "I assume you know how babies are made."

His face flushed beet red at her tart tone. "Very familiar with the process. It's our decision to wait before we start a family."

"Don't wait too long. Tabby is thirty now."

"You'll be among the first to know, ma'am," he stated calmly. "Would either of you care for pecan pie or a soda?"

My pride swelled at how Quig deflected Auntie O's probing on this delicate subject. He'd been respectful and then deftly shifted the conversation to another topic. I beamed a smile his way.

"Just soda for me," Auntie O said, "and Frankie never passes up a pie."

"Or a soda." Frankie stepped over to the basket and gazed intently inside, reminding me of my black cat Harley when he set his mind on getting a treat.

"Frankie, I apologize if this is too personal," I asked now that I had a free moment. "Are you feeling okay?"

"Been under the weather lately, but I'll come around. I bet

that pie and soda will fix whatever's ailing me."

"I'm glad you came, and I hope you're better soon."

"Oralee, apologies for my poor manners. Please have a seat," Quig said using my aunt's first name and giving her his chair. "What's the story about your grandparents being in this plot?"

I motioned for Frankie to take my seat and settled on the blanket on the ground beside Quig.

Auntie O smiled mysteriously. "You girls still can't find out anything about them can you? Shame on you for putting Quig to the trouble of asking me."

"We didn't," I said. "He's keenly interested in how they ended up here. So are we. How long are you and Mom going to protect us from the past?"

"You've got a point." She drew in a deep breath and released it. "Marjoram and I didn't choose their plot, but, by God, we chose what went on their stone. I agreed to go along with the Wayfare's insistence they belonged here, a veritable whitewash of history, but Marg took stubbornness to a whole new level with the tomb epitaph. The Wayfares threatened to redo the stone in a more traditional style though they never changed it."

"How did our grandparents get felled?" I couldn't help pushing for more answers now that she was talking.

"Might as was well tell you some of it, 'specially since you brought Quig into it now. Someone got sideways with your Grandfather Dwayne and shot him, except Grandmother Rosemary stepped in front of him at the last second. The bullet struck her lung without hitting any bones, passed through her, and then lodged in Dwayne's heart. My parents died within minutes of each other. Your Mom and I were eighteen and sixteen, respectively."

"The assassin got away with murder? Nobody knows who shot them?" Quig asked.

"Someone did, and that's all I'm saying on the matter.

Now let me slice that pie and serve everyone."

My heart raced at her revelation. I couldn't believe she'd told us anything. Sage and I shared another knowing glance though neither of us fired up our private twin-link because Auntie O could eavesdrop on us if we did, a side effect of the similar bond she'd shared with Mom. How did Quig rate an answer in his first picnic here, and we'd gotten jack squat all these years? The part about history being whitewashed stuck with me. A big secret still lurked in our past, and I vowed to unearth it one of these days. Was one of my grandparents an adopted child or an illegitimate Wayfare?

Out of curiosity, I'd researched the origins of the name Wayfare. It was British and the name meant traveler or journey. The second meaning for the name was the money used by a traveler or journey. My boundless curiosity refused to settle with that. Were the Wayfares travelers? Where'd they come from? Were they still any left in Savannah? Was money buried in this plot?

"You know who killed them?" I asked pointedly.

"I do, though he's no longer a threat to anyone in this family."

"Why can't you share the name? We really want to know," Sage said.

"I don't talk about that subject. It upsets me, and we risked our lives to return for the graveside visit. Let's speak of other things. Please."

A protest lodged in my throat. It was hard to be grateful for what she'd revealed without wanting the whole story. We were so close to having answers. But maybe we were a lot closer to her revealing everything. Practicing patience wasn't my favorite thing to do, but I was better at it than my twin.

"The T-shirt shop is drawing steady traffic," Quig said to Frankie once we'd eaten a bite of decadent pie.

Frankie nodded, his gold necklaces gleaming in the sunlight. He still looked like an aging gangster from a retro

TV show, but now his overall vibe had changed from happy to see us to tired and worn out. "Thought it would. So many teams want custom shirts and other matching items. Savannah needed a local place for that. I thought about adding trophies to the shop line, but plenty of places do those already."

When Frankie and Auntie O purchased the building beside our shop, the former shop keeper opted for retirement in Costa Rica. So now we had a new T-shirt place next door to us underneath the apartment where Frankie and Auntie O lived or had lived until they'd hidden from his crime-entangled family.

The men ate seconds of pecan pie, a feat I could never manage on a pie this rich. I savored each bite of the sweet, crunchy dessert, rolling the decadent taste around in my mouth until I craved the next bite. Conversation ebbed and flowed until the candle sputtered out, signaling the end of our visit. Frankie and Auntie O rose and insisted on driving Sage home, while I caught a return ride with Quig.

"That was nice," I said, when the two of us climbed into his Hummer. "Thanks for taking so much time out of your workday at the morgue."

He gave me a hug. "I stayed to protect you."

I stepped back to read his face, not quite catching his drift. "From my aunt?"

"From any threat but mostly from the Chicago people after Frankie."

Oh. Frankie's scary relatives. "They left town."

"That's what they want us to believe."

I didn't want to live in fear of anyone, but we had genuine concerns about that branch of Frankie's family tree. It wouldn't hurt to stay on guard.

When Quig pulled up in front of the candle shop, he said, "Don't forget our dinner reservation for tonight."

Something about his tight expression kept me from

leaning across the console for a goodbye kiss. Instead, I waved. "I'll be ready."

"So will I."

I'm certain his last words were meant to be a promise, but he sounded so grim I wondered if they were a threat. What did he know that I didn't?

Chapter Two

When I browsed in our family's black dress closet in Sage's apartment, a collection that grew with each generation, I regarded every dress with Quig's reaction in mind. "He said to wear something nice. Lot of room for interpretation there."

"Oh, yeah," Sage said. "Sexy, fancy, revealing."

"Demure, fancy, business professional, polished."

"I can't believe you picked all the boring aspects of nice. This is Valentine's Day. Flaunt your curvy figure."

"I don't usually flaunt anything. That whole blending in aspect, you know."

"You don't want to blend tonight. You're making a statement."

"The perfect dress falls in between our interpretations of nice." I tried on dresses until Sage's face lit with approval.

Sage whistled and made me twirl in a circle. "That's the one. It fits like second skin and with those sparkly heels you positively glow. You better hope he's taking you to a fast food place for dinner. Once he sees this dress, y'all aren't going anywhere for a while."

"Could be, though he's big on celebrations. We're near four months of togetherness, and Quig is all about milestones."

"Where y'all going?"

I caught her eye in the mirror. "Elizabeth on 37th."

Sage hugged her cat so tightly, Luna yowled and jumped out of her arms. "Oh! I bet my blinged-out flipflops at least three couples there get engaged tonight. You better be ready for The Question."

Quig had been sincere about marrying me ever since we'd become a romantic couple. He'd been my friend since elementary school, my best friend. I adored him, but marriage between a "normal" and an energetic rarely lasted due to our family secrets. Heck, both of my parents were energetics, and they only made it five years.

The energetic talent flowed through the female side of our family though each of us had a slightly different twist of what we could do with energy manipulation. My twin and I read auras as easily as we breathed, but her energy was of the icer variety while mine was of wholesome, life-affirming currents. I also have the ability to bend light and become invisible, though the cost of doing so zaps me hard, especially if I use white light energy instead of shadows to power the concealment.

Quig knew I had strong intuition, and he knew I had to live on Bristol Street. He didn't know how the ground beneath the shop building recharged me every night. All he knew was that it was very important to my family that we reside in this block of the city.

His intuition had previously warned him I was doing something dangerous and then he'd stood beside me in a showdown with killers, without knowing the whole of it, and I couldn't tell him. Revealing our secrets would endanger every member of our family. Despite wanting to share everything with Quig, I couldn't open up to him that way.

I wanted to marry Quig, I did. But I also didn't. Why add marriage pressure to a relationship that suited us? My twin and I had discussed this topic many times over the years. The fact we were thirty added a ticking clock to the question of marriage and family, and as Auntie O frequently harped on the subject, family is what carried on our line.

"Maybe, but I'm hoping he doesn't ask me tonight. I look forward to enjoying the ambiance of that Victorian mansion without extra pressure. I've never been there before."

"It's lovely. Wish we were accompanying you, but Brindle and I are grilling at home tonight. He's nervous about costs in his new law practice and squeezes every penny."

"It took courage for Brindle to go out on his own after being canned by his former law firm. I admire him for starting over," I said, "especially after getting spelled and landing in the psych ward."

"Looking back, I should have trusted him, but I was too hurt when he kissed his receptionist. I know now that he thought she was me but still. . ."

"Spells do weird things to people. We should know."

"Luckily, Brindle has a financial cushion to see him through this growth phase of his new firm, so we won't starve in the near future."

"Let's hope not."

~*~

Quig's jaw dropped at the sight of my dress, followed by a string of soft wows. There was a cool calculation in his eyes as to how fast the dress would come off. It did wonders for my ego as I channeled my inner vixen on the way to his Hummer. I felt sure it was only the sought-after nature of our restaurant reservation that kept him on task. Success at landing a dinner reservation at Elizabeth at 37th was akin to hitting a hole-in-one.

Sage had been right about the Valentine's Day proposals. Three prospective grooms popped the question and three brides-to-be said yes before we tucked into our entrees of spicy Savannah red rice and Georgia shrimp. Quig's eyes looked haunted each time a guy went down on one knee beside a restaurant table.

Using my other vision, I peeked at his aura to see if anything was physically wrong. His energy field looked as vibrant as usual, though there were a few erratic pulses. Maybe he felt proposal pressure. I tried distraction. "How's work going?"

"Challenging. Cops want to combine two homicide investigations near Bonaventure Cemetery. It's tricky because the means of death are different, but there's an undeniable signature component."

"What links the cases?"

"Can't share specifics." He met my gaze, and we said together, "Ongoing investigations."

Drat. I wish he hadn't said anything about those cemetery adjacent murders now. I'd rather be ignorant of a mysterious linking component. Now it was all I could think about.

"Do you like this place?" Quig asked when the silence dragged on too long.

The soft chamber music and the beautifully appointed rooms with half a dozen or so tables of couples felt like I'd been transported to a fairy tale version of someone else's life. "It's charming. I love everything about it—the food, the ambiance, and the wine. Elizabeth's lives up to the hype. Well done, my Valentine!"

His brows waggled, then he raised his wine glass to me. "The night is young."

"I hoped you might feel that way." I leaned forward, knowing my bodice gaped provocatively in this position, displaying to best effect the heart-shaped locket Quig gave me for our one-month anniversary. "Sage bet we wouldn't make our reservation."

His eyes lit up like fireworks behind his glasses, beads of sweat dotted his brow. "You always have my full attention. Tonight you'd tempt a saint in that dress, and I'm no saint. If I hadn't called in a favor to secure this reservation, Sage would've won that bet."

"Excellent." Then my ears tumbled to another delicious truth. "Is this your first time here?"

"Yes." He signaled the server and handed her his card. "Check please. We'll take our desserts to go."

I sipped my wine and wondered if I could sling him over my shoulder and carry him off into the night, a clear role reversal that had fascinating possibilities.

He lightly cleared his throat. "You're thinking about…later… too?"

"Of course. But I'm savoring the suspense. It heightens the tension…and the payoff."

"You're killing me." Quig released a slow breath. "Let's talk about something else."

A thought cropped up that had been on my mind lately. "There is something I've been considering."

"Yes?"

I settled back into my chair. "Sage and I barely knew our dad. According to our birth certificates, his name is Henry Winslow, and his address is the apartment over our shop, where Sage lives now. With visiting my grandparents' grave today fresh in my mind, I would like to find Henry Winslow. I don't know if he's dead or alive."

A man three tables down from us rose and said, "She said yes!" Patrons clapped their approval.

"Lucky guy." Quig turned back to me. "What did you have in mind?"

I winced at his sharp tone. Maybe it wasn't the proposals annoying him, though I was in the mood to say yes with all the acceptances here tonight. "Thought I'd start with a DNA test. Many of the sites that tout this service not only provide you with your countries of origin percentage, but they also compare your DNA profile to others in their database, and often match siblings, cousins, and more. It's a tool for forensic genealogists. Have you tried this?"

"My lineage is known for generations, and our genetics are a private matter. Given your family's similar stance on privacy in general, is getting a DNA profile wise?"

His aura flared. Definitely a red flag moment for him. His opinion mattered, but this was about me, about what I wanted. On the chance he knew something I didn't, I asked, "Why shouldn't I?"

"Um." He leaned closer. "By its definition, you'd create a record of your genetic material, and you would be disclosing personal information."

The bloom fell off the romantic evening with a loud clank. It must be nice to know every branch of your family. Or maybe I misread him. Maybe my spotty lineage embarrassed him. "My ancestry matters to me. On Mom's side of the family, I know her parents' names and on my Dad's side I know his name. That's it. I have no idea who his parents were or where they're buried. How would you feel if you didn't know your lineage? Wouldn't you want to know?"

He took my hand in his. "I know exactly who you are. A smart, beautiful woman who holds my heart in hers. You're the woman of my dreams, now and forever."

I softened at his touch. "You forgot creative."

"You are definitely creative." His thumb did interesting things to the back of my hand, raising the good kind of goosebumps. "Your dad doesn't matter. I love you, and I have from the first moment I saw you. That's enough for me."

"Love you too." *Here it comes.* I stared deep into his brown eyes. *He's going to propose.*

Instead he reached for the bill and said in a not-so off-hand manner, "What do you know about tallow?"

My head jerked back. *Huh?* That was not the question I expected. "Tallow?"

"You must know of it."

"Sure. It's rendered animal fat often used in making soap and candles, among other uses." Why were we talking about tallow? It wasn't like Quig to randomly mention a topic like this. Was it related to his work or the murders in some way?

"I see." His face blanched. Soft conversation flowed around us, sounding much like cooing doves. "Do you use it?"

His question didn't sound casual. It felt very direct. Was he interrogating me? If so, I'd rather not answer, not without an explanation. "What's this about?"

"Humor me, please."

The please helped. "I use some tallow."

He waved his hand in a circular motion. "Go on."

He'd never before asked about my candle and soap-making process. "At one time Auntie O made her own tallow, but it's a stinky process and so I don't make it from scratch or buy the store-bought tallow. Instead, I buy soap base with that ingredient included, depending on what I'm creating."

The planes of his face turned glacial. "Any tallow in your stillroom?"

"Don't think so. Why?"

He escorted me out through the lovely garden walk. "Curiosity."

How frustrating. Despite the excellent meal, Quig's mixed signals tonight confused me. From Sage's hints, I'd expected a proposal. Five minutes ago I would've said yes, same as the other lucky diners. Now I wasn't sure of anything.

Obviously, I'd smacked hard into the dark side of falling in love.

Chapter Three

Shop clerk Eve Seratt and I were scheduled to handle the shop today, though I'm sure my two shop cats, a brother and sister pair named Harley and Luna, thought The Book and Candle Shop was their domain. As usual, Harley supervised from the highest display shelf behind the register, reclining amongst colorful tapers, candle lanterns, and pirate statues. He had the uncanny agility to navigate the merchandise without disturbing a single item. Luna drowsed in the sunny window amidst vibrant ferns, pillar candle arrays, lotions, books on Savannah, and one-of-a-kind dragon sculptures.

Once it got warmer, say May or so, we'd move all the candles out of the northeast facing windows or they'd melt. But since we were in mid-February, candles in the front window were fine.

My first task of the day had been to gather all the Valentine decorations in the shop. We'd wait a few days before we decorated for St. Patrick's Day, which Savannah celebrated in a huge way. I had plenty of time to get everything spruced up to my satisfaction.

"Looks like we need Norah Jones music today," Eve declared as she got the sultry-sweet jazzy blues vocals dialed to background levels. A group of art students filed in and set up over in our book nook. When I drifted over to the back table with a handful of cupids, Valentine's candy, and more, Eve intercepted me. "What is it, Tabby?"

Eve's sensitivity zeroed in on my increasing sense of looming disaster. "Sorry my strange mood is giving off dark energy. Ever since last night I've felt off center. I need to keep busy today, so I don't dwell on mysteries I can't solve."

Alarm flashed in her kind eyes. "Are you coming down with something? Anything I could help with?"

Eve had studied various spiritual practices under her grandmother's tutelage. As a rule, our family steered clear of spiritualism and mediums. It angered us when people called us witches, though I supposed our energy talents appeared to be magic to outsiders. To us, the extra gears defined who and what we were—energetics. "No, not that, but..." I sighed as I sought a relevant-to-her way to describe my situation. Eve was ten years younger than Sage and me with mocha colored skin. She favored batik dresses with a turban or matching headband. And delightfully funky sandals. Her coordinating nails always looked great. In contrast, I usually wore dark pants, a solid-color blouse, and comfy running shoes.

Yikes! I'd drifted off in thought-land, and now Eve watched me like a hawk. I quickly found my voice. "You know that brooding sensation before a storm rolls in? The one that pulses underneath everything like a slow heartbeat, but it's something else? Then disaster looms as the light thins, lightning flashes, and the sky opens."

Eve nodded. "And you rush to take the clothes off the line, or carry in the groceries, or whatever you're doing, and it's too darn late because you ignored what your intuition was telling you all along. I know that boding feeling well, but there's no bad weather forecast today."

"That's the best way I can describe my mood. Has nothing to do with an actual storm."

"A storm of life?"

That made me smile for a moment. "Never thought of it that way, but yeah. A storm of life."

"With your history of amateur criminal investigations, I assume this murder discussion is about the recent unusual deaths in our town," Eve began slowly. "Grapevine says two recent Savannah homicides, one on a park bench and the other leaning against a church door, share common traits."

I lifted an eyebrow. "Really? What have you heard?"

"The bodies are posed in sitting positions. No video cameras at either site. The victims were struck with lethal objects, one by a cast iron frying pan to the head and the other stopped cold by a bullet."

"Posed? I don't understand how I missed this detail. How so?"

"Staged to look like they were alive."

"That wasn't in the newspaper." I thought back to what I'd read about those deaths. "The paper made a big deal out of how their means of death were different, so no one considered a single killer. But last night, Quig started to share something about his work, then he shut down under the catch-phrase of ongoing investigation. A little later, he asked me about tallow, specifically if I had any in the shop."

Eve sank onto the nearby stool. "Tallow? I've heard the word, but I don't know what it is."

"It's an ingredient in my soaps." I couldn't be still, so as I shared more about tallow and soaps, I grabbed my duster and headed to the wall of industrial shelving with its clusters of candles and with scents ranging from woodsy notes to crisp fruits and mouthwatering citrus. "I don't use tallow in my candles."

"How come?"

"Personal preference on my part and based on what our customers prefer. Tallow is rendered from beef fat. Lots of vegans and vegetarians don't want it in their house or their candles."

"You said it was from fat. Is it a solid?"

"It is until it heats up, then it becomes liquid."

"Like coconut oil or shortening used for cooking?"

"Good comparison. Both are solid at room temperature three seasons of the year. Add heat and both substances melt." I drew in a lungful of soothing bayberry fragrance. This was where I needed to be, in bayberry heaven.

"How does tallow relate to murder?" Eve asked.

I gestured broadly with my duster and accidentally struck the clapper on a wind chime overhead and a frenzied cascade of chimes sounded. "I don't know, but why else would he ask me about it?"

"Dontcha worry about this. If tallow matters, those detectives will scoop you up in a dip net."

I didn't care to be caught like a blue crab. Remembering my negative interactions with the police before, her comment sent my back teeth into a clench so hard I had to pry them apart. "I'm not the only chandler or soaper in Savannah." At the confusion on Eve's face, I hastened to explain. "Historically, candlemakers were called chandlers."

"Like the word chandelier?"

"Exactly."

"We sell a boatload of candles because yours are the best."

My hand strayed to my treasured locket for good measure. "Candles are bestsellers in Savannah because they're essential hurricane supplies. There's no reason for cops to think tallow use points to me, but I sense that storm is headed my way regardless."

"That's why you're emoting the blues?"

"Maybe." I ruminated on that a bit, dabbed peppermint

essential oil on my temples to fob off a headache. "I love my life, but I am stuck in a rut that's generations old. Yesterday Sage and I picnicked at Bonaventure Cemetery. It's an annual family tradition to honor our maternal grandparents. There's a mystery connected with their murder and a separate family mystery related to my missing father. Our graveyard visit got me all buzzed again, thinking about those unsolved mysteries."

Eve nodded wisely. "You have questions and no answers. You want to trace your roots. Most get that genealogy bug when they are older. Hmm." She tapped the side of her face as she studied me. "I see the why of it now. You want a family with Quig, but those lineage gaps worry you like splinters in a finger."

Her words surprised me. "That is eerily on-point, but there are few answers to be had. My family tree is as holey as a sea sponge."

"I get it. I don't know who my father is."

"Would you consider taking a DNA test to find out?"

Eve made a dismissive noise. "Not interested. My father never looked for me, so why should I find him? Mom and MawMaw raised us. Those are the elders I cherish and respect."

"Same here with my mom and aunt. However, my curiosity keeps raising its head." I stashed my duster and stood near Eve. "You're right when you said I need to know my history. I want children. Kids know gaps in their family tree aren't normal, and, besides, I also want the hereditary information for health reasons and peace of mind."

"You value answers. Do what is right for you."

I reached for my purse under the counter and showed her the DNA test kit I'd ordered. "Even if Quig thinks I should leave it alone?"

"You did not just ask me that! Girl, don't you know nothing? Start out as you mean to go on. This is your history, and you need answers. He's not a part of this."

"He's part of me. On some level, I've always known that, but navigating this sinkhole is important to me. I'm waffling because I don't want to ruin everything."

"Conflict doesn't define relationships. Dealing with conflict does."

"That's...profound." I stared at the cardboard box as if the kit were the Holy Grail of all things ancestry. Maybe I wouldn't care for the answers about origins or cousins, but I wouldn't know unless I took the test and put my results out there in a database. Not something Mom nor Quig would do. But I wasn't either of them. I needed to know who else was in my lineage. I wanted my kids to feel like they had a family they could trace if that mattered to them. Mostly I wanted them to feel like they belonged.

I clutched the box to my heart. "I'm doing it."

Chapter Four

Three days later I had just finished a double batch of bar soaps in the shop's stillroom when my weekday clerk Gerard Smith called out from the storefront, "Tabby, your best buddies are here."

"What buddies?" I peeled off my gloves and hurried out front, closing the door behind me to stand beside Gerard.

He gestured to the nondescript sedan parked in a slot in front of the door, and my breath hitched. No mistaking those cops. I hadn't seen Detectives Nowry and Belfor in six weeks. Whenever they appeared, someone in my circle of family and friends suffered. Was this the pending "stormy weather" my intuition had been warning me about?

"What do they want?" I asked, dreading the answer. Twice now I'd solved homicide cases they were working. Not that I fancied myself a cop, but I'd had no choice. They'd come after my family. Heck, Auntie O and Frankie now lived on the lam, hidden from family and friends because of news law enforcement had aired. The cops leaked Frankie's connections to a certain Chicago crime family, and unsavory relatives came looking for him in December. They wouldn't cow me.

"If you want to take a break, it's okay with me," I said to

my shop clerk. He disliked these cop visits as much as I did, thanks to them for accusing him of a crime last fall.

"I'm feeling brave today." Gerard barred his arms across his chest. "Why aren't they coming inside?"

I reached for my locket, my comfort touchstone these days. Would the cop pick up on my anxiety? Perhaps touching my locket was a tell. With reluctance I let it go. "Looks like they're strategizing. Usually Nowry charges in and Belfor brings up the rear with a smile, lulling us into thinking she's the Good Cop so we'll confide in her. Maybe we'll luck out and have Belfor doing the talking this time."

"Even if that happens," Gerard began, "I'll betcha anything Nowry can't keep quiet. That man has to be in control all the time."

A colorful bus motored by on Bristol Street, followed by a horse-drawn carriage, both full of tourists. Suddenly the detectives broke apart, and Sharmila Belfor took the lead. She represented the "pepper" of this salt-and-pepper pair in thoughts, words, and deeds. Her well-groomed appearance looked more stylish than that of her stoic senior partner. His suits looked like they were on loan from a 1960s cop TV show.

Our front door signaled when they entered, while overhead wind chimes caught air and bonged resonantly like sea buoys in rough seas. I immediately shielded myself and took the initiative. "What can we do for you today? Perhaps some candles, soaps, or our other merchandise?"

"This place always smells amazing, like a beach and forest are having a tropical drink." Detective Belfor glanced at me and then nodded toward the closed stillroom door. "You making candles and soap today?"

"I just finished a batch of soap, but they aren't packaged for sale yet."

"Do you use tallow in your work?" she continued.

My focus shifted to her face. Why was the muscle in her cheek twitching? "Some. Why do you ask?"

Tallow again. Shoot. First Quig and now the cops showed an interest in this ingredient. I couldn't mention the coincidence in hearing that word twice in the span of a few days. Not when Nowry specialized in connecting scattered evidence to build circumstantial cases. I plastered a customer-friendly smile on my face, but darn it, acting hospitable to these two after they had grilled me at length in another case pushed me straight to the barnacle-sharp edge of my patience. Most of that questioning had been at the station, so I should thank my lucky stars to be standing on my home turf right now.

Belfor's lips thinned in irritation. She must not have liked my evasion. Tough turkey for her.

"We've come across the substance in recent days," Belfor said. "Given your candle and soap-making occupation, we presume you're a subject expert. How would you describe the consistency of tallow?"

I took a few moments to stare at the wind chimes interspersed with fern baskets overhead, as if I were considering the question. It did me no good to answer their questions rapid-fire. "Firm like shortening."

"To your knowledge, is tallow solid until warmed and then it becomes a liquid?"

"Yes."

Belfor narrowed her eyes at me, cop-hard. I answered correctly. What more did she expect?

She gestured for me to continue. "Please show me your tallow so I may observe the consistency."

"Sorry, I don't use pure tallow, so I don't buy it."

Her eyebrows darted high on her brow. "You ran out?"

"Can't run out if you don't use it." I didn't miss the wistful note in her voice, nor the fact that Detective Nowry now stood beside her, staring down at me. My chin went up. He didn't scare me. Much. "I don't use tallow separately, so I don't purchase it individually. Instead, I buy prepackaged mixes of certain ingredients."

Sharmila Belfor shook her head and looked confused. "Come again? A few minutes ago you said you used tallow."

"Our signature candles are proprietary blends of fuel, fragrances, and additives, but I can share this information about the soaps I make. I start them off using a commercially-prepared base with tallow already included. It's a timesaver employed by many in our industry."

"Your soaps? Didn't know tallow went into those." She waited. I held my silence. She spoke first, a small victory for me, but who was keeping score? "What about your candles?"

"Candles can include tallow, but that's not the kind of candles I craft here. Most of mine are beeswax, though in the heat of summer, I make candles with soy as the main ingredient."

Nowry glared at me. Belfor smiled. "I had no idea candle ingredients varied so much. I thought all of them consisted of wax and tallow."

I gazed at the nearby dragon sculpture. Wouldn't it be nice to send these guys packing with a dragon-blast of fire? Again, I said nothing. So far Gerard hadn't moved a muscle. I could scarcely hear him breathing at my side. He held a zip-my-lips philosophy toward this pair. Nothing good came from volunteering extra information. So far, I'd been accused of nothing. I planned to keep it that way.

"Where would someone buy tallow?" Belfor asked.

"Some grocery stores carry it, some big box stores. Search online if you need a local source. Like I said, I don't use it as a separate ingredient."

"It's the same as suet, right?" the female detective asked.

"It's fat rendered from suet, and it can come from beef, sheep, and sometimes goats." Oops. I'd volunteered information. I had to be more vigilant. Belfor knew her stuff.

"Show us," Nowry growled.

His gruff tone ignited my intuition into full fight or flight mode. Since flight was out of the question, I donned mental boxing gloves. "Excuse me?" I said, switching my attention to his leathery face.

"Take us in the back and show us those ingredients."

Gerard stirred beside me as if he might tell Nowry where he could shove his ingredients. I caught his eye and gave a minimal shake of my head to make sure he didn't say anything. If I got caught up in this sweep, we couldn't afford Gerard to also offend the cops and get a free trip downtown. Gerard's sales superpower kept us in business.

Purposefully, I interlaced my fingers near my waist and radiated calm. "No need for that. You may verify ingredients on our products here in the store." With a broad hand gesture, I indicated a mixed display of candles and soaps.

"Forget your finished products," Nowry said. "I want to see the base you mentioned."

Not in my showroom. Not without a warrant. "Wait here. I'll bring a base package out to you."

Nowry leaned in, with his strong aftershave of citrus and kelp clogging my nose and making my eyes water. "I'd rather visit your back room."

So not happening. Besides my need for privacy, I didn't want cop energy back there. Last time I had to smudge the room with sage and lavender three times. "Do you have a warrant?"

"I shouldn't need one if you have nothing to hide."

My hackles rose. I hated his attitude, scent, and murky aura. He would never make my favorites list in a million years. "I'm not hiding anything. I know my rights. Our blended products distinguish us in a crowded market. Further, our showroom is a public area; my stillroom is not."

Nowry gazed down his knobby nose at me. "You aren't helping yourself. Your lack of cooperation is duly noted."

"What is this about?" I asked in a matching steely tone. "I don't appreciate being threatened."

Belfor picked up a candle and sniffed it. "No need for this discussion to escalate into hostility. Nowry has two voice tones, gruff and threatening. Don't take his negativity personally. It comes from dealing with criminals for forty years. Let me restate our request. We respect your expertise with tallow and would very much like to examine the package of soap base you mentioned. May we see it?"

A second ago I wanted to boot Nowry out of my shop. Still wanted him gone, but Belfor's explanation made a difference. She'd admitted her partner was a jerk. I took that as a win. "I'll be right back." With that I strode away, entered the stillroom, and shut the door behind me. I found the package of supplies and withdrew a soap base. If this made the cops go away, it was worth the inventory loss.

I carried it to the showroom and the cops. "Several companies sell soap bases, but this is the brand I prefer."

Detective Nowry whipped out a pair of reading glasses to read the fine print on the proffered soap base, then nodded at Belfor. "I'll run this through the lab."

I wanted to say no just to be contrary. The urge to say no came over me, but instead I said, "Suit yourself. Each company that makes those bases has more product information online. Note that I am cooperating with your investigation."

Nowry pocketed the base and left in a huff.

I gazed pointedly at Belfor, expecting her to follow. She shot me a wry smile instead. "Nowry is wound tighter than usual today. We found a third body at Bonaventure. We're officially chasing a serial killer."

"Another murder? Serial killer?" Surely ants crawled up and down my legs. What else could provoke that tingling sensation? Besides the creepy-crawly feeling on my skin, my belly felt like a much-abused voodoo doll. From Belfor's intensity, I surmised terrible news would follow.

Sure enough, she added, "The groundskeeper at

Bonaventure Cemetery called the body in early this morning. Sad case, for sure. I believe you knew the victim, Jerry Meldrim."

Crap. This must be why Quig left home before dawn today. Another murder. I swayed toward Gerard, and he steadied me. I'd sworn out a restraining order against Meldrim. He'd created a public disturbance in our shop before Christmas with his rowdy, brutish behavior and ugly threats. Nowry and Belfor knew that. They'd come to The Book and Candle Shop today to fish for a murderer, and I hadn't taken the bait. Better yet, I didn't have the tallow they sought. I resisted the urge to laugh in Belfor's face.

"It's on all the morning news programs. Surprised you didn't hear about the homicide already. The coverage was epic. Reporters swarmed in like piranhas, and camera crews filmed from trees. I expect this latest murder to headline the news for the next few news cycles."

"Meldrim's death is connected to the other cases, the ones with staged bodies?" Oops. Was that generally known now? Why hadn't I turned on the TV this morning?

"Absolutely," Belfor said. "His killer must've known Meldrim's love of spirits. We found him in Bonaventure Cemetery, propped against a tombstone, martini glass close at hand, as if he died toasting the dead."

Since Belfor didn't react aggressively to my gaffe about the staged bodies, I had to assume that I hadn't blabbed a secret only the Savannah grapevine and the killer knew. Meanwhile, the coincidence of our recent picnic in Bonaventure loomed large in my mind. Quig believed there were no coincidences. I risked another question. "Did he die in the cemetery?"

"From the looks of that pristine double headstone, he died elsewhere. If he were killed there, we would've found blood on the stone and on the ground, but those surfaces were pristine."

Now that prickling sensation covered my entire body. No

reason to leap to the wrong conclusion, I told myself. There were plenty of double headstones in that cemetery. "How did he die?"

"We are keeping a lid on the means of death today. But the tallow connection leaked during this morning's media blitz. We've asked a lot of people about tallow today."

Whew. A glimmer of good news. It wasn't just me they were bugging. "How does the killer use the tallow?"

"I could be as cagey as you were earlier, but I have an agenda here. The victims all have tallow in their hair, used as hair pomade. You, Tabby Winslow, know how to find answers. With each of our previous cases, our investigations only went so far and stalled. You have expertise in finding answers, and now we're hunting a killer from your world. We need to know what you know."

Did this mean I'd shifted from potential killer to trusted source in their eyes? I couldn't quite make that mental leap. Thanks to Quig, I knew there was a tallow connection for the first two victims, but no way would I volunteer that. "I told you what I know, but here's a news flash about tallow. It softens leather, skin, and more. It can replace oil for cooking. And workers in wood and metal industries use it for lubrication."

Belfor wrinkled her brow. "That may be the case, but as far as we know, no one else swore out a restraining order against Jerry Meldrim."

My breath halted at the realization. Not a trusted source. She'd as much as said I was a suspect.

With that, Detective Belfor pivoted and strolled out as if she were savoring her small victory. Oh, I didn't like being a suspect.

Gerard whooped with joy. "They came," he said. "They departed, they didn't conquer, and we remain here. Pretty amazing teamwork if you ask me. The united front worked!"

I wasn't as optimistic. Tingles like biting insects still went off on my legs. "You did a great job of staying quiet. I hope we fall off their suspicion radar immediately."

"Let's celebrate with carryout from Southern Tea. I can dart across the street and get lunch."

"Sure thing. I'd love a Shrimp Po Boy and a jumbo iced tea. It's my treat this time."

While he called in the order, I grabbed cash from my billfold to cover both lunches. I also returned to my stillroom wondering if there might be any remaining tallow here. Perhaps Auntie O had bought some when she'd been the family candlemaker?

After I searched all the stillroom cabinets, I tried the supply closet. Nothing on the upper shelves, but on the floor in the very back sat a dusty half-gallon sized plastic tub. I quickly scanned the faded label. Tallow. A cold sweat broke out all over me.

If the cops looked in here and found this tallow today, I'd be sleeping in the jailhouse tonight. I had to get rid of it, but what if the cops screened my trash? I'd play right into their hands. Worse, I'd look guilty for throwing it away.

"Did ya lose something?" Gerard stuck his head across the stillroom threshold.

I shut the supply closet door, turned, and wished I had a mind-mage talent to make Gerard think "nothing to see here. Move along." Instead, I managed a wry grin and answered in a way that didn't incriminate myself. "Double checking our inventory. I didn't like it when we ran short in December."

"Good idea but the food's out here now," he said.

"Thanks. I'll just be a sec."

Once he retreated, I slumped against the counter, overcome by dread. I'd lied to the cops about having tallow, albeit I didn't know it was a lie at the time, but I certainly had a problem. I couldn't leave the tub in here. I couldn't toss it either. I gazed across the room at the secret access for the foldaway bed, an odd relic from my aunt and mom's era with the shop. There should be room inside for this half-used bucket of tallow in the secret bed compartment. It wasn't easy, but I tapped the hidden panel, opened the bed, and crammed the bucket inside. Then I closed the cupboard and walked out to eat with Gerard in the shop.

Despite my good intentions to celebrate our victory over the cops, the awesome sandwich from across the street tasted like sawdust in my dry mouth. What a waste of good food.

The looming threat of being jailed for a crime I didn't commit crushed any chance of peace and harmony.

Chapter Five

I dashed upstairs to share the news with Sage and to see the changes in her living room. In recent weeks, my sister had been on a kick to grow native plants in her apartment. An entire wall now sported industrial racks, grow lights, and all manner of plants. The energy felt great here, with less Sage energy and more plant energy blending into the perfect mix of wholesome energy.

I knocked, then waited a few minutes for Sage to answer her door. When she didn't respond, I used my key, poking my head inside enough to say, "Sage, you decent?"

She flounced out of her bedroom in an easy fitting crop top, running shorts, and fluorescent pink nails as if it were July instead of February. "Of course I'm decent. Come in. What's going on?"

"Cops found another body." I filled her in on the morning's events.

"You're still here and that's what matters." Sage waved me to the sofa, and we sat facing each other. "Jerry Meldrim. Boy, that guy attracted trouble like a bleeder in the ocean. Wonder what got him in the end?"

"They didn't say. I'd ask you to turn on your television to listen for breaking news, but I don't see the television set anywhere. Are you anti-TV all of a sudden?"

"Brindle moved it to his new office, at my urging. Electromagnetic radiation, however slight, isn't good for plants. These suckers started to look tall, thin, and pale green when that old TV was here. Not a good start for my beginning inventory, so I nixed the TV. If I wanted radiation-absorbing plants I'd grow aloe, asparagus fern, and several others, but those aren't top sellers in the area."

I scowled at her explanation. "I thought TVs had very little radiation these days. Are plants more susceptible to bad vibes than people?"

"Don't know. I just want the absolute best for my leaf babies. And look at them now. They're-super hardy and healthy. Who wouldn't want to buy these gems?"

As directed I scanned her plants with a more discerning eye. They were full and vibrant and every shade of deep green. Sage had a green thumb, but this vibrant foliage could win prizes. Not only was our apartment optimal for us energetics, but plants also thrived here as well. "What happens when you can't squeeze one more plant in here or when mold creeps down the walls from the humidity?"

"Brindle and I have discussed buying a lot outside the city to start my nursery. I wouldn't sell from there because more buyers live in the city. However, it would be wonderful to have room to grow, natural sunlight, great nutrient blends in the soil, and an irrigation system."

I loved that she was moving forward on her nursery idea. "Any luck on your property search?"

"Not looking too hard yet. I'm only in the thinking stage

of my new plant business. I can't afford a major purchase now, but Brindle might buy the lot for investment purposes. Anyway, the first step is proof of concept. I can keep the business small scale until I get established. Maybe even hold occasional Saturday sidewalk sales in front of our shop. Like I said, everything is in the air for now."

"What about former nurseries? Any of them for sale?"

Sage nodded. "A former nursery would come with the infrastructure I need. While the price for an improved property would cost more than land coming fresh out of forestry, for instance, the net cost for a new operation would be a known factor. I should price something along those lines."

I knew of one nursery currently operating under duress — Sage's former place of employment. "What about All Good Things?"

"They're asking too much for that property. It's not for me. Besides, after all the scheming that went on there and my boss's murder, that place has bad juju."

"We can smudge away the bad juju. Would they consider a lease instead?"

"You're brimming with ideas today." Sage smoothed a hank of her dark hair behind her ear. "How about devising a company name for my sideline? The only caveat is I don't want my name anywhere in the title. I plan to sell at festivals so I don't need a storefront. I need a brand too, so people know I grew these plants."

"Less overhead without a storefront. What names are you considering?"

"Nothing so far. Brindle expects me to create a business plan, but I don't have a full vision of the scope of my operation yet. I just want to grow plants and work in our family business."

Harley trotted over to investigate, and I scooped him up in my arms. "Your reply, while interesting, didn't help me in the name suggestion department. What about The Plant Store, The Plant Shop, or The Secret Garden?"

"None of those will work. Those are already existing chain nurseries, and Savannah has a nursery named Savannah's Secret Garden."

"This is harder than I thought. Will you only sell native plants?"

"Don't know. This dream is too new, too shiny to rein it in. I need to work for myself, and the business can't be all-consuming. I want time with Brindle, with family, and with our shop."

"Oh, I see. So, something like The Bossy Slacker for a business moniker?"

Sage snorted out a laugh then covered her mouth. "Hilarious, but no thanks. Never mind. The right name will surface in due time."

"And maybe this new killer haunting Savannah has nothing to do with our family or work."

"Very funny. Somehow we've become a first stop for those two city detectives."

The air smelled forest fresh, and I loved it. "They're running out of people in our immediate family and close friends to investigate. We should get a pass this time around."

"True."

Gerard had been a suspect recently, so had Sage and Frankie, Auntie O's guy. I'd been questioned every time but released thanks to the new lawyer Quig insisted I use. "Let's hope we're all cleared now and that investigating us would be counterproductive."

"Fat chance of that," I said, "but I'll do my part and seed the shop with good vibes. That's not why I came up here." Quickly, I brought her up to date on the new victim, tallowed hair, and the heightened cop interest in my use of tallow. Then I shared that I found tallow in the supply closet.

"Don't borrow trouble," Sage said. "You didn't kill

anyone, and you certainly didn't massage tallow into anyone's hair. Worst case, they accuse you of this and you solve the case for them. It's still a win for you."

Maybe. But it felt more like that storm of life I sensed. We knew a lot about storms on the Georgia coast. They came and they went, but the powerful ones always left their mark.

Chapter Six

The next morning dawned damp and chilly. Every hour or so a fine mist blanketed Savannah, and everything slowed down. Tourists were usually out in droves this time of day, but auto traffic had slowed to a crawl, and the scant foot traffic hurried into the shelter of shops, one lonely soul at a time.

My clerk Gerard took a bathroom break, and I staffed the front counter. I dusted a few hard-to-reach nooks and crannies, hunted in vain for an emery board, and tried three music stations but nothing suited my brooding mood. I strolled around the shop to sniff our different collections of candles. I loved the citrus the most, or so I thought until I moved on to the floral section. Flowers were the most soothing I decided, until I found the woodsy scents. Ah, definitely tree nirvana for me.

Harley, my black cat, stared at me from a safe distance, the uppermost shelf in the shop, as I aligned the Savannahthemed books on the shelves. I flounced down on the wicker furniture, but I couldn't stay put. My intuition warned me to keep moving.

Looking up, I caught my cat's eye again. Harley didn't want anything to do with my nervous energy. Even so, his gaze flicked between me and the door. I paused long enough to wonder if he sensed trouble on the way.

Then a very familiar detective's car parked in front of the shop. My stomach cartwheeled into my ribs. Oh, no. I darted behind the sales counter for good measure and looked again. Only one cop in the car. Nowry. Ugh. Why hadn't I listened to my intuition to flee? My day plunged from edgy to full-on disaster mode. I grabbed my purse and raincoat from the back room and stuffed them under the sales counter, just in case, though I considered hightailing it through the alley. I had nothing to say to law enforcement.

I keyed up a text for my lawyer. "Need help. Detective Nowry just arrived. Am certain he will take me in for questioning." Took me two seconds to decide to send the message now instead of waiting. The message went to Herbert R. Ellis, as Nowry exited his vehicle.

Herbert, pronounced Herb-it, texted back. "I will meet you at the station if it comes to that. Don't tell him anything."

"I won't." I pocketed my phone after sending that message.

No time to whine. Damage control came first. I hollered to the back room, "Gerard, Detective Nowry is here. Bet I've won another interview ticket."

"Don't worry about the shop," he called through the bathroom door. "I'll hide out back here until he's gone."

"Okay, but I'll make a show of locking the door if he makes me go with him. Maybe that action will make him feel guilty about hauling me in again."

This time Detective Nowry charged inside like Uga, the University of Georgia's bulldog mascot. The pep in his step contrasted with his troubled aura as he entered the shop. What was this? He didn't want to be doing this? I should be so lucky.

I barely heard the door chime due to my loud thoughts. Again, my intuition urged me to run and hide because he came here for me. Since running would add to my perceived guilt and hiding would only delay the inevitable, I stayed put. Dang, I hated to grit this out.

I'd rather be stranded on a sandbar facing a killer rip current—or getting a root canal from my dentist.

"Ms. Winslow, we need you at the station," Nowry said. "Come with me."

"Am I under arrest?" Given the state of my frayed nerves that came out rather well.

He quartered the shop as if trouble lurked among the ferns, candles, art, and books. "You aren't under arrest. We have new questions for you based on your expertise, and Captain Haynes requested to sit in this interview."

I'd seen photos of Captain Kenzo Haynes in the newspaper. His quotes in articles seemed well-thought-out and intelligent. I doubted he'd be so even-keeled with me, a potential suspect.

"This is about my tallow soap bases? I can't believe they're relevant to your cases."

He stared at me without responding. I tried again. "How long will I be gone? I'm trying to run a business here."

"I don't answer questions from persons of interest in a murder case."

Air leaked from my lungs. This wasn't good. Mental note. I probably topped their suspect list, given this repeat visit. "You have new evidence?"

"Come with me, Ms. Winslow. You know the drill."

I did indeed know the drill. I would be treated like a person unless I refused. Then I'd be cuffed, searched, and stuffed in the back seat like the street toughs Nowry often dealt with. I much preferred to go under my own power.

As I reached for my coat and purse, Harley jumped down from his high perch and darted through the stillroom doorway. Guess he didn't care for Nowry either.

Nowy walked around the car after inserting me in the back seat. Quickly, I texted Herbert Ellis that I was in the cop car and was a person of interest in a murder case.

He replied immediately that he would meet me at the station. I sent Sage a twin-link message about what happened, and she replied with cuss words. Then she said she'd let Quig know.

The ominous silence in the car indicated this interview would be different. These cops had decided that a thirty-year-old respectable shopkeeper also had a serial killer nature. As an energetic psychic who wished to keep a low profile, I had plenty to hide, but I wasn't a villain.

Knowing I was innocent, I reviewed my appearance to make sure I hadn't accidentally dressed for the day in a dark hoodie or had a serial killer's stash of cut-out magazine alphabet letters in my purse. No worries. I wore professional attire, and my hair was secured in a low ponytail. I had, of course, remembered to don fresh underwear and brush my teeth this morning, so that covered my appearance and hygiene concerns. With a bit of luck and Herbert Ellis, this would resolve quickly.

Between the weather, stop lights and tour buses, we made poor time to the station. Herbert stood by the cop shop's door. He raised his hand in greeting, causing Nowry to let out a string of profanity, rivaling Sage's earlier swear-a-thon. "Why'd you go and do that?" he asked.

"Having three cops grill me isn't fair," I said. "I have to protect my interests. My family depends on me."

More deep grumbling came from the front seat. "Captain Haynes won't like this."

I flashed him a steely smile after he let me out. I didn't give a rip about what Captain Kenzo Haynes thought. I beamed a genuine smile for Herbert after I trotted up the steps. "Thank you for coming."

"My pleasure." Herbert Ellis and Detective Nowry did that terse manly head tilt of acknowledgment. "I'd like a few moments to confer with my client, Detective."

"Captain's really not going to like this," Nowry mumbled.

When he'd gone inside the door to wait, Herbert turned to me. "What happened?"

"Tallow is involved with the serial killer cases as hair pomade, and they're freaking out because tallow is an ingredient in some soaps and candles. Therefore, in their minds, I must be a serial killer."

"Do you use tallow in your shop?"

"Not in candles. I use a preblended base containing tallow for soaps. They came and talked to me yesterday about tallow, and I gave them a sample of my blended tallow soap base. Once I told them I didn't buy tallow by itself they left. But..." My voice trailed off as my gaze lifted to the single cloud in the sky, an outlier just like me.

"But what?"

Upon feeling my fingernails digging into my palms, I relaxed my fisted hands. "Stashed in the back of a supply cabinet, I later found an old tub of beef tallow my aunt used a few years ago. Since someone tried to frame my employee a few months ago by hiding a murder weapon in my stillroom, I panicked. I concealed the tub elsewhere in the shop because I also worry they check my trash every day."

His brow furrowed. "If they obtain a search warrant today, will they find it?"

"Probably not. I never knew the secret compartment existed until last year."

"Let's hope they don't search your place. After the interview, we'll talk about that tallow. Don't react in any way if they ask you about tallow. For that matter, don't react to or answer any questions about your family, your shop, or your boyfriend."

My turn to look startled. I couldn't quite catch my breath. Fear bit hard. "Quig's in trouble?"

"He's sequestered in a called meeting today. Rumor is certain people in county management want to make the new wonder doc the M.E. They've encouraged Chang to tattle anytime Quig shorts the county on work hours."

The fear intensified. I literally ached for my boyfriend. This was so unfair. "Oh, no. I bet Dr. Chang didn't report all the extra hours Quig works."

"Chang only advocates for himself. My take on this is the anti-Quig faction is trying to get him sidelined for misconduct or make him quit."

"Quig loves that job. It's one of his lifetime goals."

"Interesting. What else is on his bucket list?"

My heart sank. This plot to ruin our lives reeked like rotten fish. "Me. He wants to marry me."

"Well then, let's keep you out of jail. Remember, if they ask questions about the new cases, your business, or your family, don't respond. I'll take those. If they ask about previous cases, and you want to answer, look at me first. We want to give them something, but nothing important. If at any time my leg nudges yours under the table, stop talking. Got it?"

"Will they be circling me like sharks in the ocean?"

"Too soon to know. The degree of their tenacity and edge will indicate how serious this is."

"You expect me to rate that for you?"

"I'll do it. No sense in wasting an ounce of your positive energy on them. They don't deserve it anyway." His grin spread from ear to ear. "They want to know what you know, but they're oddly reluctant to come right out and admit it."

~*~

With five people crowded in the interview room, the air grew warm and stale. As Detective Nowry predicted, the robust Captain Haynes positively bristled with irritation at the sight of Herbert Ellis sitting beside me. The captain sat across from me, flanked by Detectives Nowry and Belfor who both remained standing. Guess you had to have bars on your cop shoulders if you wanted a seat.

"Did you kill Jerry Meldrim?" Captain Haynes began.

I answered without thinking. "I did not. I don't even know how he died."

That earned me a leg nudge from my attorney. "Sorry," I whispered to him.

Nowry gave me a gotcha look, which I ignored.

The captain crowded the table, bathing me with his cigar breath. "Where were you two nights ago?"

Herbert gave me the go-ahead. "Home with Quig, same as I am every night. Why don't you ask him?"

"We will."

Then he asked more questions to which Herbert Ellis answered, "No comment."

Captain Haynes shifted in his seat, then leaned forward, his cop eyes drilling into mine. "How'd you solve those other cases, young lady? I want an answer this time."

I looked at Herbert, and he nodded. "I kept turning over rocks. Eventually the right critters crawled out."

Haynes tapped his index finger on the table. "Seriously, how'd you do it? Nowry and Belfor are my best detectives, and you discovered information they didn't in their investigations."

Herbert didn't answer, so I looked over at him again. He pulled his hooded gaze from Belfor and nodded, thinking I wanted to answer. Sheesh! "I figured out who were the people in the victim's lives, and then I learned more about them. Sometimes I talked to the suspects. That's all. The clerks in our shop helped, as did my sister."

Though his eyes narrowed a bit, Haynes let the silence

yawn between us as he settled back in his plastic chair. "In other words, you got lucky."

His dismissive tone set my teeth on edge. Dangerous currents swirled inside me. "I made my own luck."

"Same difference."

"No, it isn't. That's why I discovered the actual truth, instead of a circumstantial truth your cops wanted everyone to believe." My words bounced off him like big raindrops and were ignored.

"What about those rumors concerning your family?"

If looks could kill, mine would've done the deed. "I don't know what you're talking about."

"Gossip about my client's family is irrelevant, Captain," Herbert said in a rumbling voice that would've made glass rattle in windows. I winced internally. Matching anger with anger was a terrible idea. The vibe in this room skewed heavily toward negativity now.

I showered my lawyer with calming energy, but he kept glaring at the cops. His aura pulsed menacingly. Nowry and Belfor retreated a step, but Captain Haynes met his gaze with equal determination, though his aura looked puny in comparison.

Haynes smacked his palm on the table. "I'll determine what's relevant. Answer the question, Ms. Winslow."

"I don't know what you mean, Captain." I paused for a breath. "My family are hardworking Americans who have lived in Savannah for three generations and counting. My sister and I carry on the family trade in The Book and Candle Shop."

"Not that." He made a dismissive motion with his hand. "I'm talking about the ghost stuff. My entire career has proved that where there's smoke there's fire. Savannah people are leery of the Winslows. Are you witches?"

He had no idea who we were or what we could do because witchy things weren't part of it. Darned if I would tell him anything about our abilities. Perversely, I radiated a sense of calm and bathed the room in good energy. "We are not. Are you a witch?"

"We ask the questions here. Times have changed. No one burns witches anymore. I repeat, what are you?"

"I'm a native of Savannah, Georgia."

"That tells me nothing."

Ha! He'd forgotten to ask me a question. No response was needed. I sat and continued to radiate good energy. Herbert and Belfor stared at each other with stark longing. I nudged Herbert three times under the table.

Finally my attorney stirred to say, "My client is an upstanding citizen with no criminal history. She came here willingly and is not under arrest. However, if you pull her in here again without due cause, I will file a harassment suit on her behalf against the department and your detectives."

The heck with this. The heck with Captain Haynes. I'd had enough of accusations and finger pointing. Time to be bold. I stood abruptly. "Let's go."

So we left.

Once we got outside under blue skies, I jumped for joy. "I can't believe that worked."

"You did it. Your good energy changed the outcome of that meeting. The way it looked to me, the captain expected to put you in jail tonight and declare a win before his higher ups demand he call the FBI into this case. Instead you walked out of there a free woman. Your aura is a powerful tool. If you'd studied as a lawyer, you could've made a fortune defending wrongly accused people."

Somehow Herbert knew about energetics, which meant he likely had secrets of his own. That worked for both of us. "Funny thing about that. Initially, I had no intention of neutralizing the negativity, until you lost it. I can't do that for an extended time due to the energy burn. That old saying of 'for every action there is an equal and opposite reaction' is true. In fact, that's how we lost my mom last year. She shared too much energy to a friend with cancer. She ran out of life."

"That was kind of her to help a friend." He paused for a moment. "Why didn't she draw from the universal energy like Reiki users do so as not to deplete her reserves?"

"Our talent is limited to our energy and that of others. As far as I know, we've never been able to pull from the universe at large, though we do adore a windy beach." I stopped to take his measure. "So, how much trouble am I in?"

"Not much presently, but new findings can escalate the situation fast. Whatever happens, don't write anything about this case or tallow on paper or your tech devices, especially not text messages. Even if you erase digital files, a good specialist can find them. Caution your inner circle to be extra careful as well."

"Got it. What about the old tallow I found?"

"Get rid of it. You don't want them to find it on your property."

Easier said than done, but definitely good advice. "All right."

Detective Belfor pulled up and honked. Herbert glanced up in surprise, then he grinned and waved at his former girlfriend. He glanced at me. "We good?"

"Yep."

~*~

I marched home on auto-pilot, plans churning in my head. Those detectives hadn't listened to logic and reason last year when a murder weapon ended up in my stillroom. I couldn't rely on them to make the right call if they discovered the tallow. Dumping that thick stuff down the drain would foul up our plumbing. Bad idea, but I needed a good idea.

Reading between the lines of what my lawyer hadn't said, Auntie O's tallow was a murder accusation waiting to happen. No point in harboring anything that might fuel police suspicions. That tallow needed to disappear. Forever.

Tallowed Ground

Unfortunately, I couldn't make anything magically vanish into thin air, though that would be a handy talent right now.

When I entered through the shop's front door, Gerard hurried toward me. "Spill," he said.

I circled our table of shamrocks, leprechauns, and dragons. "Routine stuff. Captain Haynes wanted the scoop on how I solved Nowry and Belfor's last two homicide cases."

He shook his head as if a bug were in his ear. "What? They asked you how to do their job?"

"Weird, I know. Listen I need to focus on a pressing issue which will take me out of the shop again. Do you mind running solo coverage in the shop for a little longer?"

"Go ahead. It's a slow, slow day."

"Thanks." Gerard didn't know about the beef tallow I'd found. Not that I didn't trust him to keep a secret, I certainly did, but why burden him with this particular secret?

A customer entered, and Gerard struck up a conversation with her. While he was busy, I hurried to the stillroom and closed the door. I donned gloves, grabbed the tallow from its hiding place, and spooned it into several small plastic bags, which I then stuffed in a drawer for the time being. Next, I scoured the half-gallon sized container until it was squeaky clean and covered the outside with the contact paper we used to line our closet shelves. It was the perfect catch-all size.

Thinking myself extra clever, I took the repurposed empty container upstairs to Sage's apartment and used her cake carrier to transport it to Quig's apartment two doors down from the shop. The cake keeper I stuffed in our plasticware cabinet until I could return it. The empty tallow container went in the cabinet under our bathroom sink. I filled it with cleaning supplies: a slender bottle of cleaning solution, long gloves, slivers of soap bars, a pumice stone, and two small scrub brushes. I even spilled some of the disinfectant solution in the bottom in the container to make it smell used.

Back in the stillroom, I considered the three bulging bags

of lumpy tallow. Dare I dispose of them now? Doing so would eradicate the problem immediately. Yes. Time for this stuff to go. I stuffed the pockets of my dark raincoat with the bags of tallow and slipped through the alley, keeping to the afternoon shadows and blurring my appearance as I deposited tallow in random trash bins several blocks away. I checked my appearance several times in windows, and I was invisible. No way could anyone see me doing this.

    I returned to the shop, tossed my nitrile gloves in the trash, and hung up my wet coat on a wall hook, hoping against hope I hadn't made my situation worse. If anyone found tallow in our apartments or shop, it would be because someone tried to frame a member of our family. Again.

Chapter Seven

When my sister declared the next day a beach day, protests lodged in my throat. I dearly loved the idea of slipping away, but should I play hooky? I'd missed work so much lately that Gerard had run the shop solo for several days in a row. Auntie O could've pitched in, but she'd taken off for a few days to visit a friend in Charlotte. Anyway, I'd worked twenty days straight a few months ago, and it slap wore me out. We couldn't afford for our clerk to burn out, not with his superpower of sales keeping us afloat.

Conversely, I couldn't afford to be arrested. Sage, Auntie O, and I were all that remained of the Winslow family. We looked out for each other, and Sage and I needed to talk about the case. We thought best at the beach. Something had to give for this to occur, and I hoped we didn't pay the price. I squared our absence with Gerard first and hopped in Sage's car guilt-free.

"I need gas," Sage said as she wheeled into a gas station on the way to Tybee.

I nodded. "Ever notice how many Berry Good places are in Savannah now?" Officially the name of these filling stations was Circle Berry, which was the company's logo of a red strawberry rimmed by a red circle on a white background. Thanks to the barrage of radio commercials about how "berry good" the gas and market were, nobody called this chain by its true name.

"This company is acquiring busy stations all over town. Makes me wonder how much he had to pay for them, and then I think only a crook would have that much moola." Sage shifted into park and withdrew her credit card. "I'm glad the gas is cheap, though that's a relative term nowadays as all prices are soaring."

I watched the traffic in and out of the station and marveled at so many Savannahians trying out the new chain. Often a new business was viewed with suspicion around here until several brave souls tried it out. Not in this case. Cars needed fuel, and people had no brand loyalty on gas. Price point always drove sales when it came to fuel.

Nearby an American flag snapped and furled in the stiff breeze. The beach would be super exciting today with all this natural energy in the air. I couldn't wait.

With a tank full of gas, Sage turned on the road to Tybee Island, our favorite beach spot. In exposed areas on the narrow causeway, wind gusts buffeted the small sedan, making me glad I'd brought winter gear for our excursion. Rock music filled the car, and it was great to see my twin smiling for a change.

Soon, we reached a deserted public parking lot and bundled up like penguins on this truly winter day. The February winds whipping off the ocean stole my breath away. A huge gust pushed us back five steps on the shore.

Sand rose from the dunes and blasted our faces, making me doubly glad of our thick, wind-repellant clothing. The cold wind crackled with life. It reminded me how much I wanted to live, and how much I had to live for. I drew deep ocean breaths inside my body, delighting in that freshness.

Like arctic explorers we leaned into the wind and plowed

forward. When Sage lost her balance on a strong gust, I tackled her to keep her from blowing away, both of us laughing like hyenas. Finally good sense prevailed, and we sought shelter from the wind in the nearby roughly-sided pavilion.

Thanks to seasonal weather, no one else had braved the elements today. We had the place to ourselves. "Brisk out there." I blinked back the wind-inspired tears. "No wonder we're alone today."

"I needed this," Sage said. "Strong wind and salt air refresh me in a way city air doesn't. You must be feeling better too."

"Oh yeah. We both need this seashore visit. Just wondering, though, will it ever feel like it isn't the two of us against the world?"

"Not as long as others blame us for their murders."

Detective Nowry had called me a person of interest. Wasn't quite the same term as a suspect but kissing-cousin close. "Technically, no one blamed either of us for the recent murders."

"It's coming. I feel it," Sage said. "Those detectives consider our shop their personal glory hole. It's a matter of time until they strike."

"What can we do?" I asked. "Nowry and Belfor are like sharks on a blood trail."

Sage waved a red-gloved hand. "Do your thing. Solve the case, which forces them to disappear, until the next time they think it's us. We're figuratively trapped in a whirlpool right now. Long as a Winslow is on the hook for a crime, we'll circle the edge until we're caught in the downdraft, plunge to the sea floor, and drown in the deep."

With a sinking sensation regarding my freedom, I contemplated my shoelaces. "You're a ray of sunshine today, Sis, but I appreciate the strong imagery. Powerful currents are whirling around our shop. We're in danger."

"So, first things first. There's no tallow at our place now, right?"

Before speaking I double-checked that no one else had joined us the pavilion. "None whatsoever. Unless someone frames us again, we're safe. Nothing links us to the crimes."

"That's good, Tabs. Not much besides tallow links the crimes to each other. According to this morning's newspaper and TV reporters, all three manners of death were different. Victim one, Jenae Pendley, died from a gunshot wound. Victim two, Butter Rawlins, entered the next life after he got bludgeoned with a cast iron skillet. While victim three, Jerry Meldrim, passed away from an arrow to the heart. If we consider something fatally struck each person, those means of death become similar."

Her listing of the victims and their manner of death raised concerns. I thought the cops were keeping this varied means of death a secret. What caused them to release that information? My thoughts veered to our family defenses, our hidden talents that allowed us to strike a person with energy. Fortunately, less than five people in the world knew our secret, or I'd likely already be behind bars for harming bad guys. Being different created challenges in and of itself, but criminal investigations kept knocking me off my feet.

The edgy sensation intensified until I couldn't draw a full breath. I carried the weight of the business and Quig's love, both of which filled me with joy. Sage and I were in a good place, especially now that we had separate living spaces in the same block. Auntie O had come home, so I felt like we were all where we were supposed to be. So why the heck was this happening now? Dang it, I had too much to lose.

Or was that the point? Could it be another powerful group trying to wrest our property out from under us? And if they wanted us gone, why wouldn't they kill us instead of all this maneuvering? That didn't make sense. It had to be another reason.

Could the cause be a vendetta against me or the family? Perhaps, but wouldn't we remember wronging someone so deeply that they picked us off individually? Again, I couldn't get anywhere with this line of thinking. It made me sad that I might have enemies I didn't even know about.

Feeling sorry for myself didn't help. I had to be proactive and stick to the facts if I wanted to solve this case. "From my admittedly limited research, most serial killers strongly prefer one means of death. Their behavior patterns don't vary because they're habit-driven. Routines are very important to them."

"That's my impression as well, though I'm sure exceptions exist."

"In other words, it's possible the variation of means of death is a pattern. Or there could be multiple killers. Man oh man alive. We barely know enough about this subject to get ourselves in trouble." I shuddered. "This case is disturbing and creepy. I hate thinking about killers."

"Let's not make this harder than it needs to be. Cops will check the multiple killer aspect. Let's focus on one killer for now. If this murderer is killing in shorter intervals of time, it's likely his behavior patterns are becoming chaotic. That means his actions may become harder to predict."

A thought whispered at the edge of my mind. "Don't disorganized murderers have another name?"

"Spree killers. Saw that in my reading. That's a possibility as well."

I stroked the white gold locket Quig gave me and felt less addled. "I don't care what he's called so long as he's caught. I've learned that each victim had their hair slicked back with tallow. According to Quig's police department source, the tallow in victims' hair is this killer's signature, the unique aspect the cops are keeping on the downlow. Whether the bad guy selected tallow usage to implicate me is another matter, but that seems to be why the cops have focused on me so much, despite the fact that tallow is available for purchase locally at big box stores and other places. I don't see why they aren't hitting local stores to check sales of tallow. Some people use it for cooking or leatherwork, and there are plenty of other uses for it."

"Perhaps they are scouring local tallow sources," Sage said. "We keep saying he. Did you have an insight I missed? Is this killer a guy?"

"It's a place holder for convenience. How could anyone know the killer's gender at this point?" Thinking about killers, organized or not, made me irritable, and with good reason. Local cops didn't solve these cases, generally, on police shows. Often a federal agency became involved. When that happened, information about the Winslow family would be available for cops everywhere. "I don't see how rank amateurs like us can outwit a complex killer. This is a bigtime case. I believe the pros took sixteen years to catch the Unabomber. As the Savannah cops keep telling us, we have no investigative training."

Sage leaned forward, her face animated "Our strength is thinking outside the box. Well, you do most of the heavy thinking for us. Don't sell yourself short, Tabs. Detectives Nowry and Belfor are clinging to you jellyfish-tight because of your crime-solving success and your tallow-friendly career. They need you on the case, whether they admit it or not."

"Appreciate the pep talk, Sis, but I'm in over my head. This case is for professional crime investigators, not a civilian like me." I huffed out a harried breath. "How'd it come to this anyway? I never had crime-solving aspirations, ever. I didn't read Nancy Drew or Hardy boys or any of those mystery books as a child."

"You didn't seek notoriety. It found you. Now the universe expects you to step up and balance the scales of justice and karma."

"I followed along until you said karma. That's when I knew you were spinning a tale. Sage, we're in trouble. This killer is a big deal. He's not some greedy Bubba who wants something he can't have."

"So? You're a big deal. I've always known it. That's why I push the limits because I'm not the main event of our generation. It's how I get attention in our family."

"You can have all the attention. I hate being in the spotlight."

She smirked triumphantly at me as she relaxed into the wall. "Too late. The die's been cast. You accepted the role when you helped Gerard last fall and reinforced it when you helped me and Frankie in December."

"This is crazy sauce. I'm an introvert. I don't make big splashes. I feel like a pogy taking on a killer whale. Why can't I make candles and beam good energy to our customers? What's wrong with that plan? Crime solving forces me to do things I don't want to do. I'm a candlemaker for goodness sake."

"You're a darn good one, Tabs, but you're much more than that."

"I'm uncomfortable discussing serial killers, much less trying to catch them. And, cops can't consider paranormal explanations. Sometimes those are the only explanations, especially in a city rife with practitioners like Savannah."

Sage held her silence for ten seconds, then she tapped her watch. "Done venting?"

The figurative hole in my stomach deepened. "You won't give me a pass?"

"No way. If our roles were reversed, you'd pressure me to do the right thing. This is important work, and because we're energetics, we're drawn into the fray. I'm beginning to consider our energy abilities attract trouble. We're better off staying aware of the world around us and protecting what's ours."

Oh, to be two years old and throw a temper tantrum. I would love to kick and scream out my frustration. Childish, I knew. Now that Sage mentioned it, I sensed the strong current of power connecting us, even understood the basis of Mom's protectiveness. She'd kept the world at bay as long as she could. She didn't want us facing hatred and lethal threats as kids.

Little did she know we dealt with schoolyard bullying in our own ways. Sage had knocked the meanies down and run them off. I'd practiced avoidance and kept an energy barrier up to protect my personal space. But I'd never realized we'd drawn the bullies by our very nature of being energetics. Now bigger bullies wanted us out of the way so they could take what they wanted from our town. We thought we'd stopped them cold last year when their ringleader passed away suddenly, but it could be that they hadn't stopped, merely reorganized.

If our secret energy manipulation talent drew the wrong sort of attention, our problems wouldn't go away. They would keep coming and coming like ocean waves until they forced us out or they drove us to take action.

I hated bullies as a kid, and I cared less for them as an adult. Heck, I'd rather noodle for catfish with my bared arms than confront a serial killer. Maybe I could be like Biblical Jonah who ran away from his life, only where would I go? My very existence depended on me living here on Bristol Street, where the shop's location naturally rejuvenated me each night.

Protests aside, I couldn't determine a plan based solely on my welfare.

Sage depended on me, and I depended on her.

The family business needed both of us to survive.

Bristol Street had to be protected for us and for the next generation of Winslows.

Crap.

I needed to release my frustration, so I stood tall and kicked the pavilion wall. Repeatedly.

Sage scrambled to her feet, her eyes round as sand dollars. "What's that wall ever done to you?"

"Wrong place, wrong time for this wall."

"Get your head in the game, Tabs. A killer stalks our city, specifically in the Bonaventure Cemetery area. According to the newspaper, we've got three victims, all Caucasian, of ages twenty-something, fifty-ish, and retired."

"Looking for another connecting factor besides murder and tallow?" I asked. "Very well, I thought of something. We have a young woman who works at a fancy club, a fiftyish male fired from Bank by the Sea, and a retired male accountant who played in a rock and roll band. Thus, the band guy probably played music for bankers at the private club."

"Weak, Tabs, but I like that you're brainstorming. Keep it coming."

"Okay. Try this on for size. They handled money in all three places. Nope. That idea's no good. Money also flows through shops, stores, and movie theaters, etc. The suspect pool becomes too large."

"Money is a sound motive for murder," my twin said. "I trust that you'll save the day, and you'll be the hero. I'm content to have the role of quirky sidekick."

"I don't like being exposed. Competitors aim for the frontrunner."

"Not on my watch. You lead, and I'll zap our enemies."

Chapter Eight

After immersing myself in that seaside energy boost, I felt compassionate and grounded, something I'd been missing of late. Feeling generous, I gave Gerard and Auntie O the rest of the day off. My aunt decided to spend the afternoon with Gerard's grandmother, so Sage and I had the place to ourselves. All went well until mid-afternoon. A gaggle of cops arrived at our shop door. One handed me a warrant. It included the shop, the stillroom, and Sage's apartment, where I used to live. It also included Quig's apartment, where I currently live.

All the positivity I'd been radiating crashed headlong into the steel bars of reality. I glared at the intruders wishing they weren't here.

Detective Belfor looked weary when she served the warrant while her partner sported gleeful disdain. "No hard feelings," Belfor said. "We have to eliminate you as a suspect."

I gripped my hands together in the classic athletic photo pose so I didn't strike down the nearest cop with an energy spear. "You upended our lives on the last case, and I didn't appreciate it then either. To be fair, you had better conduct the same search at every candle-making shop in town. I'm calling my attorney regardless."

"This is harassment," Sage said. "I won't keep quiet about the way you keep targeting us."

"You can't interfere with the search," Nowry said, "so make yourselves scarce."

"We're not leaving until my attorney arrives," I said. Negative energy pulsed throughout the shop with every cop that came in the door. Every square inch would need to be smudged. Lemon and lavender most likely.

"In that case, Officer Willis will keep you two company by the shop door, and if there's any flap you'll be secured in police custody for officer safety until the search is concluded."

Sage growled at the senior detective, but we allowed Willis to escort us to the door. When I couldn't get hold of Herbert R Ellis, I left him phone and text messages. Sage had the right of it. This was harassment. I wanted to sue every cop on the force.

Sage called and texted her lawyer boyfriend. No luck finding Brindle either.

We watched cops comb through the shop. Five officers searched my stillroom in protective gear. What the heck was that about? Did they think I made explosives in there?

Of the two detectives, Belfor was the bigger threat. She appeared more approachable than her cranky partner, and a couple of times in the past I'd opened up to her without realizing it. Detective Nowry acted like a jerk all the time, and I never doubted that he meant to put me behind bars.

Are we good on the tallow jug? Sage asked.

Absolutely. I told you so earlier. No tallow in our shop. Took care of that yesterday and thank goodness. I know they won't find any pure tallow here. But if they're diligent, they might find the empty tallow container I repurposed for holding cleaning supplies. Should've thrown that sucker away, but a lifetime of frugality wouldn't let me.

I need fresh air. Let's get out of here.

What happened to our stand against injustice and persecution?

Screw that. If these are my last minutes of freedom, I want to be outside near plants with my feet touching the ground.

Good idea.

Sage and I retreated to the fountain wall at Johnson Square, watching the ant hive of activity in our homes and place of business. Officer Willis turned customers away at the door.

Even if we were allowed inside our shop before the day's end, the premises would be unfit for customers. There'd be fingerprint dust, emptied drawers, disturbed closets, and cabinets rifled through.

Mindful of foot traffic and a crowd in the square, Sage and I continued conversing via twin-link. *This sucks,* Sage began.

Majorly. If we didn't need to earn a living and if our energy didn't recharge every night on Bristol Street, I would move to a friendlier town. One where different people fit in because everyone was different. But we can't move, can't find another place like this one.

Can't escape either of those ifs, Sage said. *I wish our energy didn't naturally attract this kind of attention. Further, I wish they'd leave us alone.*

I wish I knew what they were looking for besides tallow.

Suddenly, cops emerged from the shop and gathered on the sidewalk, their excitement tangible. My throat felt as dry as day-old toast. *I've got a bad feeling about this.*

You and me both. Wonder what they found? Sage asked.

The chill from our concrete perch seeped through my trousers, numbing my bottom and thighs. I tried to project positivity, but my thoughts were locked on that empty, camouflaged tallow container. Had it shone like a beacon for the cops to find? Why oh why didn't I throw it away? Why had I given into my thrifty gene?

When Brindle and Quig walked up with ice cream cones

for us, Sage and I tucked into ours like it was the Last Supper. Butter pecan had never tasted so good. Maybe the sugar fix cancelled my worries, or possibly the distraction worked. All I cared about was the creamy delight on my tongue. Taste ruled my thoughts for a few hallowed minutes.

"Looks like they're done. I'll handle the exit paperwork," Brindle Platt said with a lawyerly nod toward the Big Exodus. "I'll scan the inventory list and make sure they didn't remove the shop's cash register system or other electronics that keep you ladies in business."

"Thanks," Sage and I answered in unison, then Sage added, "I'll join you."

After they left, I glanced at Quig. "I'm glad you're here, but I'm concerned for your job. Shouldn't you be at the morgue?"

"I'm where I need to be. First time I've ever had a search warrant served on my home. I hate their broad-sweep tactics."

"Me too," I said.

He drew me close and spoke softly in my ear. "You're the common factor of the search locations. They're gunning for you this time, love. Soon as I heard about the search warrant, I texted our attorney."

I whispered to him. "Thanks, I texted him too. This is so strange. I did nothing wrong."

"Doesn't matter in today's guilty-until-proven-innocent world. If they escort you to the station, I'll spring you, one way or another. Say nothing except Herbert's name. I'll call him again."

"Did something else happen?" I tensed, and he stroked my back. Oh, his touch felt good. I sank into his caress. "Why focus on me?"

"Far as I know we're still at three murders."

"Jerry Meldrim is the only victim I've met."

"I remember him as the intoxicated man who damaged

your shop property. Does booze link the victims?"

"You're the Medical Examiner. Did the victims have high blood alcohol levels at death?"

Would he hide behind his official answer of ongoing investigation? I felt adrift in a sea of monsters. Why didn't he say something?

"That," he said as his eyes bored into mine, "is an interesting question. While I can't answer specifically, they likely frequented the same parties in town. The other two might've had belligerent personalities like Meldrim. Heck, for that matter, few people drink or party alone. It might tell us the victims knew each other and/or their killer."

My jaw gaped. I hadn't gotten that far in my thinking, though his reasoning included several assumptions. "You're good at spit balling ideas. Ever think of becoming a cop?"

"Wasn't on my horizon. I prefer the puzzle of an autopsy. The wear and tear on a body reveals how a person lived and often helps in solving the riddle of how they died."

"Are there times you can't tell why someone died?"

"Sure. There's a category on the death certificate for that manner of death. Undetermined."

Without warning, he kissed me. Not a quick buss on the lips, something more, something I wished were private so I could be myself. I sagged against him, needing him. He broke off the kiss and whispered in my ear. "Not a word to anyone, love. I'll call Herbert myself."

I met his worried gaze and nodded. Then I realized we had company. Half a dozen cops and two detectives.

"Tabby Winslow, you're coming with us to the station," Detective Nowry said, grim as ever.

"Am I under arrest?" I asked from the safety of Quig's arms, dread rising like a tidal surge. From their serious faces, it would be days or years before I saw my bed again. If ever.

"You're a person of interest in the death of Jerry Meldrim. We're detaining you for questioning."

Rotely, I followed the detectives and sat in the back seat of their sedan. During the short drive to the station, I wondered what they'd found. What incriminating evidence was in my residence and shop? The empty tallow container came to mind, but so what if they found it? There was no raw tallow in my shop or residence. I'd made sure of that.

What else prompted them to run me in?

Chapter Nine

After they checked my purse and phone into the property room and escorted me all the way down the hall, I maintained a semblance of calm. Panic edged in once I entered the interview room. Except for the fact that there were solid walls instead of partitions, this small space could've been a work cubicle. It took everything I had not to cringe at being caged in here like a wild animal. *This isn't really about me,* I realized. *This is them trying to hang this on a scapegoat. All I have to do is wait them out.*

Wistful thinking as it turned out. Right away the negative emotions in the room clobbered me. The despair and pathos in here pulsed with ferocity. I barred my arms across my chest and shielded my senses, wishing the residual energy attack would cease. Good grief. I didn't even want to breathe this tainted energy inside me. I envisioned shooting micro darts filled with peace at each bubble of negative energy.

That distracted me for a while, and then I realized my intentions to clear the bad vibes had worked. The room no longer felt like a boa constrictor squeezing the life out of me. I could breathe again. Well, hallelujah. One thing was going right for this interview.

Tallowed Ground

But I was here, so that raised a few questions. What did they find to incriminate me? Was something planted in my home or business?

Ten long minutes passed before Detectives Nowry and Belfor came in along with the Eastside Police Captain Kenzo Haynes. Haynes sat in the chair across from me. His two detectives stood behind him. While Nowry and Belfor were very familiar to me with their salt and pepper personalities and looks, Captain Haynes was an unpredictable variable in the interview equation.

"We meet again, Ms. Winslow," Captain Haynes spoke in a voice that sounded as if it had been shredded by gravel.

"I invoke my right to be silent," I began. "I wish to have my attorney, Herbert R. Ellis, present during questioning."

He gave a curt nod. "I figured as much. In the interim, I'm placing our cards on the table. No response is needed from you. But first, I'll have Nowry read your rights in case you change your mind about speaking."

Weird. My attorney would want to hear their information, but they weren't waiting. If I protested, I'd waive my right to silence. I wasn't born yesterday and wouldn't be tricked by this ploy.

Detective Nowry recited the Miranda list, every right clanging like a jail cell door ominously closing in my ears. I acknowledged I'd heard them and repeated my intention to remain silent until my attorney arrived.

Captain Haynes shrugged. "Understood. Again, I'm sharing information here, and you aren't expected to answer. I respect your right to be silent. Here's where we stand. Our previous search of your home showed a long bow in the inventory list. We searched the same closet today and confiscated the hunting weapon. We also found a tallow container in Dr. Quigsly's bathroom. Pardon me, the apartment you and Dr. Quigsly share. Tallow and familiarity with archery are key elements in Jerry Meldrim's murder, a man you had a confrontation with in December. We don't believe in coincidences."

My bow? His words faded as I thought about that dumb bow. That relic was left over from Archery 101 in college, six years ago. A classmate and I took archery after watching "Hunger Games" at the Student Center. Though I tried my best to hit the paper targets, I found it hard to get the arrow launched and into a bullseye. I tried to return the bow I'd borrowed from the classmate, but the gal said to keep it. After that, I stuck the bow in my closet and forgot about it. I didn't own any arrows.

My responses threatened to come out, but I knew their strategy. They hoped I'd talk and waive my rights so they could start in with stronger tactics. As for that tallow container, I now wished I had thrown it away at first sight. I mentally railed at my heritage of thriftiness. Worse, by placing the repurposed container in the apartment I shared with Quig, I'd inadvertently implicated him in a crime neither of us had committed.

Why would they speak without my lawyer here? Wasn't that illegal for them to stay in here once I said lawyer? None of it made sense unless this was a loophole to exploit. A sneaky loophole to trick a naïve candlemaker. How depressing. The interview hadn't even started, and I already felt out of sorts. But no matter what, I wouldn't step into their trap.

Could I object to having two cops staring at me while the captain talked? I didn't want to hear anything without Herbert, but even a single objection would land me in trouble because that would be a spoken word. Argh! Keeping my mouth shut was hard work.

With a placid expression on my face, I stacked my hands before me on the table. I tried to summon good thoughts but that proved downright impossible with three stern cops cataloging every nostril quiver and cheek twitch. If I had the archery skills of the main character from that blasted movie, I'd use arrows to pin their clothing to their chairs and saunter out of here like I owned the world.

"We appreciate you coming in today, Ms. Winslow," Captain Haynes continued. "If you set the record straight right now, you could be out of here in no time at all and be back home with Dr. Quigsly."

Yeah, right, I said silently. Anything I said could be used against me in a court of law. Oh, how I wanted to touch my locket for comfort, but I wouldn't let them read my tells. I didn't want them to know I was rattled.

The captain cleared his throat. "Speaking of Dr. Quigsly, I'm sure you don't want any suspicion attached to his reputation a minute longer than necessary."

They thought they could get me talking by saying Quig's career was on the line? I'd heard about that power play already. Moreover, these cops couldn't fix what was happening in Quig's world. Quig broke no laws. Neither did I.

Sharmila Belfor stepped close to her captain. "By refusing to answer, you could sink your business, lose your home, destroy your boyfriend's career, and your sister's boyfriend's career, as well as put your two employees out of work. Uncertainty will resolve once you fully cooperate with us."

Her fake smile riled my temper. I could hurt everyone in this room energy-wise, but to what end? There'd be a video recording of what happened. I could fuzz the camera because it used energy. Probably not a good idea though, since they could then attribute that mechanical failure to me and Sage, since Sage had done the same thing last time she'd been questioned. One time with a bad feed could be a fluke, but two or more times indicated a pattern. In their eyes, a witchy pattern.

Where was my lawyer? How long did I have to wait for him? Worse, I couldn't stop the flow of questions in my mind.

Would I go home tonight? Would I be arrested? I didn't want that. Every cell in my body cried out for me to use my energy talent to escape.

Escape. Now that was something positive I could focus on as the cops alternated between talking and glaring at me. As if I could escape this fortress of a building. I was good and stuck, and they knew it. Better keep my wits about me, or this could be my new residence.

A quick knock sounded at the door, and Herbert Ellis strode inside. "There was a long delay processing me into the building. Sorry for my tardiness." He made eye contact with the captain. "My client and I wish to confer privately."

"Of course," Captain Haynes said.

As the detectives shifted to the corner of the room so the captain could stand and exit first, Herbert and Detective Belfor stared at each other. Raw emotion flared between them, charging the air.

Neither seemed comfortable near the other. Being caught in the middle of their staring contest felt prickly as all get out. Yikes!

Herbert waited until we were alone, and the camera light winked out. "Talk to me."

I drew in a breath through my teeth. "Thank you for coming. What took so long?"

"Can't prove it but there was a suspicious issue when the scanner at the security checkpoint needed a visit from maintenance. Felt like they were stalling on purpose, but maintenance was performed on the instrument, and it worked again. They scanned me for weapons, and I got here as fast as I could."

"They tried to trick me by talking to me after I requested a lawyer. Is that legal?"

"I'm sure they skimmed the line of legality. I'll request the interview tape to be certain. Captain Haynes is very results-oriented. You didn't talk, did you?"

"No, but it was hard to stay quiet. That must be what they count on with that tactic."

"Catch me up."

"During the search of our premises earlier today, they seized a long bow from my college days, six years ago. A friend offered it to me since she had several. We took an archery class, then she didn't want her bow back afterward. I kept it in case she changed her mind."

"You must be good at archery."

"I'm a terrible shot with the bow. It doesn't matter though. I don't own any arrows, and that thing must've been dusty as all get out. Look at my fingers." I held out my right hand, showing him the smoothness of my skin. "No calluses or blisters from shooting arrows or contact with the bowstring. I haven't touched that bow since college."

He shook his head, light glinting off his owlish glasses. "They hauled you in for that? Unbelievable. Belfor is so vindictive. I apologize if my capsizing relationship with her caused you undue distress."

Oh. They were on the skids. That was bad news. "Well, that bow and one more thing. They found an empty plastic tub I repurposed to hold cleaning supplies, the one we'd *discussed* before. But there wasn't a drop of raw tallow in the shop or apartments. I don't use that individual ingredient, never have. The empty tallow container is a holdover from my aunt's candlemaking days."

He nodded as he digested my information. "Sounds like a reasonable use of a plastic tub to me, but I'm not a cop. Still, this is much ado about nothing."

"Their show of force at Johnson Square where they took me into custody made it appear I was a dangerous felon, both with the search warrant and the *invitation* downtown. I didn't kill anyone, and I'm being unfairly targeted. This bears repeating. I'm not the only candlemaker in town, nor is mine the only local business that uses tallow."

"They must need an arrest. Regional newspapers have whipped the public into a frenzy about a serial killer on the rampage. You're the patsy this go-around."

From the dust atop that tallow container formerly buried in my supply closet, no one had been in it in a long time. I hadn't done anything wrong in tossing it. I threw out expired supplies routinely. "I repeat, I didn't kill anyone, and I don't use pure tallow in my candle or soap making. I barely remember how to hold that bow, much less shoot it. How can they detain me like this? Why don't they ask where I was the night Jerry Meldrim was shot? I was with Quig the entire night."

"Let me worry about that. Anything else I should know?"

"Captain Haynes was present again, which seemed odd. When I requested you by name, they said they would talk to me until you arrived. Talk at me is what they meant. They said if I didn't cooperate Quig's career likely would be collateral damage. That angered me, but I held onto my temper. They can't hurt Quig, can they?"

"Don't borrow trouble. Quig has more than enough problems already. Let's get you extricated and back to your shop." He opened the door and waved Detective Belfor over. "We're ready to proceed with the interview."

"Nowry will notify Captain Haynes." She stepped forward, advancing into the interview room, forcing Herbert to retreat to my side. "He's lead on this interview."

Herbert Ellis braced his legs as if he faced gale force winds. "Has my client been charged with a crime or read her Miranda rights?"

"She's detained as a person of interest right now. We've read the Miranda rights. This is a high profile case, and all of Savannah expects it solved yesterday. They want answers. So do we."

My attorney shot her a tortured look. "Let me expedite the process. Prior to the interview, I'll give a statement on my client's behalf. I promised reporter Liz Bryan an interview once we're done here, so you better believe I'll talk about the entrapment ploy that occurred before I arrived. Liz will print every word I say."

"You're making this personal, and it doesn't need to be." Belfor's words were clipped and tense.

"It is personal. Out of this entire city, you've singled out my client. You're harassing her to get a press sound bite and in the process opening the department up to lawsuits."

"Don't do this, *Herbert*."

I drew in a breath as she pronounced his name in the standard way, with a strong "rt" sound to end the word. He preferred it when people used his name as if the second r were silent.

His face flushed bright red. "I'll do as I see fit in the name of justice and freedom."

"Squabbling, children?" Nowry asked as he returned with Captain Haynes. "Thought you'd be bigger than that, Mr. Ellis. Shame on you for picking on a woman."

The cops shuffled into their earlier positions with Captain Haynes sitting at the table and the two detectives standing behind him.

"You're one to talk, Nowry. You pick on her every day and often all day." Herbert R. Ellis' aura flashed and sparked in chaotic dissonance as he sat beside me. Instinctively, I sought the bands of chaos and tweaked them into a regular wave pattern. Within a few seconds, he stopped glaring at Nowry and Belfor to give me a nod, as if he knew I'd pulled him back from the brink of anger.

I didn't know what to think about his sudden scrutiny. No one ever noticed me fooling with their auras. I'd done it for years, helping people feel better. Occasionally, I'd done it for Sage, of course, and a few times when Mom was failing and she'd used all her energy for transference to another person's aura.

I'd long suspected Herbert had paranormal sensitivity, mostly on the basis of his comment to Quig months ago that I was special. He'd been very happy to take me on as a client, and if Quig and I weren't a couple, Herbert had said he wanted to date me. While it seemed like the "Twilight Zone" to have two men wanting me in their life and beds, I did my best to look like an innocent nobody in the midst of cops and my powerful lawyer.

Belfor leaned forward to catch the captain's eye. "Mr. Ellis requested time to provide a statement before we question Ms. Winslow."

"All right," the captain said. "Make an audio tape with your phone in case the room camera malfunctions."

The detective tapped on her phone and prefaced Herbert's statement with her name, the date, the time, and place as well as a reference to the serial killer cases. She turned to Mr. Ellis. "You may begin."

Herbert also set his phone to record. Then he stated his name, firm's name, date, and his legal representation of me. "My client is innocent of the accusation you've leveled against her. Tabby Winslow is a Savannah native in good standing, and her family has lived here for a hundred years or so with no hint of trouble with the law.

"Ms. Tabby Winslow and her twin, Sage, recently assumed ownership and operation of a family business that has been on the same premises for three generations. She does not use raw tallow in her business, and the empty tallow container you found is unrelated to your case, and in fact is a relic from the thirty-plus years her aunt was the candle and soap maker.

"Further, the long bow you confiscated was a gift from a fellow student in Tabby Winslow's college archery class years ago. My client hasn't used that bow in over six years. In addition her hands show no calluses or blisters that occur from use of archery equipment.

"On the night Jerry Meldrim was killed, she and Dr. Quigsly remained together the entire night. Further, she's been unfairly targeted by Savannah PD, and I'll make sure the public is aware of this persecution. This concludes my statement on her behalf."

He fiddled with his phone and pocketed it. Detective Sharmila Belfor did the same. They glared at each other.

"May I go now?" I asked.

"Yes," Herbert said. "She's done nothing wrong."

I started to rise, my eyes on the door.

"No," the captain said sternly, rising to stand between me and the door.

Chapter Ten

The police interview began in earnest with Captain Haynes asking questions about the bow and tallow, all of which my lawyer answered with "No comment" or "That was covered in my statement."

The cops excused themselves, leaving us alone with the camera rolling. "You want the camera turned off to confer again?" Herbert R. Ellis asked me.

"No need on my part. You know what I know at this point."

"We'll wait on-camera then."

Five minutes ticked by and then ten. Were they trying to see how patient I was? Or possibly they thought I'd get bored and discuss case-breaking details. I was tired of waiting, tired of feeling like I was in a cage. Dark emotions swelled inside me, so many I couldn't handle them. So I released the energy for self-preservation. The surge of rightness lasted but a heartbeat.

Our interview room flashed from light to dark in a single heartbeat.

What? I did that? How was that possible? *Think about it, Tabby. You released an overflow of energy as a current. There are electrical receptacles in this room as well as electronic equipment. You are out of control.*

I drew a few breaths as the emergency lighting came on. That was a first, but it was nothing I should brag about to anyone. This needed to be my secret. Forever.

"That's a first," Herbert said, illuminating the room with his phone display. "It's dark as midnight in here."

"It's a first for me as well," I said innocently.

Footsteps pounded in the hall. Detective Belfor opened the door, with faint radiance from additional emergency lighting in the hall brightening our tiny room. "Everyone all right in here?"

"We don't appreciate the long wait or the harsh darkness tactic," Herbert said with a glare. "Sensory deprivation is not acceptable for an interview. I will report this."

"This is unfortunate situation," the detective said. "Sit tight for another minute."

The overhead lights flickered, then returned to full illumination. So much for my new hidden talent. It barely caused anyone any inconvenience.

Rapid footsteps approached. "Evacuation protocol is in effect. Leave the building in an orderly fashion," an officer shouted, Nowry hard on his heels. "Leave the building now."

"Get up, Winslow, and follow us," Nowry said, gruff as usual. "Much as I'm tempted to leave you here, I don't want that kind of heat focused on me. We'll wait for the all-clear outside."

"Am I free to go?"

"Your purse and phone are secured. I don't recommend leaving without them."

Though all the lights were shining again, and there was no

smell of smoke, I joined the throng in the corridor as we calmly exited the building. Outside, police cruisers blocked the street from vehicular traffic, and we were directed to a parking lot where others were already waiting.

Herbert and I stood together for a bit. Then he strolled over to Belfor. From their body language, their private conversation fared poorly. Herbert rejoined me. He seemed so down, I shared energy with him, a slow process since we weren't touching. Though he'd noticed my efforts earlier, right now he didn't do much except retreat into himself.

When they allowed people into the building, Belfor headed the line. Minutes later she returned with my purse and phone. "You're free to go. We have no further questions at this time."

"Thank you," Herbert said in a flat tone.

"Thanks," I echoed.

"What did you say to her?" I asked Herbert after she'd gone, and I'd shouldered my bag. It was dicey getting in between these two, but I couldn't help myself.

"I reminded her I loved her, and work shouldn't come between us. She doesn't want to see me socially again."

Poor guy. I'd hug him, but he looked like he'd aged from his boyish thirty-five years to twice that in a few minutes. "If it's any consolation, she seemed miserable the whole time you spoke to her."

He winced as he nodded, light glinting off his wire-framed glasses. "Higher ups put heat on her to end our relationship. Since we're on opposite sides of the interview table, our association is seen as fraternizing, although it wasn't stated so bluntly. They used terms like appearances and perceptions."

"I'm grateful she let me go. Thanks to her, I'm headed home this afternoon. Maybe she felt sorry for us, and that's why she retrieved my bag and phone."

"You. She feels sorry for you. If she cared for me, she would've responded when I poured out my heart to her and begged her to take my calls."

"I'm sorry. That is harsh, but you never know. Perhaps things will work out. Don't give up hope. Will she get in trouble for releasing me?"

"Nah. They planned to release you anyway. An urgent matter required Captain Haynes to be elsewhere, so he left the building."

We all left the building because of their evacuation procedure, but I let that pass without comment. "Am I no longer a person of interest?"

"They didn't arrest you, so that's a plus. Further, they don't have a legitimate way forward with a case against you. Their so-called evidence is flimsy, and it won't hold up in court. It would be a waste of taxpayer money to arrest you."

His words didn't reassure me. Quite the opposite. I gestured with my hands. "Innocent people go to jail all the time."

"Not on my watch. They may harass you again, but I'm off to talk with reporter Liz Bryan in hopes she'll cover the way they targeted you."

Some tension eased from my shoulders. "I thought that was an empty threat. I'm glad you're holding them accountable."

"Don't get too excited. She could write the story and the editor pull it, for one reason or another. All I can do is try."

I felt mentally battered from all the dark energy generated today, though no one had laid a finger on me. I looked for my boyfriend and didn't see him. "Did they haul Quig in for questioning too?"

"The cops aren't after him," Herbert explained. "It's the behind-the-scene folks in county politics who have a bead on him, and they're using his record of taking leave without prior approval against him."

"Why? Isn't he good at his job?"

"He's exceptional at his job, but he has political savvy and experience now, so he costs the county more than a guy freshly credentialed. There's a push for Chang to be the new M.E."

I saw red. "How is that possible? Quig is an elected official."

"He's also out of the office more in recent months than he used to be. Time he's spending with you, Tabby. You're his priority now, not his job."

Ouch. That was often true, but he made up the work time. "I don't encourage him to duck out of work, but he takes personal leave when he is out of the office for anything unrelated to work. Most nights he does M.E. work for at least an hour after dinner, not to mention the times he's called to the crime scenes after hours. And because I work Saturdays, he does M.E. work on Saturdays, often at the office, to stay on top of things. Whatever perceived absence of weekday time he has is more than compensated for during his after-hours work sessions. That man easily works sixty hours a week."

Herbert rubbed the back of his neck as he studied the sidewalk. A siren wailed in the distance. "Let's hope he accounts for his time to everyone's satisfaction. Chang would be a disaster at M.E. His social awkwardness would cripple him in front of a camera, and Quig heavily edits all his reports to bring them up to par. No one understands how much Quig helps him. They don't want to know. If past behavior runs true, political rainmakers are probably salivating about how they'll divert the cost savings in salaries to their pet projects once Quig is fired."

What I knew about county politics would fit inside a minnow. I hated that Quig had to fight for his position. "This is terrible. He could lose his dream job. I never imagined he would be targeted because of me."

"These influencers have a system. First, they'll rake him over the shoals to justify their accusations. Then he'll go on administrative leave pending review. Chang will be

Tallowed Ground

appointed acting M.E. in Quig's absence. Then they keep jerking Quig around until he resigns his position. That's the script, according to my source."

Poor Quig. If someone came at him, he'd push back hard. That would be catastrophic in this situation. It needed subtlety. "I need to talk to him right away."

Herbert scanned the area. "He's not here, so he's tied up elsewhere. When we spoke about today's interview, he planned to wait here for you. Trouble found him. Nothing else would keep him away."

The truth tasted bitter. Our relationship put Quig's career at risk, not only from his association with me but by distracting him from the approaching storm at work. I drew in a shaky breath. Both of us were vulnerable, with the cops nipping at me and the politicos barking at him.

I wanted to be with Quig and turn off the world for the night. These rainmakers, whoever they were, better watch their backs.

Blinking back tears, I tried to speak without weirding out my lawyer. "I'm heartsick Quig's job is under fire. The county is making a mistake. They're lucky to have him."

The need to act intensified until I couldn't ignore it. Though there was no proof Quig and I shared a telepathic link, in the past I'd shared an image with him that he saw. I sent an image of him with his seat belt strapped tight, a symbol I took to mean "be safe."

"Agreed. May I offer you a lift home?" Herbert said. "For obvious reasons I'd rather not remain here."

Those reasons most likely being his breakup with Detective Sharmila Belfor. I wasn't the only one having a bad day. In that interview room, Herbert had to sit across from the woman who dumped him for her job. "Go ahead. I'll call my sister for a ride."

"I don't mind running you home."

"Please, resume whatever you were doing before this

interruption. I wouldn't be breathing fresh air without your help, so you're much appreciated. I can't take up more of your time."

With that, Herbert waved and departed. I sent a twin-link message to my sister. *Sage, I need a ride home from the station. Herbert Ellis kept the cops on their toes, and I'm free to go. I need to get out of here.*

Can't break free right now. Catch a ride, and guess what?
What?
There's a big surprise waiting at home.

~*~

I grabbed an Uber and as soon as I let myself in to Sage's apartment, my aunt turned off the kitchen faucet and grinned at me. I was so surprised I stopped moving. "Auntie O! You're the best surprise ever. How lucky we are to see you again so soon!" I pushed forward for a hug and she obliged. I delighted in all of us being under the same roof again. My aunt had been a second mother to us twins, and with our mom gone, she was all the family we had left.

She smelled faintly of the rose-scented lotion she preferred, and her petite and slender body felt sturdy and radiant through the trendy tunic top she wore over leggings. In this moment, she embodied everything I needed most: compassion, support, confidence, loyalty, and love.

"Welcome home," I said when I let her go. My voice broke with emotion.

"Land's sakes, you're a sight for sore eyes." Auntie O patted my arm and ushered me into a seat at the kitchen table. "We have been worrying ourselves sick in here. Sage thought sure you'd be arrested. I was fixing to bake a cake with get-out-of-jail tools inside of it."

I smiled at the idea of that cake. "My lawyer tore their circumstantial case to shreds, and I remain a free woman. Thank goodness. Someone else killed those people. Not me."

"Of course not," Auntie O said, echoed by Sage who

Tallowed Ground

strolled out of her bedroom towel-drying her long black hair.

"Glad you're home, Sis," Sage said. "Sorry you got swept into a rip current of persecution." Sage blistered the air with cuss words, then she grinned. "I had to get that out of my system. Those detectives get under my skin."

"Mine too. I had a bad feeling headed to the interview, but I'll take freedom over jail any day. I'll prove them wrong because they made me mad. I'm doubling down on the investigation as of now, and I'll find that killer."

"I know you will. You're that good." Sage scooped up her kitty and flopped down beside us at the table. "Brindle didn't take offense you went with Herbert again as your attorney. Said if anyone could get you off, it was the man sleeping with the detective on the case."

"If only that were true." I stopped to gulp down the iced tea Auntie O handed me. It tasted like nectar of the gods. "Thanks for the tea. Where were we? Oh yeah. Herbert and Sharmila Belfor broke up. For this interview, their disconnect worsened my odds of freedom."

"Wonder what happened to them," Sage said.

I looked around for my cat. He sat on the sofa watching us, giving me cat stink-eye for the earlier intrusion of the cops. "She got pressure from her job about it, but don't quote me on that."

"Did the cops return your archery bow?"

"They kept it. I'm still under suspicion. How could they tell anything from looking at that bow? They can have it as far as I'm concerned. I'm unlikely to suddenly have hours of free time to practice archery." I noticed Auntie O's male friend wasn't around. "Where's Frankie?"

Auntie O's entire body seemed to lose shape for a moment, shocking me. "It isn't safe for Frankie yet. I sensed the gathering storm surrounding Tabby and I couldn't stay away. I had to come home."

Her fading was a bit like my invisibility talent. Did she

share the same extra ability? My racing heart began to slow as I reasoned this out. She wouldn't answer a question about her powers if I asked her directly. That was engrained in all of us from the cradle. *Do what you have to do to survive. Hold family secrets near and dear.*

Speaking of talents, I had a way to snoop on hers. I switched to my other vision to view her aura, and dark bands snaked through her normally serene currents, prompting wailing alarms in my head. My heart galloped again. What was going on with her? She was the picture of health today and yesterday, unlike Frankie. I'd never seen her aura like this.

Aware the silence had lasted too long, I said, "So, you're here to stay?"

"Sitting idly on the sidelines of life didn't suit me. I need to be with the people I love here on Bristol Street. My hands need to stay busy."

"Frankie didn't mind being left behind?"

"He came around to the idea, though he'd rather I remained in hiding. He's worried he can't protect me if we're apart. We contacted the tenants in our apartment, and they offered to cancel the short-term lease. Turns out, they bought a place on Wilmington Island and can vacate in two weeks. So I won't cramp your style for long, dear."

"I understand, but Frankie didn't look too good at the cemetery. Will he be okay without you?"

"Frankie is doing his own thing. Men, you know. They balk like horses if you try to lead them around on a short leash. We're taking a break, that's all. Hope it's okay if I use Tabby's room until I can move into my apartment next month."

"Of course," Sage and I chimed together.

"How do you manage?" I asked. "Sage and I can't live anywhere but here without suffering energy-wise. How'd you make it Florida for months and then wherever you've been hiding with Frankie?"

A muscle in Auntie O's face ticked as she turned to face me. "Good question. I have ways to supplement my energy, and the urge to stay rooted fades as you age. It's easy to figure out ways to not only survive but to thrive."

"Like what?" Sage asked.

I wondered if Sage was already planning her escape from Bristol Street, but I didn't wonder too hard because I was fairly certain our aunt wouldn't share her energy-substitution plan. A light flashed in my head. Was that why Auntie O's aura looked different? She'd done something different to gain the energy she needed?

"Like none of your beeswax, girlie. We all have our secrets." Auntie O made a show of brushing the flour off her hands. "Moving on, what's next on the case?"

Sage gave me a pointed look. I couldn't switch gears as quickly as they both did. I wanted more answers from Auntie O. Her secrets notwithstanding, she'd called their apartment hers just now. Was that a slip of the tongue or a throwaway comment of no import?

I shook my head. "Sorry, it's been an intense day. I'm having trouble taking everything in at regular speed. As for the investigation I'm running in my spare time, Jerry Meldrim's graveside service is tomorrow. I plan to attend as inconspicuously as possible. The cops can kiss my cheese grits if they don't like it. Jerry's daughter, Fawn, is a frequent customer at our shop, so I'm actually going to support her and do a little snooping."

"I remember Fawn. She changes her hair color a lot. Poor thing." Auntie O's brows knitted together for a moment. "This serial killer is all a bit shocking for me too, and I'm having trouble understanding what's happening in our city. Please refresh my memory, Tabby. Did you know the other victims who died near Bonaventure?"

This time the answer boiled out of me. I hated feeling out

of control, but for now I had to roll with it as it seemed to be my new status quo. "I swear by all that's green and fried, I didn't know Jenae Pendley or Butter Rawlins. The paper said Jenae worked at The Oaks Club. Pretty sure none of us has ever been to that swanky place. And Butter, his death makes no sense to me. He was a corporate accountant with a passion for singing in an oldies band."

"What do we know about them?" Auntie O stood, opened a cupboard, and pulled down flour, baking soda, and other baking necessities.

I dared to hope she was making a cake after all. "Nothing. I hadn't investigated either Jenae or Butter until now. Due to my history with Jerry Meldrim, I worried the police would misinterpret our fraught connection and they did. So I didn't focus on the other deaths until now, didn't think they had anything to do with me. That was a mistake, but I had no idea the cops would think I'm a serial killer. I need information about all the victims. Sage, can you ask Brindle for addresses for Jenae Pendley, Butter Rawlins, and Jerry Meldrim?"

"Oh. 'Fraid not." Sage blushed. "That utility I used last time we needed information came through a paid subscription at his old firm. Now that Brindle has his own practice, he pays for individual searches as needed, so that's a no-go for us. I'll search for their addresses online. Failing that, I'll find their obits and read them. Sometimes physical addresses are listed in obituaries."

"What about the phone book?" Auntie O asked, mixing eggs and oil in a clear bowl.

"Not such a big help these days with all the cell phones everyone prefers, but we can try that as well. Every little bit helps." I cleared my throat. "I have other news to share. Quig's in trouble. I've been texting him and he's not responding. Because Dr. Chang went the extra mile on that poisoning case, political influencers want Quig out and Chang in. My lawyer said Quig was undergoing a similar gauntlet at the county as I am experiencing with law enforcement, only his bosses are also questioning events at the morgue and Quig's daily attendance. It seems the interest in removing Quig stems from people behind the scenes, as in the big contributors to election candidates."

"My stars," Auntie O said. "I knew we hadn't seen the last of trouble, but I never thought they'd come after you girls like this. People have taken leave of their senses. Again. Or still. Way back when your mother and I were your age, something like this occurred and put our family pod at risk, Marjoram impressed upon those folks to look elsewhere for their empire-building schemes."

"What?" I shut my mouth. Took another breath, but my head still felt muzzy from this unexpected revelation. I'd heard "pod" used before to describe an energetic family unit, but the danger our pod faced through time astounded me. "You and Mom went after influencers? I thought y'all only had the run-in with Moxley McAdam Sr."

She nodded solemnly. "That we did. We chopped off the snake at its head."

"Details," Sage said, her face alight with interest. "I need details."

Auntie O combined her wet and dry ingredients and then shook her head. "That's in the past, and I won't disturb those ghosts for any reason. Besides, no two situations are similar, and this one will play out differently."

"How do we discover who's behind this?" I asked.

"Easy. Go to the funeral and take pictures surreptitiously. Find connections between the three victims. This is an urgent matter. Good thing I returned today. I'll run the shop with Gerard and Eve's help so you two can get out there and ask questions all over town. Once we identify the killer, we'll unite to remove the threat. Meanwhile, Tabby, you must run interference for Quig. Find out who's making waves, and we'll address that issue as well."

"All right." I secretly sorted out the numerous items on my to-do list: figure out what darkness tainted my aunt's aura, help Quig thwart this witch hunt for his job, avoid being railroaded for three murders, unmask the movers and shakers, and prove who the serial killer was. Why had Savannah's latest power group, after previously targeting Sage, Gerard, and Frankie, used the cops to rattle me? Now, it seemed, Auntie O wanted to help fix my problem and Quig's.

I appreciated and welcomed her help, but this was my problem. I shouldn't draw the only remaining elder of our family into danger.

The nauseating truth flashed blood red, as tacky as those Berry Good gas station signs cropping up all over town. Fact: Mom and possibly Auntie O had killed in the past to protect our family. The room circled around me figuratively as I considered the next question. In the game of kill or be killed there was only one winner.

If our pod's survival depended upon it, could I destroy an enemy?

Chapter Eleven

Decked out in my belted raincoat, rainhat, boots, and umbrella, I felt sure no one other than my family would recognize me at Jerry Meldrim's Greenwich Cemetery graveside service. Mercifully, thunder and lightning took a powder, so funeral-goers had only a downpour to contend with. I shivered at the dampness invading my bones on this chilly February day as buckets of rain pelted me. Jerry's service couldn't end fast enough.

In the same way my outerwear concealed my identity, most of the dozen attendees were similarly shielded from the inclement weather. However, Jerry's daughter, Fawn, was instantly recognizable with her blue hair, piercings, and Goth clothing since she wore no rain gear.

I'd visited this cemetery previously for other funerals. Eye-catching statuary, monuments, angels, fountains, and headstones filled the area. Oak tree branches formed a cathedral-like canopy over lanes, along with peaceful Wilmington River views to soothe the troubled soul. But while this graveyard served its purpose, it lacked the prestige of Bonaventure. Not that it mattered to the dead.

At the last minute, Sage opted out of this spying excursion, claiming she needed to accompany Brindle to an appointment, so I came alone. Since I wasn't family, I didn't seek shelter under the small tent for loved ones. Instead, I huddled under my umbrella to stay as dry as possible. Approaching the plot, I'd been mindful of where I stepped, hoping not to disturb spirits. So far, no animal spirits had mugged me, and I considered that a win.

A decorative urn of Jerry's remains perched atop a sturdy pedestal. The service was led by a guy dressed in a burgundy suit that coordinated with the other funeral home employees. Afterward he invited family and friends to speak.

Fawn stomped up in her chunky black boots. Her knuckles gleamed like pearls as she gripped the podium, looking more like a young teen than a nineteen year old college student. "My father led a troubled life, stumbling through addiction, loss, and more. As a kid I blamed him for his failings, but now I realize we all stumble and fall. His issues made him vulnerable, and I wish I could turn back time to help him. Funny isn't it, how death puts everything in perspective. He didn't deserve what happened, but I hope he's at peace now." Her chin quivered. "Thank you for coming today. Your presence means everything to me."

Fawn returned to her seat. People shifted uncomfortably in their seats. Had her heartfelt words shamed everyone?

"Would anyone else like to speak?" the service leader asked. There was a long pause while the man searched for movement. "With there being no other remembrances, the service is concluded. The family will inter the ashes privately."

Mourners expressed their condolences to Fawn and fled. When I stood fast, she approached, rain flattening her blue hair, soaking her black clothes, and running in rivulets down her gaunt face. "Thank you for coming, Tabby. Your candle shop is a safe haven for me and my friends."

"You're always welcome at the shop, Fawn. I'm sorry

about your dad. It's hard to lose a parent, even one with issues. That suddenness of a violent death or disappearance gives rise to questions."

"Yeah, I keep wondering what I could've done to help him. My mom hated what he did to our family, and I grew up indoctrinated with a litany of his shortcomings. I wish I had made an effort to reach out to him after high school, but I was too afraid of being vulnerable."

"I understand." This wasn't the place to share about my missing father, but I knew where she was coming from. "At some point we all have to figure out who we are and how to deal with people who make us feel bad. While this is hard, please understand you are not alone. You've got friends."

"Sounds like you've been through this. I'm old enough to think for myself but it came on so gradually I didn't notice. My tendency is still to react like my mom."

"We can talk about that later, if you like. I can't and won't tell you what to do, but I think you are handling this quite well."

"I appreciate that, more than I can say. My friends at school have traditional families, but my mom is still so bitter and angry. I can't talk to her about anything. Jerry broke all three of us before he left this life. I keep wondering, will I grow up to be like him?"

"Let's see. Are you rude, crude, intoxicated, irresponsible, or oblivious of the effect you have on others?"

"No."

"Relax. You're not your father. You are yourself. Hold onto that when dark thoughts come. You're a different person with different values and goals. And before I offer unsolicited advice, I'll change topics, if that's okay with you?" She nodded so I continued. "I'm concerned by the rumors that I had anything to do with Jerry's death. I assure you I didn't do it."

"I know you, Tabby, and I trust you."

"Thank you." Though I was relieved by her statement, I immediately felt bad for mentioning death. Fawn looked bereft and done in, so I stepped forward, hugged her, shared a quick pulse of healing energy, and turned to depart.

"Wait!" Fawn said, catching my arm. "Don't leave yet. I want to hire you. Um, I hope to hire you. Because I've spent so much time in the shop, I know you're a whiz at figuring things out. I need to know who killed my dad. I didn't help him in life, but I won't fail him in death."

"I'm not for hire, but lucky for you, I'm looking into his death to clear my name. Once I have an answer, I'll share it with you. Would you like my coat?"

"Nope. The cold numbs the hurt inside. I need to get through this before I feel anything."

"But getting drenched in February is bad for your health. If you're not careful, you can wind up with bronchitis or worse. Finish up here, dry off, and change into dry clothes."

"You sound like a mom now, but in a good way. Thanks for caring about me. See you at the shop."

I left, though I wasn't in a hurry to call for a ride so I walked for a bit. Poor Fawn. Her relationship with her dad had been troubled in life and death. Now their possibility of reconciliation had vanished forever.

The statue of a girl holding a shell-shaped basin caught my eye, and my steps slowed for a moment. Today's rain pooled in the nearly full shell, providing a welcoming oasis for songbirds. As someone who observed nature, I knew birds were huddled in trees and bushes waiting out the storm. Only when hunger drove them or they sensed a large predator bearing down on them would they leave their perch.

Perhaps Fawn had been like those birds, sheltering from the showers of her life, and now she'd missed her chance to know her father, and the chance for him to know her. That must've been a sobering realization for someone so young.

Like Fawn, I had a father-void in my life. My few

memories were of him tossing me in the air and both of us laughing, but he'd stop tossing me in the air before he left. He had been too tired to read to me or play with me. All he wanted to do was sit in his easy chair and watch TV. Then one day he was gone. He just wasn't there.

No explanations, no nothing. Mom wouldn't allow us to speak his name, and she donated his chair to a thrift shop. Sage and I adapted to his absence, but questions about him lingered. Was he dead or alive? He had no grave marker in Savannah, though that didn't mean he wasn't in an unmarked grave elsewhere.

Gosh. What maudlin thoughts. Must be because I truly empathized with Fawn. We both experienced loss and disappointment with our fathers. We shared a hollowness inside that we hid from everyone. Now cops were investigating me, and my future was shrouded in mist. I had to stay the course and hold threats at bay. Only I didn't know whom to fight and that made me feel vulnerable and anxious.

Worse, trouble rolled in as regularly as the tide.

If I didn't find the right answers, the Savannah district attorney would come after me with a vengeance. Given the bias people felt about those who were nonstandard, as my energy manipulation talents made me, my odds of fairness and presumptive innocence weren't high.

One oddity about today stood out. No cops stood among the mourners. TV show cops turned up at funerals and had blinding insights. Unlike those fictional characters, I'd walked away from Jerry Meldrim's service no wiser than before.

The hair on the nape of my neck snapped to attention.

Someone was watching me.

I scanned the area casually, as if I strolled through rainy cemeteries every day. No one lurked nearby, though I saw a glint of something shiny where it shouldn't be. Like a prey animal, I stilled, watched, and waited, using the cloak of immobility as camouflage. I didn't see it again. Was my imagination in overdrive? Or was I devolving into paranoia?

A few heartbeats later, a familiar dark sedan stopped beside me. The passenger-side window lowered. "Want a lift?" Detective Belfor asked.

Belfor. I sighed in relief that I hadn't attracted a stalker. So much for no cops being present. She must've huddled in her cars to watch the proceedings. Despite the automatic cop-inspired lump in my throat, I declined. "No, thanks. Last time you offered a lift, I spent hours in the interview room."

"Not my doing," Belfor said. "I'll run you straight back to The Book and Candle Shop, promise."

I shook my head. In addition to my innate caution, Belfor and my lawyer had a personal relationship. Perhaps that was in the past, perhaps not.

"You're a smart gal, though not smart enough to come in out of the rain. Sit in the front passenger seat this time."

Another cloudburst opened up making it hard to see. Though I was covered from head to toe, I felt vulnerable against such a force of nature. I grabbed the door handle and jumped in the car. An odor like old tires and yesterday's supper prevailed. Windshield wipers fought a losing battle against the deluge.

I covered my hesitation by saying, "I'll give you a second chance."

The detective laughed. "I'll take it. I strongly believe in second chances."

Her response struck an odd chord with me. "Coming from a cop, that's a strange philosophy."

She sighed as she eased out of the graveyard. "I don't feel that way about seasoned criminals, just beleaguered candlemakers."

"No offense, but Nowry's a tough bird. How do you stand being around him?"

"That's true about my partner. But, along those same lines, you're an odd duck yourself. I can't figure you out."

I tried to act natural but caution and fear battled in my head. "How so?"

"You're smart. You're creative. You're loyal to your family. You snagged the county's most eligible bachelor."

"My personal life is private. I don't talk about it."

A light turned red, and Belfor braked for the signal. She eyed me as we waited. "People made bets at the station."

"About what?"

"About how long you'd last. Quig's pattern is he dates someone a coupla times, then he's done with them. He moved you into his place two months ago. Nobody else ever spent the night there. Every woman in Savannah wants to know your secret."

Had Belfor dated Quig? How'd she know so much about him? I knew the secret of our relationship and his previous dating history, even if he'd never articulated them. Those other women weren't me. Not that I would brag about how long Quig wanted to date me. That was his business, and this detective was fishing. "First, I didn't know until this week that anyone else cared about our relationship. Second, it's none of anyone's business."

"Why do you say it like that?"

Again I hesitated because this woman wasn't my friend. Then I decided knowledge was power, and she needed to know this, if she didn't already. "Mr. Ellis told me there's a movement afoot to oust Quig and install Chang as the M.E. That isn't right."

"Herbert shared that with me as well. I agree with you. Quig does a good job. He's competent, professional, and thorough. Ever since he's been elected, autopsy reports stream out of his office like, well, the tide. The guy before was the opposite of Quig."

I stared at my hands. It was weird to be chatting with the detective, weirder still we agreed on anything. "I know what it's like when people try to get in your business, but I couldn't help notice you and Mr. Ellis were distant to each other during my recent interrogation."

The light turned green, and the detective punched the accelerator. "Workplace romances always go up in flames. At least for me they do."

I checked Belfor's aura out the corner of my eye, and she seemed off. Less vital, less engaged. My intuition flared. "Did someone in your command structure tell you to walk away?"

Belfor inhaled sharply. "Back off."

"The shoe's not as comfortable when it's on your foot, is it? I suppose lawyer-detective fraternization is frowned upon."

"I fought hard to get where I am today. Everyone has an opinion about my life, and the likelihood of pillow talk."

"Screw 'em." I clutched the armrest as she made a sharp turn. "They're miserable sourpusses anyway. Life is short. If you want to be with Herbert R. Ellis, do it."

"I could lose my job if I openly date Herbert."

I glanced at her bowed shoulders. "More to life than a single job. You'll figure it out."

"I wish you didn't make good sense. It's hard to be objective about murder suspects you like and respect."

Ugh. My gut knotted.

I still topped their suspect list.

Chapter Twelve

The next day, I rose with Quig. Once he left for the morgue, I turned on the computer with plans to dig into the first victim's online life. As I waited for the machine to boot up, I reflected on Quig's homecoming last night. He'd been mum about the behind-the-scenes jockeying at the morgue. All I'd gotten from him the night before was a brusque, "I'll handle it."

If I knew their identities, I'd snatch up those power brokers and punish them for making Quig miserable. He didn't deserve that. In the past, I'd avoided meeting trouble head-on because I didn't want to hurt anyone, knowingly or unknowingly.

Some twenty years ago, I aimed my talent at a teacher who watched other kids bully me and never intervened. I lost control of my powers that day and zapped her hard. She got a hunted look in her eye that stuck. A few days later she took a leave of absence for health reasons and never returned. Though I got a new teacher who didn't look the other way, seeing that my actions hurt my teacher stung. Of all people, I knew exactly what it felt like to be picked on in an unfair fight.

How'd I get on this tangent? I cleared my thoughts and

focused on the present. I needed background in the first two victims' lives. I started with the first victim, Jenae Pendley, the woman fatally shot near Bonaventure Cemetery. When her death hit the news, I paid little attention since it didn't affect me. After all, we have shootings in Savannah for various reasons.

Now that three homicide victims were linked by tallow in their hair and I was in the hot seat, I had to move fast. The more I knew, the better chance I had of identifying this killer.

I went to work. According to her social media profile, Jenae Pendley had worked as a host at The Oaks, one of Savannah's most exclusive clubs. She had the sleek feline beauty and luminous skin of actor Halle Berry. Proud eyes gazed out from her symmetrical face, capped by a head of short, tousled dark hair. In every image, she looked polished with nice clothes, makeup, and nails.

Like the actor, her smiles were lips only. No teeth showed in any of her online photos. I sipped my coffee and pondered that. She could be close-mouthed as in she didn't like to talk. But if she was introverted, why take a job where she interacted with people all the time? Or it may have no meaning at all.

Thanks to her online presence, I knew she had been in her late thirties, though she easily looked ten years younger. I studied her brown eyes. They had an old soul quality to them, as if she'd seen things beyond her years and seemingly insulated lifestyle. She had had her looks, her health, and a good paying job, going by appearances.

She must be into plants. Each day she'd posted an image of a plant leaf, everything from fern fronds to magnolias to banana leaves. Sometimes insects appeared on the foliage, but mostly a sea of greenery filled her feed.

I found no video interviews of her, no podcasts, no mention of her in subgroups. She didn't appear to be crafty as she had no products listed for sale on the artsy-crafty sites. I

Tallowed Ground

took a moment to stretch, stand, and pace to consider the information. Jenae appeared to have had a good life, one with rich rewards and beautiful things.

The analytical side of my brain brimmed with questions. *What got you killed, Jenae?* What did you see or overhear that cut short your future? Were you snapping leaf pics in the wrong place?

The blinking cursor held no answers for me. I searched for Jenae's phone number and found a listing that gave a partial address. My eyebrows inched up. She lived at The Retreat? Swanky neighborhood. Must've made very good money at her job.

What about her family?

I pulled up the newspaper's online obituary archive. No other Pendley in the records, but the digital archives didn't stretch back past the 1990s. The only Pendley death notice I saw was Jenae's, and it was as barebones as you could get, *"Jenae Pendley, 38, of Savannah died on February 20. Arrangements are pending."*

Hmm.

Did she move here in recent years? If her parents weren't around, who raised her? I made a note to ask Quig if her body had been claimed yet. Other than her leaf photos and the police blotter report of her death, Jenae felt like a ghost. That disturbed and intrigued me.

No doubt in my mind, Sage and I should visit Jenae's place tonight.

I shot Sage a message on our twin-link. *Let's begin with Jenae Pendley. She lived at The Retreat. See if you can nail down her address through your contacts.*

I'm fine with scoping out her place tonight, but you have the best contact on your speed dial, my sister replied. *Her address is on her death certificate. As the Medical Examiner, Quig is the Answer Man.*

I grimaced. *Bad timing. I can't bother him with this now.* Quig *is under tight scrutiny at work. He has to keep his head down until the problems resolve.*

It's up to you. If we don't know her address, I can't unlock her door, and we can't read the residual energy there.

My sister's boyfriend taught her to pick locks last year. Since then, we've successfully used her new skill to learn more about murder victims. Initially I'd wrestled with our breaking in hobby, though technically we weren't breaking anything. We left places as we found them. Thunder rumbled outside. Another storm approached. It should blow over soon so we'd have a shop full of customers.

Wait. A storm. Ideas glimmered.

May I borrow your car for an hour? I asked.

Sure. My key is on the kitchen counter. Brindle and I aren't going anywhere in the next hour or so.

From her smug tone, I had a clear idea of her preoccupation, and it worked in my favor. *Thanks.*

I jumped into dark clothes, darted up the steps to grab Sage's key, and hurried to her car. Before I cranked the sedan, I shot a text to Gerard. "Something came up. I have to go out and may be a few minutes late, but I'm working in the shop today."

"Take an umbrella," he texted back.

"I've got Sage's car and rain gear. I'm good."

Easy enough to say. I prayed it would still be true in an hour.

Chapter Thirteen

Odd how I never noticed the lack of tall vegetation at the morgue entryway before, but then I'd never tried to sneak inside this building before. The small facility not only housed the morgue, but there were offices for other county personnel inside too. Quig once told me fifteen people worked in this building.

With an eye toward blending in, I parked Sage's car in a side lot two blocks over so no one would notice this vehicle in the area. I decided against the umbrella as it wasn't a stealth tool. Instead I raised the hood of my raspberry raincoat. I checked for cameras and saw none. Good. I didn't want any record of today's activities. I strode through a misty rain with a purposeful gait as if I knew how to get inside that locked door.

Unbidden thoughts gained traction in my head. Quig would never forgive me if I got caught sneaking into the morgue. No problem. I'd make sure I didn't get caught.

I glanced at the dark sky again. Thanks to cloud cover, the ambient light tended toward thin, pale. I could work with that.

My plans for searching the morgue were loose. I truly

regretted I hadn't paid attention to the electronic paperwork trail on a previous morgue visit. It would've been nice to go right to the recent death certificates. Quig would know the location, but I was on my own today.

A man approached from behind, muttering to himself. I slowed my steps and to the side as if checking my phone. Dr. Chang hurried past. Perfect! No one else was around. When he was ten steps from the building, I faded out, drawing on the muddy hues of storm light to fuel my concealment. After I became invisible, I hurried to catch up with him.

Still muttering to himself, Chang started at the sound of my approach and turned. Seeing nothing, he quickened his steps.

He reached for the outer door, and I crowded close so that I could enter with him. I had to be close enough but not too close. I prayed my vinyl raincoat didn't make a sound to give me away and I crossed the threshold right behind Chang. Then I stepped into the central hallway. My nerves pinged at hyperspeed, making it seem as if time flowed differently around me. I hugged the edge of the bright corridor, and my energy burn accelerated without shadow energy. I needed to pass thru this bright light quickly, or the heavy energy drain would force me to become visible again.

Chang marched straight to the morgue, and I tailed him, step for step breathing as lightly as possible. When he unlocked the morgue's inside door and antiseptic-scented air wafted out, I hurried behind him again before the door closed. I paused just inside the entry way to get my bearings. Chang sat at a countertop desk, so I crawled under Quig's desk and hid in the shadows to conserve energy, though I remained invisible. Chang punched up something on his monitor screen, taking notes on a pad of paper. Suddenly, he pushed away from the counter, hurried to the refrigerated wall of corpses, and withdrew a tray.

After folding back the body bag, Chang examined the

corpse as if he were looking for something. Seemed like he did that for hours, but when I checked my watch, only two minutes had passed. Then he returned the body to the wall unit and left the morgue.

I drew a full breath. Alone. Time to move. I darted over to dim the lights so I could keep using shadow energy to hide. Then I hurried to Chang's computer. He hadn't been gone long enough for the screen to lock. Lucky me. Donning gloves, I searched until I found the information I sought. I memorized Jenae Pendley's address, then returned the screen to the page Chang had been studying, the timesheet records for morgue personnel.

Boy was I tempted to mess with his recorded hours, but no, I couldn't do that. It wasn't right. If Chang survived or failed in this system, it would be on his own merit.

Curiosity is a terrible burden at times. Since I knew where Chang had viewed a corpse, I trotted to the refrigerated wall of body lockers. Jenae Pendley was the only name I recognized in the area. Without warning, the door to the corridor snicked open and fear of discovery made me seek cover, even though I was invisible. I dove under the nearest autopsy table.

"What the heck happened to the lights?" Chang asked aloud as he brought them up to a full radiance.

Crap. And more crap. He was literally killing me by immersing me in a sea of bright light so that I no longer had shadow energy for concealment. What a dirty rotten skunk. Unaware of my presence or predicament, he sat at the desk, picked up the landline phone, and made a call.

Shamelessly, I listened his conversation, closing my eyes to hear without distraction.

"Hey, it's me," Chang said in a low voice.

After a few beats of listening, he continued. "He hasn't returned from the informal inquest." Another pause. "Yeah. I put the strip of paper in her throat as you requested, but I can't do that again. It goes against everything I've worked for."

Squawking came through the phone. Chang held the receiver away from his ear. "Yes, we're all working for a different outcome. I understand, but I resent destroying a good man's reputation. He's in there right now straightening out his hours. I don't know how the man works so many hours. He's like a machine. I won't do that when I'm M.E. No future in it."

More squawking. "I understand." He dropped the phone into its base. The clatter made my eyes open in fear of discovery, but he never looked my way as he stormed out again.

My ear tips burned with fury. He'd planted evidence in Jenae's body? I couldn't let that stand. I wouldn't let him frame Quig or anyone else for that matter.

Good thing I still wore my gloves. Heart thumping wildly at what I needed to do, I opened Jenae's unit, rolled out her corpse, uncovered her, and stopped cold.

Hurry, my blood sang to me. *Do it now.*

"My apologies, Jenae. I mean no disrespect," I whispered as the pungent scent of preservative and death filled my lungs. I summoned courage and realized I had burnt too much energy. If I didn't borrow energy immediately I might not make it out of the room.

I squeezed my eyes shut at what this choice meant. It was a badge of pride that I'd never taken energy this way. Good people didn't do that. They went home and rested until they recovered naturally. Screw that. My extra senses engaged and drew energy from living people in this building, squeezing my eyes to slits so I only focused on the woman's mouth. I parted her lips and reached inside, shivering with chills, not bothered by the cloying feel of the cold flesh, but from my grand theft of energy.

Nothing on the tongue or in the cheek pockets beside teeth

and gums. This was exhausting. I quested out again to get more energy. I siphoned energy ruthlessly from the building occupants and extended my fingers to the back of her mouth, trying hard not to gag. There. I felt something. I kept reaching until I had it. My knees trembled in relief. Then I covered the murder victim up and sealed her inside the locker.

The slip of paper went inside my used gloves, and then I stashed them in my back pocket. I desperately needed to exit by going invisible, or in mere minutes I would be too tired to leave. I hurried to the door. Through the glass upper door panel, I noted the clear hallway. I eased out of the morgue and ran through the corridor to the front door.

Once again I checked behind me and outside. An office woman approached. I retreated slightly, using her entrance into the building to disguise my exit. I raced through the driving rain for a full block before I dared show myself.

I hurried to Sage's car and drove away. My knees trembled with fatigue. I needed more energy, fast or I would collapse. I circled a different office building, parked, and reclined my seat until I was partially hidden. I allowed my energy currents to quest outward until I found someone. I siphoned a surge of energy from him, moved on to someone else, and so on until my body tremors ceased.

A dark place inside me whispered to keep going. I could sate myself on all these strangers, and they'd never know it, but that wasn't me. It would never be me. I wasn't a person who stole energy from an unknowing person. I never ran out of energy.

Until today.

I'd been invisible too long, nearly fried my body with the high rate of burn. I couldn't do that again. I'd come too close to the line. I might have gone into a coma or died.

But I'd saved myself and that mattered.

It had to matter or I was a monster.

With the car heater running full blast and the wipers

beating a steady pace on the windshield, I returned Sage's car to the lot and her keys to her apartment. Then I went home and showered twice. Wrapped in a thick robe and wearing more gloves, I unfurled the slip of paper. When I saw the spindly handwriting and the spots of blood, my heart fluttered.

I read and reread the words, hoping they'd say something different. But they never changed. *"To light a candle is to cast a shadow."* Ursula K LeGuin

Chapter Fourteen

Somehow I made it to the shop and tried to work. Despite my best intentions to act as if nothing happened, I couldn't pull it off. I kept startling at shadows and dropped my duster twice. The note, safely tucked into a plastic baggie in my pocket, was a constant, burning presence in my mind.

Those words incriminated me, not Quig. I was the one with candles and the one that used shadows. Whoever was running Chang had to be the killer. They wanted me and Quig out of the way? But why? It made no sense.

After my third oopsie, Auntie O sent Gerard across the street for an early lunch and pulled me aside. "Anything you want to talk about?"

I couldn't drag my aunt into the investigation, not for any reason but especially not when her aura was off. "The strain of being on a suspect list got to me. My sleep is so fitful now. I keep wondering if each night will be my last one at home." A yawn slipped out. "Sorry, I need more coffee."

"You need to go home and take a nap. A long one." She leaned close to whisper. "Your aura looks off."

Of course it did after the morning I'd had, the energy I'd had to steal to restore my baseline currents. "I'm not surprised."

"Go home and nap. When are you and Sage planning your investigating?"

"Tonight."

"Even more reason to rest today. Go home. Gerard and I can cover the shop."

"You're sure?"

"I'm certain you can't infuse therapeutic candles in your current state. I'll catch you up on inventory."

"I should fuss because you're doing so much for us, but now that you mentioned it, all I want is to lie down."

Auntie O made a shooing motion with her hands. "Go."

Fifteen minutes later, I was tucked in bed. My eyes wouldn't close, though I lay still and tried to rest, my thoughts remained in overdrive. Even though someone appeared to be forcing Chang's hand, one thought looped through my head. "What'd I ever do to Dr. Chang?"

That slip of paper he'd planted incriminated me. If someone else found that, I'd be having an intense conversation with the FBI and the Savannah detectives. Dr. Chang was a treacherous man, and he'd betrayed Quig. I hoped karma bit him where the sun didn't shine.

His complicity tarred him with the same brush as the killer. Not only was his handler intent on utterly destroying Quig's career and reputation, but he also intended to ruin my life.

While I couldn't identify this faceless enemy, I knew what Chang looked like. Dark thoughts welled and for once, I thought about embracing them. Every part of me wanted to race down to that morgue and drain every ounce of life from that evil man. I could do it. Except taking him out of the picture wouldn't take the heat off Quig or me. I yawned, surprising myself that I felt sleepy, and snuggled under the covers until I drifted off.

~ * ~

Sage knocked on my door right at five. When I opened it, she asked, "You okay? You look a truck ran over you."

I'd washed and dried my dark clothes and now wore them again. Sage was similarly dressed. "I'm fine. I have information to share. My day veered into wild and woolly territory. Want to come in? I'm almost ready."

"I'll wait out here. My day's been packed with fun," Sage said, "but probably unlike yours, unless Quig took the day off."

"No such luck," I answered, my voice catching in my throat as I added a flashlight and gloves to my snooping outfit. I pocketed my gear. "He called earlier and said he'll be late tonight. Some big muckety-muck insisted on a second autopsy on Jenae Pendley, and Quig had to observe, along with our favorite detectives and the feds."

Sage leveled her finger at me as I stepped onto the landing. "Tell me what you know."

My toe caught, knocking me off balance. I caught myself on the stair rail so I didn't careen into her. I had clumsy episodes from time to time, but this felt different, like something had changed inside me. Had I contaminated my body with stolen energy? Sage lived on stolen energy, and she never tripped over her own feet. "In the car. Not here. We need privacy." I shivered at the chill lingering in my bones. "But first I need to grab some towels. Gimme a sec."

"Why? The rain stopped," Sage said.

"Yeah, but I drove your car soaking wet this morning. Thought you might appreciate sitting on a dry towel."

"Yes, I appreciate a dry butt. Hurry. Tell me everything, and I'm not as patient as I look."

I snorted and then hustled. Once we sat on our towel-covered seats, I shared Jenae's address and how the new doc under Quig was conspiring to oust Quig. Then I told her exactly how they tried to trap him and me today.

"I don't believe you put your hand inside a dead woman.

That is too creepy," Sage said. "I need proof."

A lifetime of living with my twin prepared me for her show-me mentality. I pulled the sealed evidence from my pocket.

Sage glanced at the bag then met my gaze. Her jaw dropped to her chest before she could gather herself. "Wow. These mud-bellies are serious. This is all true. No wonder you're acting so weird."

Her truth comment smacked into me like a fish in the face. I'd never lied to my twin about anything. Ever. "Of course it's true. I don't lie."

Her eyes rounded. "My apologies. I'm shocked. Your news rattled me. You're a target. So is Quig. What can we do?"

I breathed easier. "Solve the case, the faster the better. If that doesn't discredit Dr. Chang, I am certain his handler will turn on him like a snake."

"What about this slip of paper? It's proof of Chang's betrayal. If you show Quig, he'll want the how and why of it. Worse, he'll realize you made an unauthorized entry into the morgue."

My hands strayed to the heart-shaped necklace Quig gave me and I felt a wave of comfort. "I hate keeping anything from him. But he's loyal to his superiors, and he'd tell them what I did. Even Herbert R. Ellis couldn't finesse me out of that pickle."

My need to clear my name led to this mess. Though we weren't married or even engaged, Quig was family to me. I protected him from Chang and Chang's puppet master because family is everything. Chang, it seems, would do anything to have Quig's job. Quig was my all, but he wasn't an energetic. His loyalties included me, but I ranked lower than his career.

Lying or omitting the truth, both of which he'd consider a lie, could ruin everything. I could lose him over the decision I made right now. Ohhhh. My jaw flapped a few times until the right words emerged. "I can't tell Quig about the evidence I found. Too many pieces of the story involve my hidden abilities."

"I agree. You must protect our family secrets. Tell him nothing about his vindictive coworker. We can't afford to be distracted by his reaction to our illegal entries, even if he already suspects how we enter people's homes."

I understood her logic, but this was about Quig. I had to protect him too. "I have to warn him about Chang's betrayal. I can use lawyer-client privilege and have Herbert tell him that Chang is taking active steps to get him fired."

"Herbert won't ask the wrong kind of questions?"

"He is sneaky good at what he does. He reads people and know what's what. He'll believe me without a long explanation."

"He's like us? An energetic?"

"Not sure, but he's way luckier than a lawyer should be. I'm tempted to say he has extra gears, but he keeps them tightly under wraps."

"Do whatever you think is right but make sure the family is protected."

"I will."

"Let's go have some fun. Time to scoot over to Jenae's place. We'll scope out the neighborhood before we engage."

"I'm ready. And thanks for not making me chose between Quig and the family."

"Of course, Sis. I'm not heartless." With that, Sage switched on the car and the radio. A Berry Good gas station ad came on. "Enough with the commercials, Mr. Berry Good. We got it already. You're a big deal in our city, so what? You can't make me buy your gas."

"Those commercials annoy you too? He is syrupy happy about his product, and it sounds false to my ears. No one should be that ecstatic about gas."

"He can probably buy and sell half the town now," Sage added. "Must be nice to be dripping with money. Maybe that's why he's happy, Tabs. He can buy anything he wants."

"Old Savannah will flush him down the drain one way or the other. I'm sure they hate his business strategy of mass domination, and his bright signs are tacky."

"Agreed. They'll send that carpetbagger running with his tail tucked between his legs."

Soon we cruised through the parking lot of Jenae's building. A sleek black sports car occupied the numbered slot for her condo. "Is that her ride?" Sage asked. "Looks high dollar."

"I don't know. I never met her." I paused to watch a woman unlock the door to access the three-story building and the unattended lobby. No guard out here, either.

The parking lot filled in more every minute. Lucky we'd scored a guest slot. "People are coming home from work," I continued. "If we go invisible and sneak in behind someone, entry will be easy."

"Scratch that. It's too bright outside," Sage observed. "I worry about you concealing us for as long as needed, especially when you had that close call earlier today. I wish I had your invisible skill to help with that."

"You have plenty of useful talents, like lock picking. I can hide both of us because you'll be picking that lock like the wind. Once inside, assuming there are no cameras, we can be visible again."

"Refresh my memory. What are we hoping to find?"

"Anything that looks out of place or doesn't fit with what we know about Jenae. Anything that connects her to Meldrim or Rawlins."

"Got it."

As I pulled white light to conceal our presence, Sage made fast work of the lock. Then we slipped in the building, summoned the elevator, and left the lobby. I saw no cameras

Tallowed Ground

in the elevator or inside the building, so I quit shielding our bodies in the elevator.

We were silent on the elevator ride and kept our hoodies up. Neither of us wanted to draw notice to our presence should the elevator stop on the second floor Jenae's place was the first door on the right. Since we'd hear if someone entered the corridor, I didn't hide us a hundred percent. Instead, I blurred our faces, which used minimal energy.

We opened the door and crept in. There were no sounds inside. Everything looked shipshape in the driftwood white kitchen. I opened appliances, while Sage checked the furniture in the living room and dining room combination. I found nothing of note in the kitchen drawers, cabinets, or appliances. Many lighthouses adorned the counter.

As I joined Sage in the large bedroom, I saw more lighthouses. Some were framed photographs; some were miniature replicas of different lights in various media.

I shot Sage a message on our private twin-link. *You finding anything of interest?*

Other than a bazillion lighthouses?

Yeah, I noticed that too. I admired the replica of the Tybee light station. It was the oldest and tallest in Georgia, having been commissioned by General James Oglethorpe in 1732 and rebuilt after hurricanes, sea encroachment, and a fire.

You found anything to explain why this gal was shot? As in something to keep you out of jail?

I glanced at the fancy closet chock-full of clothing, shoes, and purses. Nice stuff. Designer labels. Whatever charity received this donation would make out like crazy. I shook off my drifting thoughts. *Not that I know of, but what's missing strikes me as significant. Remember Jenae's social media posts? Leaves of every shape and color dominated her media streams. Not one plant here, except that dead husk on the balcony. If she loved plants, they'd be everywhere.*

That used to be a camelia bush. Sage nodded. *How odd. Seems like she would've posted pictures of lighthouses instead of leaves.*

Unless the leaves were some kind of code.

Trust you to make something sinister about plants. What if someone stole her plants?

No fertilizer under the kitchen sink, no gardening gloves, no stacks of empty pots here and there. Not only that, but no water rings are on the floor, by the windows, or in the sink. I stepped in her closet and scanned the racks of shoes. *And no gardening boots or sneakers.* I picked up one set of impossibly high heels. The bottoms looked pristine. *Look at this. These shoes were never worn. Maybe she loved to shop.*

Sage joined me in the closet. She checked several outfits. *You're onto something. Most of this formal wear has store tags.*

I wandered out of the closet, careful to keep my flashlight beam angled toward the floor. The large picture window drew me, and I switched off my light. What was her view?

Not much. A wide expanse of brown marsh, typical for February.

There's nothing controversial here, I answered on our twin-link as we left in invisible mode. *Worse, we found no leads to follow.*

Sage trailed close on my heels. *Jenae Pendley took her secrets to her grave.*

Maybe. I wish we could talk to her coworkers, but I don't know any members of The Oaks.

Me either. What a waste of time.

She pushed passed me to open the exterior door. Once we were safely in my sister's car and visible again, I spoke in a soft voice, "Butter Rawlins is the second victim, and before you ask, I don't know much. He was an accountant with a local rock 'n roll band named Southern Nites."

"How'd he get a name like Butter? Did he eat sticks of the stuff as a kid?"

"We'll find out."

Chapter Fifteen

That night Quig surprised me by taking me in his arms as soon as I returned home. At first I was relieved that he didn't comment on my all-black sneak-around attire, then I became distracted by his passion. We fell asleep entangled.

The next morning as he was leaving for work, Quig gave me a light buss on my lips as if we were an old married couple. I sat up in bed and caught his hand, needing answers. "Can you talk about yesterday's meeting?"

"My grandfather warned me this job could be like this, but until now, it was easy. Too easy. Empire-builders take no prisoners, and they caught me off-guard." He sat, grimaced, and looked away. "I won't go down without a fight, and yesterday's called meeting woke me up. Luckily, I document my weekly hours, more than sixty hours per week on average, to Human Resources even though I am on salary. That clear paperwork trail defused their allegations of any impropriety. Now they've called for an all-out audit over my years in office."

"You'll do fine," I insisted loyally. "You're thorough in everything you do. I'm sure they won't find deficiencies in your records."

"Nothing missing in my death certificates, that's for sure. But as M.E., I'm also responsible for the work and performance of everyone whose work contributes to my autopsy. I could've missed something in those tangential records I review and sign off on. All it takes is a moment of distraction to slip up, and I have been quite distracted lately."

My cheeks burned. "I feel bad about that. I don't want you to lose your job because of me."

"Don't fret, Tabby love. I wouldn't change a second of our time together. You are the best thing that ever happened to me, and I intend to spend the rest of my life proving it to you. But right now, I need to quench this fire at work. I'm pushing back, hard, so they'll get the message to leave me alone."

"Good. Bullies shouldn't win. How can I help?"

"Nothing. I want you far from this mess."

"Too late. My gut says your troubles and mine are related. The cops keep crowding me into the serial killer corner. They intend to arrest me, but Herbert Ellis has kept them at bay, for now."

"Don't give Nowry and Belfor ammunition to use against you. Listen to Herbert and stay safe. For me. For us."

Whew! He didn't ask me about the "my gut" comment I snuck in there. "I will, trust me. I would love to just be a candlemaker again." I had drawn the covers high and tucked them under my arms when I sat up. They must've slipped a bit because Quig drew his fingers across my chest to touch my locket, eliciting thrilling sensations from his caress.

"You certainly light me on fire," Quig murmured.

Only the thought that his career was at risk kept me from reaching for him. "Halt that rebellion at the office, and then come home to me," I said.

Quig took his time with the next kiss. "Always."

~*~

Once I was alone in the apartment, I donned Quig's robe, topped off my coffee, and fired up my laptop. Like my boyfriend, I had to get my life in order, and that involved research on victim number two, the man who'd died by a cast iron frying pan to the head.

Each member of the four-man band Butter Rawlins played in had a bio on their website page. As I listened to snips of Southern Nites' peppy oldies, I discovered the murder victim's singing voice had been dubbed "smooth as butter" at an early age and the name stuck. He'd changed it to Butter legally in his twenties, which he must've felt was hipper than Claude.

In the newer photos, the men in the band looked stockier and more hair-challenged than in their younger shots. They sported clothing styles from tuxedos to suits to beach shirts and khaki shorts. Their gigs ranged from Savannah to Hilton Head at the big name hotels, but they also played class reunions and other private events in the Low Country region.

Private parties. Hmm. Did this band play gigs at The Oaks? Possibilities cycled through my head. With nerves tingling, I searched the internet for Southern Nites and The Oaks and found nothing. Zilch. Nada. Zipperoo.

My soaring hopes crashed like waves on a sea wall, without the resounding roar of the watery collision or the explosive splashes. I was grasping at straws here, and it showed.

I sat back in my chair and stared at the dawning sunshine brightening the kitchen window. I'd been so sure I was on the right trail. Did someone scrub all online connections between the victims? Tech-savvy villains on TV did it all the time. Another flimsy straw of an idea, but it was possible.

Moving on, the obituary for Butter listed two heirs, a son and a daughter. One lived in Albuquerque and the other in San Francisco. Since Butter had been the band's point of contact on the band's social media pages, I had his phone number. When I plugged that into a search engine, I discovered a Georgetown address. As I recalled that

Savannah-adjacent neighborhood had strict covenants and tidy properties. I started to jot down the house number and street, but Herbert Ellis' warning about not writing anything down echoed in my head. I memorized the address.

The Rawlins funeral occurred a week ago, so I assumed his heirs had come and gone. Perhaps neither intended to move here. To test that theory, I searched for the address and the words "for sale." Satisfaction welled as my hunch proved true. His four-bedroom brick home was listed with one of the top-selling agents in Chatham County, and she was holding an Open House there this afternoon.

Hmm. Maybe I should go to that. I'd call Quig and invite him along. What better cover than a couple posing as home buyers? Then I remembered he needed to concentrate on his own problems right now, or he would lose his job. Drat. I could still go and use the excuse that I was unable to make an offer without him seeing the place.

On the other hand, I could view the Rawlins home in the sales photos without leaving home. Exterior photos showed a spacious lawn and a house in good repair. Each interior room displayed barely furnished areas to indicate the function of the room. To my eye the bamboo floors looked zebra-striped, and the glossy black kitchen cabinets, stainless steel appliances, and granite countertops shrieked bachelor to me. The bedrooms and baths, while functional, were unremarkable. If I'd been truly considering this location, I would've taken a hard pass.

Plus, all personal items had been removed. The bare bones furnishings looked so bland as to be sterile. Nothing of Butter Rawlins remained inside those walls.

What got your head whacked with a frying pan, Butter? Did you file someone's taxes incorrectly? Were the band members feuding? What were you doing all the way across town, prowling midnight streets near Bonaventure Cemetery?

Wait. The scope of my questions was too narrow. I tried

again. What did Butter Rawlins have in common with Jenae Pendley? Both worked in exclusive clubs. Perhaps Butter was Jenae's accountant.

Even if private clubs or accounting connected those two, how did Jerry Meldrim, by general consensus the town drunk, fit into this picture? Even if Jerry tried to crash The Oaks while Jenae staffed the door and Southern Nites played the room, what were the odds the three of them and the villain had been there at the same time? Pretty unlikely and highly coincidental. Not good odds to ensure my freedom.

Clearly I needed to chat up Sherry Doolittle, realter extraordinaire, to learn about Butter Rawlins.

Since Sage was helping Brindle with a drapery installation in his new office, I borrowed her car for the Georgetown excursion. Much to my delight, Auntie O offered to ride out to the dead man's Open House with me. The stop-and-go traffic on Abercorn did us no favors. I didn't come this way often, as anytime I wanted to travel south it was easier to take a different route.

"Where's Frankie hiding?" I asked my aunt after hitting three stoplights in a row. "Auntie O? Shouldn't we check on him to make sure he's improving? Your hideout must not be too far away since you went there and back in less than a day."

Auntie O busied herself with picking an invisible piece of lint off her patterned pants. "He's…in the wind, dear. For his safety and yours, I can't reveal his whereabouts."

My aunt's aura flared when she spoke. The dark bands previously threaded through her energy field seemed fainter after a few days at home, and she acted more like her usual self. I took that to mean that Bristol Street and family nearness had wrought their usual restorative magic.

Finally we reached the neighborhood, turned in, and located the house. Sherry Doolittle hustled out to greet us in the driveway. We introduced ourselves, and I said, "My boyfriend and I are looking to move out of downtown, and we'd like more tranquility than city life allows. He couldn't make it today, but when I saw the Open House you'd scheduled, my aunt and I drove out to take a look."

Sherry tapped the side of her face, sizing up the situation and my potential purchasing power, no doubt. "Will one of you be making the purchase or both of you?"

"I hadn't thought that far ahead, to tell you the truth. However, I'm keenly interested in seeing this house and the neighborhood amenities. Once I have an in-person feel for it, I'll know if we'll want to make an offer."

The realtor beamed her approval. "Excellent."

Since I'd seen the stark interior photos online, I expected a lightly furnished house. What I hadn't expected, despite everything being shipshape, freshly painted, and spartan, was the "tired" feeling of the house. Butter Rawlins must have been an unhappy person to imbue this house with so much weariness.

In case the agent had inside information on Butter, I tested the waters. "I read in his obituary that he played in a band, but I don't see any instruments here."

"The daughter took his guitars, the son called dibs on the keyboard. That's all they wanted of his personal property. I couldn't believe they weren't sentimental about their father. To tell you the truth, both kids will sell the instruments. Neither of them are musically inclined."

I shuddered. "That's cold. My sister and I kept most of my mother's items, and she's been gone for months."

"Not everyone gets a loving family," Sherry said, continuing to spill the beans in hope of a contract. "Both were open about their windfall from his estate. The daughter wants a boob job. The son dreams of upgrading his pickup truck."

"No one asked my opinion," Auntie O said from beside me, her voice very much instructional in tone, "but I feel compelled to share it. Disposing of a loved one's belongings is difficult. People react to death differently. Those kids may appear distant and cold based on their actions, but they did what's right for them. Tabby, I know you're interested in this location, but I don't see you in this house. Not now, not in a million years."

I glanced around Sherry Doolittle, wondering what my aunt was doing. Being critical could shut down the flow of information. That wasn't the right strategy.

The agent scowled at my aunt, then flashed me her best trust-me smile. "Let's not get sidetracked, Ms. Winslow. This neighborhood is highly sought after. The property values will increase here due to the property owners association enforcing the covenants. Plus, the demographic here skews toward couples your age. There are pickle ball groups, book clubs, and more."

Did the realtor take my aunt's criticism as a challenge? I could toss her a bone. "My boyfriend will love the kitchen."

She nodded. "He's the cook, eh?"

"He's very serious about meal preparation."

The listing for this real estate was just under four hundred thousand. These modern homes lacked the character of our historic neighborhood. Even though I wasn't interested, I tried the "what if" game. I did love the back porch, and it's marsh-side view. It would be wonderful to find a place suitable for energetics and on the water.

The realtor guided us through the kitchen and into the garage where a jumble of boxes were piled to one side. "What's all this?" I asked. A glint of blue caught my eye. Something small made of royal blue glass sat on the transom window's sill.

"The remnants of Butter Rawlin's life. A charity has already collected the furniture we didn't need for the Open House. These are personal items from his closet and dresser. The first charity wouldn't take that stuff. I have another one coming to get the rest of this, but they couldn't schedule a pick up until tomorrow."

Sherry's phone rang. "Excuse me while I catch this."

When she went outside to take the call, I asked my aunt, "What was that all about?"

"A warning. This place reeks of bad vibes. More layers of it than the house is old. Don't even pretend you want to live here. Something very bad happened here."

"I understand. My interest in this real estate stems from my investigation of Butter Rawlins, and how he connects with the other serial killer victims. If I find the link, I'll find the killer."

"Even so, when we arrived you genuinely seemed interested in this place. The realtor bought it, and so did I. You're very good at selling the story."

"Sorry if I made you uncomfortable, Auntie O. I'm highly motivated to solve this case. I despise being the target of a police investigation."

She nodded toward the pile in the garage. "If there's anything to be learned out here, it's in these boxes."

"Exactly. Let's see what's inside."

I rifled through the contents of the open boxes. "These are a mess. She dumped his clothes in here. Nothing's folded or stacked, but it's just clothes. I glanced around the two-car garage with fresh interest. Odds and ends of lumber filled one corner. There hadn't been a fireplace, and these boards weren't big enough to build with. The lumber scraps made no sense.

"What's that atop the window trim?" Auntie O asked. "It's too high for me to reach."

"I wondered about that too." I stood on tiptoes and pulled it down. The blue glass felt cool in my hand. "Looks like the neck of a wine bottle."

Auntie O examined it upside down. "Could be a funnel."

I returned it to the windowsill. "For a small volume. Not useful for transferring a large volume."

In recent months, I'd snooped in several homes of deceased people. Some had houses filled to the ceiling with stuff. Some, like Butter Rawlins, traveled light. No art to speak of, no sound system, and no car either from the pristine condition of the garage floor.

"Sorry about that," the agent said. "Now where were we?"

"Just curious after seeing the garage. Where's his car and the yard tools that fill most garages?"

"The garage was empty when I listed the property."

This man had been Auntie O's age. He still worked as an accountant and played in a band. Nothing about his home suggested the kind of wealth that came with a driver and a limo.

The lack of a car concerned me, even though I didn't own a car by choice. "No stores are in walking distance. How'd he get groceries and run errands?"

"Probably rode the bus or hailed a ride," Sherry said. "Everyone is into those phone apps these days."

Oh goodie. I was trending by using an app. That was miraculous in itself.

The realtor withdrew some pages from her tote. "Let's step back inside and fill out this contract."

"Not today," I said, disliking how pushy she was. "I need to think it over."

A frown flitted across her face. "This place won't stay on the market long."

The realtor fenced with me about the urgency of an offer, then she realized I wouldn't budge. She peeled out before we even got our seat belts clicked in place.

"She sure wanted an offer," I said. "I pity the person who buys that place. It needs more than a smudging with sage. What happened there? Do you know?"

"I didn't pick up a specific sense of what went down. However, a rowdy crowd lived out here for years. The nicest way I can put it is that they bent people to their will."

Her comment had me hitting the mental brakes. "They were energetics like us?"

"Nope. Just some folks pretending to be civilized lived in this area. They looked down their noses at city people. Now they couldn't afford this neighborhood if they tried. It surprised me that they lost this place all of a sudden in the 1970s, but I never heard a peep about them after that."

"Unless the history, fascinating as it may be, is relevant to the homeowner's murder, I need to stay on task. Butter Rawlins had no known passions other than accounting and his band, but I knew that before I drove here. This trip was a waste of time."

"Maybe not. You've visited Jenae Pendley's and Butter Rawlin's homes. Now, you'll know if you find something relevant at Jerry Meldrim's place."

"That's just it. I don't know if he had a residence. He might have lived in his car."

"What about his daughter? The blue hair gal."

Why didn't I think of that? Fawn might know things about her father she hadn't shared before. "I haven't seen Fawn Meldrim since his funeral."

"I've got time to speak with her today, if you like."

Everyone seemed pushy today. I checked my aunt's aura and it looked normal. How was that possible?

Chapter Sixteen

"Whatcha doing?" Gerard asked the next day as I stood statue-still behind the shop counter stargazing at my phone. My DNA test results were back in what seemed like record time, but I couldn't bring myself to open the message on the app.

I studied the notice with a peculiar mix of dread and fascination, glad Auntie O hadn't come downstairs yet and also glad we were in a customer lull. Though talking with Jerry Meldrim's daughter Fawn topped my to-do list, my ancestry results might connect me with my missing father.

I needed the answers this could tell me, but the backlash of what I'd risked with DNA testing could be huge. *Not that again. Buck up.* I controlled my data. Nothing would leak unless I changed the privacy settings, and that wouldn't happen. Besides, all I'd done so far was check into my ethnicity.

"Tabby?" Gerard moved into my personal space with rounded eyes, concern etched into his face. "You blanked out on me. We were discussing ideas for St. Patrick's Day sales."

I shook my head to clear it. "Sorry. Didn't mean to alarm you. I was checking to see if my test results were in. I'm okay with the two thoughts you proposed, but I lean toward 'A Magical St. Patrick's Day Sale.'"

Gerard got a knowing look in his eye, ignoring my sales theme comment. He also eyed the phone like it might be the Holy Grail. "Aren't you going to look? I know how important that testing is to you."

I put down the phone and stepped away from it, shaking my hands. "It's weird how anxious I am about this. I need to know the results, but what if it's bad news? I could be descended from serial killers, cannibals, or dastardly space pirates. I only considered the upside of doing this, not the potential for undesirable kin."

"Millions of people do this. It's not like the company will say you have Martian DNA."

"Knowledge can be as scary as ignorance. I didn't even think about that before." I countered. "The thing is, I wanted this too much to be objective. Those results are a big deal to me. I used up all my courage to send in the test sample."

"You're the bravest woman I know. You took on the detectives when they thought I killed Blithe McAdams. You got this."

He was trying to help, but his positive attitude in the face of my floundering rubbed me the wrong way. "You didn't take a DNA test."

He pointed to his face. "Look at my skin color. My people came from Africa. I don't need a test to discover that."

"The genetic information might narrow down the region."

"To what end? I have MawMaw and more cousins than I can shake a stick at. I don't need more relatives. On the other hand, I understand why you did it. You've got Sage and Oralee and that's it. Wanting to know about your extended family is human nature."

Even though I'd made a calculated risk to find my missing parent, I suddenly dreaded the results. "Except Mom told us repeatedly to keep our heads down. She said the world is full of haters and being different makes us a target for bullies."

"Girl, you're preaching to the choir about keeping a low profile. You think I want to attract notice from the wrong sort? No way. It's bad enough that the cops have our shop on speed dial. I prefer to stay out of the limelight forever."

"On that we agree."

He pointed to the abandoned phone on the counter. "Are you going to open the link?"

I tried to shake the tension from my hands. Didn't work. "The longer I delay, the more scared I am. My intuition is telling me to walk away from this, but how can I?"

"Taking the test and sending it off was the hard part. Reading the answers is easy."

Harley walked over and leaned against my legs. I picked up my cat. As I stroked his soft fur, his purring soothed us both. Finally, I felt composed enough to face this potential storm. I nodded to Gerard. "I'm ready, but would you do the honors? I need Harley to ground me right now."

"Glad to help out." Gerard tapped the phone and clicked to the right screen.

I studied the phone display. The words blurred. I blinked the moisture from my eyes. Intense ringing filled my ears. I couldn't hear myself think. Was my internal alarm warning me against reading this?

I turned away and had a serious conversation with myself.
Do you want to read this or not, Tabby?
I do.
No, I can't.
I must.
This is about your father. Be brave.

I took a deep breath of forest-scented candles and leaned closer.

There was a table with different nationalities listed. The information was also displayed in a colorful pie chart. My gaze drifted to the bright colors of pie slices. Some Scottish ancestry had been detected, but the majority of DNA indicated Scandinavian and Egyptian heritage. I'd long thought my grandparents' presence in the Wayfare plot meant we had a tie to English ancestry, but that wasn't the case. So I came from Africa and Europe, specifically Scotland, Egypt, and Norway.

As my vision sharpened, I noted an asterisk next to an uncolored section. That extra information notice concerned me. I read the footnote to myself. "Some aspects of your profile suggest a limited heritage from Egypt, but a few of our test results were inconclusive and non-repeatable. We encourage you to make your results public and upload them to similar sites for more comps. Further, one cohort of your DNA was atypical. We'd very much like to discuss your results with you. Please contact us at your earliest convenience." A phone number followed.

Oh no. Gerard was wrong. I might as well have Martian blood. My DNA was flagged as abnormal. This was awful. Who knew psychic abilities could manifest in DNA? I thought DNA related to eye color, height, body type, susceptibility to some diseases—a person's physical traits. Because in every visible aspect, my family looked absolutely normal.

However in other ways, the intangible ways that made Winslows unique, we weren't normal. For generations, our family had kept our differences a secret. I could scarcely draw in a breath. Hackers could get into any database, even private ones. What had I done?

My aunt bustled into the shop in a cloud of scent and a tinkling of wind chimes. "Here I am, ready to take on the day."

Quickly, I palmed the phone and hid it in a pocket. I couldn't tell Auntie O about the test or the results. Like Mom, she preached keeping a low profile. No way would I upload this any place else or make it public. Now I had a new concern. How could I get my DNA wiped from that company's database? Could my attorney help me do that? I made a mental note to call him as soon as possible.

"Why's it so quiet in here? This place feels like a boneyard. We can't have that. It's bad for business and employee morale." Auntie O continued with sunny cheer in her voice and step. "We need music and bright scents to counteract the negativity in here. What gives, you two?"

Gerard met my level gaze, and I barely shook my head. He got the message.

I'd had experience pretending to be normal, so I drew on that. This needed to be the performance of my life. "Good to see you looking so chipper, Auntie O."

Her infectious grin eased my troubled soul. "Feel like a million dollars ever since I returned. Dorothy from "The Wizard of Oz" had it right all along. There's no place like home."

"You wear it well." Gerard waved toward our sound system. "As for music, it's your day to make a selection."

"Of course." She trotted over and selected a jazz station. Peppy music filled the air waves.

Much to my delight, Gerard swept Auntie O into his arms, and they danced to the music with fancy footwork, tight spins, and a dip or two. Their vibrant energy distracted me enough to shrug off my dark mood. Though I still worried about my new secret, Harley and I settled on a stool to watch the show. Luna, Sage's cat, joined us, sitting beside us on the spare stool.

The test result didn't hold a candle to real-life interactions. Moments like these were what life was about. Sure, they each had their place, but my world of energetics thrived with human contact. Years from now, I'd remember today as the day Auntie O and Gerard cut a rug in the shop. It wouldn't be the dark moment I leaked my family's weird DNA to the world.

I hoped.

My phone rang. I fished it out of a pocket and earned a feline evil eye as my actions jostled the cat on my lap. I glanced at the unfamiliar number, silenced the call, and placed the phone on the counter next to a new release from a Savannah author.

No good reason why I had a call from the city of the DNA testing lab.

"Aren't you going to get that, dear?" Auntie O asked.

Automatically, I rubbed my locket, seeking comfort. "Not today."

~*~

Auntie O left the shop early that afternoon to prepare a war-room dinner for everyone. Quig and I reserved most evenings for us, but with the clock ticking a countdown on my freedom, I craved family time. Until the last six months of my intimate friendship with Quig, family had been my all. It felt natural to seek them out for counsel and comfort about the case. And as much as Quig appeared a tough guy, he needed tender loving care too.

"Why am I under suspicion?" I asked over a delicious meal of lasagna, salad, and garlic bread. "I never met the first two victims, and I barely knew Jerry Meldrim. Not that I would kill anyone, but why kill strangers? I had no reason to harm them."

"Herbert R. Ellis will make sure we both stay out of jail," Quig said loyally.

"I appreciate our attorney," I said, "but I've mulled this over. There's a chance we're looking at this case wrong. What if this harkens back to our ongoing struggle to hold onto our property? Another land grab for Bristol Street would explain why someone is coming after me and Quig."

Brindle cleared his throat. "Herbert is a good lawyer. He's well-respected in the legal community. He'll stay on top of it."

"He'd better." Sage topped off everyone's wine and refilled her glass. "I will go berserk if Tabby is in this witch hunt."

"Funny you mentioned that." I sipped my wine. "Captain Haynes asked if our family were witches."

"Haynes and his minions can suck goose eggs," Sage said. "New Age shopkeepers aren't necessarily witches. Local artisans supplement our product lines with handcrafted one-of-a-kind wares. We're artists, not witches. Tabby and Auntie O's candles are the best around. That's talent. Others are jealous and resent our success."

Auntie O looked stern.

I shrugged. This topic couldn't be addressed in depth with Quig and Brindle present. Neither of them were family per se, and neither were energetics. Hence neither were privy to our darkest secrets.

"Captain Haynes' interest prompted this strategy dinner," Auntie O said. "He bullied Tabby, hoping she'd react to his accusations. Since she's a free woman, she calmly listened to her lawyer. We have to stay alert. I agree with Tabby that there's a chance this might be another land grab. Developers want this street for the location."

"If so, let's shut down the land pirates permanently," Sage said. "These tribulations are getting old. How'd you and Mom stop them last time?"

Auntie O moved the food around on her plate for a bit. "Your Mom spoke harshly with them, and they left Bristol Street alone after that."

"Wonder what she said," I mused, glancing across to the sofa where both cats watched us with unblinking gazes.

"Doesn't matter. She instilled fear in their hearts. Follow her example."

"You're the elder and wiser member of the family," Sage said. "Shouldn't you reach out to the deal makers? You have more experience in this area."

"We don't know who 'they' are," her aunt said. "Can't have a conversation with someone you can't identify."

"How do we cut to the chase?" I asked. "My neck's on the block, and I hate the view."

Auntie O sat taller in her seat, resolve stamped on her rounded face. "Last time it was Old Savannah that wanted us gone. Not only did they have a grudge against us, but they also had blueprints ready for this street. Rumors implied the new build would've been an enclave."

Light caught on Quig's dark-framed glasses as he studied my aunt. "What do you mean?"

"It was to be a deluxe resort-style community in the city reserved for wealthy people. They wanted to squeeze everyone else out of the historic area."

Her cutting words drew outrage from deep inside me. "They have no right to steal our homes and businesses. If I'd been an adult then, I would've taken them on, same as you and Mom did."

"It was more Marjoram than me," Auntie O said quickly. "She got their goat, and they never bothered us again in her lifetime. Now she's gone, I feel as if the hell hounds have been released. Until we make a stand, they'll keep coming for us."

"If we knew Mom's tactics, we could use them. No need to start from scratch."

Auntie O shook her head sadly. "She took those secrets to the grave."

"We could ask a medium," Sage said.

"No!" Auntie O said. "That's not our way. Don't open that can of exploding snakes."

Sage looked like she would say something. I poked her with my foot under the table. Our family had a zero tolerance policy for mediums, though we'd never known why. We couldn't talk about this now. Not with the guys here.

I swore silently, aware of many mysteries Mom never explained. She'd been protective. Now our safety was in peril, and her surefire defense was lost to us. "She claimed the world was a bad place and added we'd figure it out if we had to. She meant well by sheltering us, but we're running blind here."

My summation met with mixed results. Auntie O nodded. Brindle and Quig looked puzzled. Sage radiated boatloads of toxic anger. I sent out a few cancelling currents of energy to freshen the air.

"Mom hobbled us in a field of predators," I continued. "If this 'attack,' for want of a better term, is like the last time, we need every defense we can muster."

"Did she expect us to invent new options for protection?" Sage asked.

"Marjoram never confided in me, but I interacted with her when I was a boy and not at all as an adult." Quig said. "I've never been in a turf war before, and therefore need pointers."

I squeezed his hand. "I don't want you hurt or your career derailed if this is the age-old struggle about our real estate. We have to figure out it this is new money or still Old Savannah that's after our prime real estate."

Brindle leaned forward, catching my eye. "Does it matter? If you won't sell and they can't buy your property, trouble is likely. Given the past land grab attempts, they won't take no as a final answer. Perhaps we can track recent land acquisitions nearby, observe who might be buying the parcels, and come up with names. Following the money is a winning strategy in court defenses, and it'll work for this too."

Sage beamed. "Excellent idea. If we freeze their assets or render them otherwise unavailable, they'll tuck tail and run."

It would be magic if we managed that. Deep-dive tech skills weren't in our wheelhouses. "Maybe. Or they'll come after us twice as hard. They'd have nothing to lose."

Auntie O clapped her hands. Both cats perked up as did the rest of us. "These are fine ideas, and we'll watch for a secret cabal to thwart, but the immediate problem is clearing Tabby's name. They'll have an easier time of gaining the land if they divide our family."

"United front," Quig said. "I'm all in."

A chorus of "me toos" followed, and my eyes misted. I stroked my locket, feeling the love in this kitchen. "Thanks. I appreciate everyone's support. Which brings us full circle to the three murders. Question is, how do we flush the killer?"

"Bring us up to speed on what you've learned, dear." Auntie O rested her chin on her hands.

I nodded. "The first victim, Jenae Pendley, worked as a host at The Oaks Club before a bullet ended her life. She literally had dominium over who entered the club and when they left. Her social media feed puzzled me. She posted a leaf photo a day, never any pictures of family or friends, never any photos of herself. For someone in a traditionally low-paying career, she lived at The Retreat, which is very upscale, and drove an expensive car. Next, Butter Rawlins, the guy who got coshed with a frying pan, worked as an accountant for a mid-level firm and moonlighted in a band for most of his life. Southern Nites played in hotels and clubs throughout the region. Lastly, Jerry Meldrim, the victim felled by an arrow, had a booze problem. He was estranged from his grown daughter, his ex-wife, and most of Savannah."

"Nice summary," Brindle said, "but those victims are quite different."

"I've been considering that angle," I said. "Perhaps Jenae and Jerry hired Butter as their accountant and met in his office lobby."

"Wait a sec." Sage snapped her fingers. "Jenae works for a club that serves alcohol. Jerry drank alcohol. Butter's band sang at clubs. What if The Oaks ties these three together?"

That seemed a stretch to me, same as my idea of an accountant link. We didn't know if these people had been acquainted.

"Brilliant," Brindle said, apparently having no reservations about my twin's idea. "Wish I'd thought of it."

"Perhaps," Quig said, his tone cautious, "but life is rarely so straightforward. How would we prove that theory?"

"Maybe we should come-by the club's roster. Or their financial records. We could see dues payments and any payment to Southern Nites." Auntie O stared at me. "Think you could wrangle that?"

Oh joy. More breaking and entering. We have done enough of that already.

"Maybe we shouldn't look into The Oaks Club members or owners," Sage said. "We can share our ideas with Detectives Nowry and Belfor. They have the resources and authority to do a deep dive on the club and financial records."

I finished my wine and set down the glass. "Actually, I had a different approach in mind. Jerry's daughter Fawn was a frequent visitor to our shop. She's been a no-show since his death. What if I make a gift basket of our products and drop it by her place tomorrow? Hopefully, she'll invite me in, and I can ask her if her father and The Oaks are connected."

"That's a good plan," Quig said wryly. "There's no breaking and entering involved."

Brindle looked like he might add something, but Sage elbowed his side and silenced him with The Look, a certain cast of the eyes that mothers used to hush their kids. We'd learned it from Mom, and she'd learned from her mom.

Ack! How much did either man know about how Sage and I investigated cases?

Sage shot me a twin-link message. *Does he know?*

I met her level gaze. *I didn't tell him.*

Rats. I don't like anyone knowing.

You think I do?

Outwardly we both smiled. Not even so much as a wobble occurred in Sage's aura. She always could beat me when it came to lying, though in this case we were in a lie of omission.

I rose, stacking empty dishes atop mine. "Sounds like tomorrow will be a busy day. We should be going soon."

Auntie O held up a hand. "Not done yet. What about the

FBI?"

Quig shifted in his seat. "What about them?"

"Captain Haynes invited their help on the case. He announced their acceptance on the evening news."

"I heard a rumor that might happen," I began slowly as I sat back down. "Does it matter?"

"Depends on which agent gets the case," Auntie O said. "If an investigator wants to make a name for themselves, they might stick to the current theory of the case, which keeps Tabby front and center, even though she had no motive or opportunity to kill those victims. On the other hand, if the feds find another suspect, that will benefit Tabby."

"I didn't kill anyone. It's frustrating that no one outside the people at this table believe in my innocence. It's ridiculous that I've lived under this dark cloud for days."

"The wheels of criminal justice creak forward slowly," Brindle said. "You can't hurry love or investigations."

"Have patience, Tabby," Quig said. "We're believers. Others will believe too."

"Got your back, Sis," Sage said. "Always."

"Thanks for the show of support. I'm feeling jammed up by the local cops, and now I've got feds joining the chase. I'm running out of options."

"Nonsense." Auntie O's gaze focused on the horizon for a long moment. "You can finesse the situation. I have faith in you."

If only it were that easy.

Chapter Seventeen

Stormy skies blew in the next morning and dampened my mood. Auntie O, despite her professed intent to help in the shop all the time had slept in, exhausted by yesterday's events. Gerard had asked for today off because his boyfriend had outpatient surgery, so Eve and I staffed The Book and Candle Shop.

I sputtered invisible fire when she escorted two well-dressed people with government badges into the stillroom where I worked. Or tried to work. My thoughts wouldn't settle enough to make candles, so I'd shifted gears to blend a new scent...until this ghastly interruption.

The FBI agents wore dark suits, industrial-looking black shoes, and slicked back short hair. This agent pair could have been matched under the same stars as Detectives Nowry and Belfor, as he looked dour while she gleefully inhaled the room.

His loose-fitting suit was charcoal grey, with a white dress shirt and a black tie. Hers was a fitted version in navy blue. Both wore gleaming badges on their hips.

Darkness and light threaded their auras. I'd rather they had kinder, gentler personas, but given their profession, that was an unreal hope. They weren't here for a social call.

Eve cleared her throat and gestured to my unwelcome visitors. "Tabby, these FBI agents asked to speak to you privately."

The male agent nodded and said, "Special Agent Oxley."

"I'm Special Agent Easton, Miss Winslow. We have questions for you."

My plan to visit Fawn Meldrim later might be on hold indefinitely if the feds nabbed me. "About what?" Just in case they pounced, I shifted my stance to a ready position with my weight forward. Not that I expected they'd pounce, but the active position kept me focused.

Eve backed away, mouthing "I'm sorry."

Cripes. Feds in my stillroom. Eve and I would discuss this breech of shop policy later..

"The Meldrim case," Easton said, taking the lead.

My right hand fisted around the glass stirring rod I'd been using to mix fragrances. Did I need to call my lawyer? Maybe I should see what they wanted first. The blends of tree-derived essential oils wafted up my nose. The woodsy scent suited my dark mood, and I took refuge in the combination of cedar, fir, and cypress punctuated by after-notes of sweet balsam.

"We understand you knew Jerry Meldrim," Easton continued as if I'd lobbed the ball back in her court.

All I had to do was recite the facts already on record and they'd leave. "He visited my shop once, when he'd had too much to drink. I'd never heard of him before then. I wouldn't call that knowing him."

"You got a restraining order against him."

My spine stiffened. "Upon the advice of the officer who responded to the call. It was the officer's second time of having to remove Meldrim from a place of business."

"We read the grounds you stated. Disorderly conduct. Criminal Mischief. Menacing Behavior. It sounds like he had a prior beef with you."

"Neither I nor my family had prior contact with the man."

"I see," Easton continued. The agents exchanged a glance, then Oxley spoke. "We're intrigued his body was found on your grandparents' grave. Do you have any idea why?"

I drew in a considering breath. Should I call my lawyer now? Maybe I could still finesse this. "No. My family is mortified by this desecration."

"Please put down your magic wand," Easton said dryly.

Magic wand?

I glanced down and realized I'd been gesturing with my hands while talking. I'd forgotten I held the stirring rod so I placed it on a clean paper towel. "It's for mixing. I was blending scents when you interrupted me."

"You mix beeswax granules into scents?" Oxley asked in a wry tone.

"I craft candles with wax. I stir essential oils into melted wax or into prepared soap bases."

Easton sniffed appreciatively. "Smells like a forest back here. No offense intended, but you're awfully young to be running a business."

Lightning flashed and thunder rolled outside the window. Oh goody. A thunderstorm and a fed storm.

"I grew up in this business, ma'am. I'm a third generation chandler."

"You're a light fixture?" Oxley asked, arching a brow.

Focusing on my stillroom's robin egg blue walls centered me. I would gain nothing by being snarky. "Candle and soap maker."

"That's not a profession you hear much about these days."

"I'm not the only one in town, sir."

"Did you know the other victims?" Easton asked, without missing a beat.

"I did not." So far I'd recounted information shared during my police interviews. I'd stick with that policy.

"What's with the tallow?"

"What do you mean?"

"Why does the killer smear it in his victim's hair?"

"How would I know?"

Oxley shifted and part of his shoulder harness showed. As did the ominous gun he wore. I didn't want to talk to these agents. "I've answered your questions, and now I'd like you to leave. This area of the shop isn't open to the public. My new employee forgot that visitors aren't allowed back here."

"Only one more question," Oxley said. "Why does Captain Haynes believe you killed Pendley, Rawlins, and Meldrim?"

"It's a mystery to me."

They left, and Eve skittered back once the shop door closed fully. "I'm so sorry. I panicked when they entered the shop."

"I don't allow outsiders back here, Eve. Not for fear of discovery, but to keep the energy right. Cops give off negative energy from the craziness they are immersed in every day. I don't want contamination in here."

"I understand," Eve said. "And I apologize for my mistake. All I could think was to hand them off to you as soon as possible. I can't promise to be a perfect shopkeeper if they return, but I won't allow them back here. I'm a grown woman, and I've done nothing wrong, but my innate fear of law enforcement is crippling at times."

Because I worked with her cousin Gerard all the time, I didn't think of him or Eve as black. I thought of them as people. But I understood and hated that cops often profiled people based on their race. I ought to cut Eve some slack.

Harley wandered in, sniffed the room, turned around, trotted up to the apartment's cat door, and vanished inside. He didn't care for cop mojo either. I'd need to smudge the room with sage and lavender before I made candles again. First, I needed to come to an understanding with Eve.

I leaned against the counter. "It's never good when law enforcement officers appear. True confession time, I also fight the strong urge to run and hide every time. An ancestor or two of mine must've had a bad encounter with law and order."

"Someone in my family did with deadly results," Eve began slowly. "I never knew Uncle Rueben, but he died in his twenties during a false arrest. He told them they had the wrong guy, and they wouldn't listen. People keep saying times have changed, but discrimination is worldwide. I was glad to learn my grandmother's spells so I have a defense if I'm targeted unfairly. What I didn't consider is the knowledge I learned makes me as much of a target as my heritage."

"We're on the same page. Captain Haynes believes my family are witches. Maybe he considers any paranormal person to be a witch. I still hear about arrests gone wrong. Cops are quick to charge in and single out people in the name of justice."

"I feel ya." Eve nodded. "You're brave to meet them head on. I've never stood my ground like that. Too scared because my people were mistreated for generations, right up through the present times. We have long memories too."

At least she had family memories. "My mother barely mentioned her parents, and we have no family records or oral history beyond that generation. Mom said we were better off not knowing, and I always felt she didn't trust us with that knowledge. She shielded Sage and me from the world, but school kids bullied us. Now, as an adult, I help those in need." I shot Eve a knowing smile. "Of course, not everyone is worthy of help."

"You're my kind of people." Eve doubled over laughing. "Since I messed up the mojo back here, I'll remove the negativity."

"I accept your offer. Thanks. I'll leave you to it. I need a few minutes out front to collect items for a gift basket for

Fawn Meldrim."

"She loves our lip balm," Eve said.

"Thanks." I slipped out front with a small blue basket. Earlier this morning I'd sprayed it the same color as Fawn's hair. The aerosol paint covered the St Patrick's Day green in one coat, and I'd already checked to make sure it was dry. Now I needed the rain to stop before I ventured outside.

Chapter Eighteen

Fawn padded to the door when I knocked. The door didn't open. "Fawn, it's Tabby Winslow. I brought you a gift."

Silence met my words at first, then Fawn spoke. "Go away. I don't want to see anyone."

"I'm sorry you feel that way. Now that the thunderstorm's over, maybe you'll take a short walk with me. I would like to see you're okay. We miss you at the shop."

I heard a few sniffs. "Really? Not even my mom came to see me. Nobody cares my father died."

"I'm sure that's not true. Your dad had friends and business associates too. Surely some of them miss him."

"None of them came to his funeral service. I was glad to see you."

I sagged against the door. "I came to support you, Fawn. I lost my mom a few months ago. It's hard to bury a parent. May I come in?"

"No! I don't want anyone to see me."

"I don't care if you look a mess. I need to see you. Please. Would you rather I ask the police to do a wellness check?"

"You'd send the po-po?"

I crossed my fingers. "I would but only because I'm

concerned. No one's seen you in days. Please open the door. I have a wonderful gift basket for you."

"Did Gerard select the items?"

Her voice tinged with wistfulness. "His cousin helped. Gerard is off today."

"Any chocolate in there?"

"Yes."

The lock turned, and the door opened. Fawn stood there, her hair a tangled mess, the grey color of her sweats extending to her skin tone. I stepped inside and opened my arms. She hurled herself at me, wrapped her arms around me, and sobbed for five minutes straight. I showered her with good energy.

When her tears subsided, Fawn snatched the basket and dug for chocolate. I was glad I kept a stash in the stillroom to add to the soaps, lip balm, lotion, votives, and a book from a local author. I'd added a few bags of peppermint tea because that always hit the spot. I followed her inside.

"I failed him," Fawn said around a mouthful of chocolate. "I didn't want to see him once Mom kicked him out, and when he came to see me after school, I blamed him for everything. For Mom's crying jags, for losing our home, for debt collectors pounding on our doors. He came to my high school graduation high as a kite and stumbled all over the bleachers. I've never been so embarrassed in my life. I'm surprised you still allow me in your shop after what he did there."

"We're a business, and customers are welcome as long as they respect others and our property. Have some more chocolate, and when you feel comfortable, I'd love to hear your memories of your father."

Fawn gestured to a chair full of discarded clothing. "Sorry about the mess."

Her color already looked better. The energy boost and chocolate were working. "No worries. I've been in your shoes before. Healing is a process."

I followed her to the kitchen. When she began moving dirty dishes to the sink, I grabbed a mug of what looked like flat soda. "I'll do it," Fawn said. "Please sit down."

"Okay, I understand. But you don't need to clean up for me. I surprised you with a visit. Please sit down and talk with me. I'd love to hear what you loved about your dad, if you're open to sharing."

Fawn took a long moment. "When I was little my father used to toss me in the air. I liked that, and I liked him reading to me. One day he brought home a dog from the pound. I loved it and played with it until Mom returned. She started sneezing and pointed to the backyard. 'Out,' she yelled. She had a pet dander allergy. I never knew until that moment of any allergy. But my father knew. He had to have known. He argued with her about keeping the dog, even said I loved it already. Mom put her foot down hard. Allergies made her miserable."

"Sure, but it must've been devastating to give up the dog."

Her voice took on a distant quality. "My father took it outside and turned it loose. The dog bounded away. We never saw him again."

"You could get a dog now."

"Guess so. Though I'm scared I have Mom's allergy."

I thought about that for two seconds, the answer coming in a flash. "With our shop cats, you'd already know if you had a pet allergy. Cats trigger more allergies than dogs. But to be sure, you might consider volunteering to help with dogs at the shelter and see what happens."

She brightened. "Didn't think of that."

Dare I push for background on her father? Might as well try. "What other memories do you have of your dad? Did you ever go to work with him?"

"No. It wouldn't have been appropriate."

"Was it top secret?"

"Not hardly. He got fired twelve years ago from a company that made big machines."

"He was an engineer?"

"Pretty sure he majored in booze in college, but somehow he earned an MBA. He was very good at talking people into whatever story he was selling. He started in sales but moved up the ladder until he got a job in what my mom called the wine-and-dine department. He truly embraced the client entertainment aspect of his job, but his work suffered because of the booze. The company gave him several second chances before they cut him loose. He couldn't kick the booze, and it ruined everything. My mom started typing medical dictation, and she kicked my father out of the house after he kited checks all over town. She was humiliated. Worse, because they were married at the time, she had to pay off his debt. She never got over that insult."

"I'm sorry you grew up in such a volatile situation." Hoping I read her correctly, I tried a different tack, much like a sailboat changing course. "Now your father is paired in death with Jenae Pendley and Butter Rawlins. Did he know them?"

Fawn sniffed. "I don't know. Those aren't names I recall from my childhood."

"What names do you remember?"

"Unfortunately, there were no famous people around like Juliette Gordon Low, Flannery O'Connor, Paula Deen, or Jack Sherman."

I knew about the first three famous locals. "You lost me at Jack Sherman."

"He's known in music circles as the second guitarist for the Red Hot Chili Peppers. My mom loves rock music."

"Funny, my mom was the opposite. However my twin sister adores rock music. What are some names from his former work life?"

She grimaced. "His big boss is in a nursing home now, and

Tallowed Ground

the guy that got his wine-and-dine job moved to Denver a few years ago. Those were the only people he mentioned. If someone hated my father, why wait so long to come after him?"

"Good point." I paused to see how she was holding up. She looked better than when I came in a few minutes ago so I continued digging for information. "I'm sorry for all the questions, but I'd like to help find out who killed your father. Is that still all right with you?"

"Yes. I need to know that his killer is caught."

"All right, then. Did he find another job?"

"He worked in a bank for a year, then he left to start his own business. He convinced another man to go in with him on a yogurt shop. He wheedled a bank coworker into loaning him and his business partner, Joe Block, enough money to build their own place. It was a terrible location, and within six months of opening, they declared bankruptcy. That was another 'worst' day of my life. At least by then they were divorced, and Mom wasn't saddled with that bill."

I made a mental note of the partner's name. "Gracious. I'm so sorry all that happened to you. It must've been awful."

"It was. My father drank heavily, but after the yogurt shop failed, he drank even more. The thing is he'd try to see me, and I secretly wanted to see him. He made drunken promises that I clung to. It took me a year to realize my loving father was gone. The drunk who stumbled around in his body never delivered on a single thing. Eventually I pretended he wasn't family. It was easier that way."

"Dads are hard to figure out sometimes."

"You have father trouble too?" Fawn asked.

"Vanishing father trouble. He left to get eggs when I was five and never returned."

"Did you look for him?"

I didn't know Fawn well enough to confide about the DNA test. "Mom said there was no point looking for trouble.

I didn't know what she meant at the time, but he rejected us when he abandoned us."

"But you're smart. If anyone could find him, you could."

"I might not like the answer." I sighed and reached for my locket again. Touching this gift from Quig reminded me I was loved. Quig wouldn't desert me.

"At least you'd have an answer. I don't know who shot my father with an arrow or why."

"I'll find that answer for you."

~*~

That evening, the chain on my locket caught on a blouse button and snapped as I undressed for bed. I gasped, horrified at what I'd done. This precious keepsake from Quig that I treasured...I'd *broken* it. I was upset, even though it was an accident. Tears blurred my vision as I cradled it in my hand.

I'd repair the chain. I had the pieces. A jeweler could fix it.

Should I tell Quig?

He'll hate you for breaking it, a dark voice in my head whispered. My guilty conscience shrank from the drama of an angry man. Another voice countered with Quig was level-headed, which I knew to be true. Why was I so emotional? Must be from all those years of living with Sage. If anyone was an expert at drama it was my twin sister.

The dark voice whispered again. *Don't tell him. He's under too much pressure at work. This is a bad time to confess you broke his gift.* I sighed, not wanting to be a drama queen, but Quig had a heavy workload. Why complicate matters? If I didn't tell him and repaired the chain, he would never the difference.

Problem solved.

After placing the necklace in a dresser-top dish with other jewelry, I donned a shawl-collared pajama top to conceal my bare neck. I would repair the necklace immediately.

Chapter Nineteen

Auntie O and I stood side-by-side in the shop to face the oncoming detectives, Nowry and Belfor. Though our united front felt like a sand dune fighting off a nor'easter, I girded myself with protective energy, and my aunt did the same. Our combined currents twined together to create an invisible barrier. I prayed it repelled cops.

Of all the rotten luck to be here now. This wasn't even my day in the shop, but Sage had a dental hygiene appointment first thing this morning, and Gerard's grandmother had a medical appointment. I did not need to see detectives so early in the day, or at all, for that matter.

Worrying about the broken necklace, I'd slept fitfully. Now a low-grade headache pulsed under every thought, so I wasn't up to skirmishes with law and order. Why were they here? I had assumed the detectives were off the case since Captain Haynes invited the local feds to find the killer. Obviously I assumed wrong.

Was it just me or did our pleasant door chime have an evil undertone today?

"Good morning," Auntie O said, cheery as today's sunrise. "What brings you in this fine day?"

"Morning, Ms. Colvin." Nowry gave her a polite nod before addressing me. "Got questions for your niece."

Annoyance trumped my usual commonsense policy of limited speaking to these detectives. I would love for this man to stumble, and I wasted a millisecond considering it before I dismissed the action as too overt. I hit him with sarcasm instead. "Haven't you asked me all the questions in the world yet?"

"Tell me about your archery skills," Belfor said.

Aack. This was about the case. Prudence interceded. "If this is about you wanting to railroad me into something I didn't do, I shouldn't respond."

"Nothing official about our visit. We have gaps in the information you provided before." Nowry whipped out his small notebook and read from it. "For instance, how often do you use your bow, where do you shoot it, and why do you have a bow?"

The need to speak bubbled up inside of me, not hard and fast but determined and assertive. "Why?" They hadn't been here a full minute and already their negative energy battered our safety barrier. It shouldn't be influencing my thoughts, but the mere sight of these detectives triggered my fight or flight instincts.

Nowry huffed as if he'd climbed two flights of steps. Belfor grinned as she took the question. "The feds gave us make-work questions to keep us busy while they're leading the Tallowed Killer investigation, that's why."

My confusion was genuine. "The what?"

"Didn't you see it in today's paper? Liz Bryan, that reporter your attorney favors, coined a nickname for the killer, and the feds are beside themselves over this development. Naming this criminal empowers the killer and diminishes the victims. The feds tried to contain the reporter's story, but the tag got legs immediately. Regional news and podcasters adopted the killer nickname in their morning coverage. The feds worry this will go viral, and then they'll get blamed for losing control of the situation."

I gazed at Harley who reigned supreme on the upper wall shelf. My black cat was surrounded by pirates, jars of seashells, and our textured, sand-rolled Savannah Sunrise candles. He regarded me steadily from his lofty perch. No answers up there, but this was the first time he didn't run from the cops.

Before I could figure out what the cat's altered behavior meant, the entirety of what Belfor said sunk in. If this case went viral, every armchair sleuth and crime podcaster in the nation would nose around my shop thinking they could solve the case. No one in my family sought notoriety, ever. Our mantra had always been to keep a low profile, something I was finding harder and harder to do. I wanted the case solved. Most of all, I wanted to go weeks, even months, without seeing these detectives.

"Answer the question," Auntie O said, poking me in the ribs. "I've got a good feeling about this."

Didn't see that coming, but my aunt's *feelings* were rarely wrong. "You already know the basics. Six years ago a college friend convinced me to enroll in an archery class with her. We watched 'The Hunger Games' at the campus center, and she thought I would enjoy archery as much as she did. The way she talked about how easy it was, I thought it would be a breeze. Skilled archers make the sport look deceptively simple, but it is very hard. I got so discouraged I never tried archery again after that class. I kept the bow because it was a loan from that same classmate, and someday she may want it back even though she said to keep it. That seems like a lifetime ago."

Nowry snorted. "Lifetime? Thirty is still young. I'm twice your age and counting."

"A lot has changed in my life since I tried archery in college. The truth is I stuck that bow in the closet when I returned home and never gave it another thought."

"You ever practice archery at a range?"

"Nope. I don't plan to hunt game, ever, so why spend my limited free time in an activity that causes immense frustration? That bow is a relic from a former life."

Belfor made a sweeping motion with one hand. "Bam! She told us."

A related idea surfaced. "If you need names of archers, request user lists at area ranges and cross-reference them."

"If only we'd thought of that," Nowry bleated like an ornery goat.

"Been there, done that," Belfor said. "Your name isn't listed."

Their denseness made me want to stomp my foot, and my voice rose higher than I'd planned. "Because I don't practice archery. Ever."

"We're wasting time." Nowry jerked his thumb toward the door. "Let's go.

They left, and Sage breezed in immediately after. "Hey, everyone. Quiet morning?"

"Not so much." Relieved that her presence meant I could leave, I grabbed my purse and headed through the stillroom for the alley door. Sage followed me while Auntie O greeted incoming customers. The combined weight of the case, the broken locket chain, and a sleepless night squeezed my heart. I slowed by the back window and tossed a sour comment over my shoulder at my twin. "Great timing, Sis. You missed our persistent detectives."

"I missed nothing because I saw them arrive, so I waited until they left to come downstairs. Good riddance to them."

My out-of-sorts mood didn't improve by stepping inside the stillroom, my go-to happy place. Still, I shouldn't take my bad mood out on my twin. After all, she'd taken advantage of me plenty of times before, and I'd let it go. Consequently, everyone walked on eggshells around my twin because they didn't want to set her off.

My needs and wants should be as important as hers, but did I want to deal with Sage fireworks today? To err on the side of caution, I gave my response in a neutral tone. "You were gone longer than expected. Everything okay with your teeth?"

Sage plucked brown leaves off the hanging ferns. "The dental hygienist found a cavity, and they had time to fill it. Getting the filling done today saved me from making another trip, and another day of having someone cover for me here. Now that I'm also working for myself, time is at a premium. Hope you didn't mind subbing longer for me."

She acted so casual, as if this happened every day. Who was I kidding? It occurred whenever the whim struck her. If I didn't make a stand one day, she would take advantage of me for the rest of my life. The cauldron of thoughts welled up in a boiling frenzy. Why should I cater to her whims and ignore what was best for me?

I crossed my arms and glared at her. "Actually, I did mind your tardiness. I have a life too, and this is my day off from the shop, my *only* day off this week. If I were delayed, I wouldn't leave you hanging an extra hour without first touching base. I would've appreciated knowing about the delay."

Sage scowled at me, flipping into her other vision to view my aura. "But you had nothing else scheduled. I don't get why you're upset."

Her aura check felt intrusive, and my patience shattered. Angry words steamed out of my mouth. "You took advantage of me. I never call you out on it, but it's high time I did. I have plans for today. Important plans."

"Why are you making this into a big deal?" Sage glared at me. "It's barely eleven. You have plenty of time to run an errand."

I matched her intensity, pushing my aura into hers. "My

free time is mine. Not yours."

She stilled at the intrusion, her mouth gaping. "It's not like you to complain."

I leaned toward her, wanting to be sure she heard my every word. "Right. I give you the benefit of the doubt, you take advantage of me. It has to stop. You are my beloved twin and sister, but we must redefine the boundaries on our relationship. If I'm subbing for you, I expect to be notified if your plans change. You shouldn't assume your plans or convenience carry more weight than mine."

Sage retreated a few steps. "That's harsh. I didn't do that."

Something dark flared deep inside me, something that urged me to press her harder. But this was Sage. If I did that, she'd dissolve in a puddle of tears, storm upstairs, and sulk for hours, and I'd be stuck in the shop. I barely wrestled my emotions under control. "Yes, you did."

I turned to go, but Sage lunged forward and caught my arm. My aura roiled and pulsed full strength with charged energy. Sage let go as if she'd been burned. "I'm sorry," she said. "I never set out to disrespect you. You're right about me being selfish and thoughtless. I promise to contact you if I'm delayed in the future."

The air pulsed between us as prickly as a sandspur. I had aired my feelings, and she apologized, so why did I feel like a brute? Standing up for myself came with its share of perils. Wanting to cease hostilities, I released the caustic emotions and took a cleansing breath. "Great. I'll do the same."

I made my way over to the apartment I've shared with Quig for the last two months. Much to my surprise, Harley shot out behind me and followed me home. Wonder of wonders, he wanted to go inside. I'd never discussed having Harley move in with us, but Quig never had a problem with my cat elsewhere, so he likely wouldn't object. I unlocked the electronic door lock with my palm print, and Harley darted inside and explored every nook and cranny.

Tallowed Ground

Mindful of the conversation with Sage about her taking advantage of me, I realized I had overstepped my boundaries in our shared apartment by allowing the cat inside. Immediately, I phoned Quig to run this development past him. The call rolled to voice mail, so I left a message. "The oddest thing happened. Harley followed me home from the shop. I let him in to explore our place, but I should've asked you first. Do you mind if Harley visits our apartment? I know it's a lot to ask, but do you think it would be okay if he lives with us? Please contact me about this when you have a chance."

While I was speaking, Harley darted out of sight. I found him on my side of the bed, curled up and purring. Overjoyed that he looked so relaxed, I cuddled next to him. For me, it was a dream come true. When I'd moved, I considered it cruel to split him up from Sage's Luna, his littermate, and deprive him of his home. Now he'd chosen to visit, and he looked right at home.

In general, cats had good intuition about people. As a shop cat, Harley had been around customers every day for over ten years. He usually ignored them. He'd never ignored the cops before. Instead he'd stuck by me. Now he was on the bed I shared with Quig.

Practicalities crowded in. The way stuff kept happening, it would be prudent to run my errands sooner rather than later. If Harley stayed with us, I would need pet supplies. If Harley's presence wasn't okay with Quig, I could return everything. I'd hit a supermarket right after I found a jeweler to fix my necklace.

When I rose from the bed, Harley didn't stir. Knowing he conserved energy, he'd likely be in that same spot when I returned from the store. I freshened up and hurried to the dresser to collect the necklace.

It was gone.

Chapter Twenty

It couldn't be missing. The room spun, and I wobbled with it. I drew in quick puffs of air, until my horizon settled and I breathed easily. How could my locket and necklace disappear? Quig and I were the only ones who had access. He had a lock override feature on his phone he'd used to admit the cops on search warrant day because there were no physical keys. He and I used palmprints to enter.

No way it could have been Sage or Auntie O. They weren't on the electronic entry system for our secure fortress. That left two choices. Either I didn't remember moving it, or...I didn't want to consider the other choice.

I patted the dresser top to make sure I hadn't dislodged the keepsake when opening the drawers this morning to get dressed. I lay on the floor with a flashlight and checked under and behind the dresser. Clean as could be and no trace of my missing necklace.

Only one choice here. Quig took the locket with the broken chain. Would it cause our first fight? I reached for the touchstone usually around my neck only to come up empty-handed. No locket and no self-soothing comfort.

My cat watched as if he understood my dilemma. I stroked

his head. "Thank you, Harley, for knowing I'm too emotional and insecure right now. This is my first live-in relationship and I don't want it to end. I have a headache, argued with my sister, and can't find my necklace."

An incoming text message chimed on my phone. "I'm fine with your cat living with us. I'll be home early today."

A complete sea-change of attitude happened as a smile filled my body. "Thanks so much," I replied via text message. I almost added a query about the locket but hesitated. That conversation would work best in person, so I could better read his body language and reassure him the broken chain was unfortunate.

With Quig's approval secured, I scooped the cat into my arms, vibrations of his purring connecting us deeply. Quig loved me and my cat. For many years of not having more than one date with anyone, I'd found my guy. One who ho didn't question my family secrets. I'd be a fool to let him get away.

My cat couldn't live here without a litter box and food. So I ran out to a big box store, purchased the necessities, and returned laden with cat gear.

Harley supervised my efforts, then tried out everything before he curled into a nap.

I should be tracking down new leads about the serial killer case, but I needed "me" time. I baked Quig's favorite dessert of chocolate cake, and then I soaked in the tub. I was drying off when Quig arrived.

He sniffed the air and then he nuzzled me, reminding me of my cat, though I'd never admit that. He whirled me in his arms, holding me close. "You smell good enough to eat."

Harley darted from the bedroom, giving us the privacy we desired.

~*~

"The reason I'm home early is I got suspended," Quig said when we came up for air at twilight. "The advisory board implied I was too close to the Tallowed Killer case to be effective. Six people stood up and demanded I resign due to improprieties. One loon even insisted I killed the murder victims." His arms tightened around me. "I had thoughts about killing him at that moment."

"What? You had nothing to do with the murders."

"Doesn't matter. That's what they think, and others agree. The truth appears irrelevant."

"I'll march down there tomorrow and give those jokers a piece of my mind."

"No need. I take responsibility for what happened."

I planted my hand on his chest and soothed the troubled currents in his aura. No way could I mention my necklace now, not when his career hung by a thread. "What does this suspension mean? How soon can you go back to work?"

"I believe it's the step one of getting fired. This was an inside hatchet job. I won't resign. They expect Chang to be the M.E., but they'll soon discover their mistake. Herbert learned Chang spun the false rumors to force me out."

I silently thanked Herbert for keeping me out of that conversation. Even so, I hated Quig's situation. "I thought Chang was getting better."

"It seemed so, but he backstabbed me. When I return, I'm firing him. I'd rather be overworked than having to look over my shoulder."

"He's incompetent?"

"Incompetent and opportunistic, like a swamp leach."

"Ick."

"Right. My people intuition failed me. I never saw this coming. I'm upset about the suspension, but you've helped me by listening."

Compassion filled me, as well as the need to comfort him. I gave him another hug. "Go easy on yourself. We've all misjudged people at times. For instance, I've had trouble reading people because Mom's idea of parenting us was to shelter us from the world."

"Your mother..." He stacked his hands beneath his head and smiled for the first time this evening. "She couldn't keep me away."

I studied his shadowed face. "Truly?"

He nodded. "She told my parents I should be playing sports instead of carrying you piggyback around the park."

I remembered how much fun that was. He'd been my only friend, and I never gave our slight age difference any thought. "Wow. I had no idea. What did your parents say?"

He barked out a harsh laugh. "Dad bluntly said I was too smart for my own good. He explained I genuinely liked you. He must've persuaded her because we spent time together as kids."

My history was being rewritten as we spoke. I was very glad Mom allowed Quig to be my friend. "Why did your parents send you to private school?"

"Dad added some just-in-case space between us when I hit puberty."

"Come again?"

In answer, he kissed me. "You have your family secrets, and I have mine."

"The one where you identify your mates on sight?"

"Something like that."

Chapter Twenty-One

"Though I'm worried about the havoc Chang will wreak inside my morgue, the upside of being on suspension is now I can spend every day with you," Quig announced early the next morning.

He pulled me into his arms again as if we had no responsibilities in the world. While that was his reality right now, my daily activities hadn't changed. I had a business to run, though today was Sage's day in the shop, and a case to solve. "I have places to go, people to see. In case you've forgotten, Savannah cops and the FBI have me topping their persons of interest list in the Tallowed Killer case."

"I'm unlikely to forget any threat to our future happiness. Let's make that problem vanish."

"Working on it," I said, "which is why I can't be with you all hours of the day and night."

"Why? I'm changing my status from investigative assistant to full-fledged investigator. I've got the time, and you need the help."

"True and true." I needed a clear head for this discussion and a different location than nestled up to his side. If he became my constant shadow, I'd be too preoccupied to make aromatherapy candles.

Though he was right about the case, and he was brilliant. Could I delegate leads to him? That idea held merit, but he was a born leader. This was my freedom we were talking about. I needed to be in charge of my fate.

We were charting new territory as a couple, and I wouldn't walk on eggshells around him. I rolled out of bed, reaching for my robe. I began in a gentle tone. "I appreciate your offer of help."

Quig sat up against the headboard, and I noticed a slight narrowing of his eyes. I drew a deep breath. "However, I have my own way of investigating. I'm totally invested in the outcome, and I need to stay in charge of my efforts."

He raised his hands in surrender mode and grinned. "Fine with me. I'm totally invested too. What's happening today?"

His face looked so eager, so brand-new-puppy fresh. I would kick myself to Florida and back if I hurt him. I wanted his help. Did I trust him enough to reveal a few secrets?

Yes. "I have names of two people Jerry Meldrim's daughter Fawn identified as being upset with her father. There's Joe Block, his former business partner, and Randy Myers, his banker. I planned to visit Randy today. The institution where he worked took a big hit when Joe and Jerry's yogurt shop closed, and they declared bankruptcy."

"Okay, we'll start at the bank."

"Nothing is ever so simple. I called the bank, and Randy retired soon after that bankruptcy. Claimed he wanted to spend more time with his family, from what the helpful woman in Human Resources told me."

"She shouldn't be releasing confidential information like that."

"Apparently, the woman owed my mother a favor, so she bent the privacy rules. It was nice to catch a break like that."

"Very nice." He gazed at my robe which now gaped open and then he reached for me. "Speaking of nice..."

~*~

Over a late breakfast of mouthwatering French Toast and strawberries, I changed my mind about the usefulness of visiting the bank. After all, if one employee had been chatty on the phone, maybe that was the culture of the bank. Quig and I created a cover story of a young couple interested in borrowing money to build a home and then drove to the bank.

The bank lobby walls and floors were made in several shades of marble and had an echo component that no amount of area rugs could soften. Cameras in the ceiling covered all comings and goings. After we asked a chirpy teller who to see about a loan, we were shunted to a different waiting area, where artwork hung on the walls and soft carpet covered the floor. If cameras were back here, they would be concealed. In short order a loan officer, Ms. Clay, escorted us to her office.

She bore the calculating smile and battle-hardened gaze of a used car salesperson. Much to my annoyance, after we were seated she spoke directly to Quig. "What brings you in today, Dr. Quigsly?"

Quig nodded politely. "We're considering building a home and wanted to familiarize ourselves with construction loans. What's your process for that?"

"I'm happy to help you with that," Ms. Clay said. "Do you have an account with Bank by the Sea?"

"Didn't know that was a requirement," Quig said. "We currently bank elsewhere."

"It isn't a prerequisite to apply. Just more paperwork involved up front. Once your loan is approved, your draw is deposited in a Bank by the Sea construction loan account." She brought out a tablet, opened a form, and began uploading our information. "Have you already purchased your lot?"

"We're still looking," I said, deciding to wrest control of the conversation. I noticed there were no obvious cameras in her office. "We don't plan to apply for the loan today. We want to know hypothetically if we could get a loan, how much we can borrow, and what your loan rates are."

Ms. Clay gave off an academic vibe of one eager to impart knowledge. "Many people don't realize that it takes longer to get a construction loan than a mortgage. You'd be wise to apply now and get pre-qualified. After we have your financial information, we run a credit check and determine if you meet our criteria. Your credit score will dictate the amount we'll offer. The loan approval process may take seven to ten business days, depending on the time of year."

"I see." If we were actually applying for a loan, my business was solvent, and Quig had a county government job, for now, so that shouldn't take long at all. The fact that his job might be on the line wasn't commonly known yet, as far as I knew, so that shouldn't matter.

Ms. Clay reached into her top drawer and withdrew a couple of brochures for us. "Our loan rates vary with the product, the economy, and whether you qualify for a specialty package. To finalize your application, we'll also need copies of your property contract, and your building plans. We'll need to talk with your builder and obtain a cost estimate from him. Once we have those in hand, we'll order an appraisal of your property at your expense."

I leaned forward and gave her an earnest look. "That sounds like a lot of paperwork. Do you ever streamline the process? Quig is the County Medical Examiner, and I co-own a Savannah business with my sister."

Ms. Clay stopped fidgeting and shook her head. "We don't skip steps. We use a check list of tasks in our evaluation process. If those boxes aren't all checked off, we can't proceed with the approval process."

"That's different information than we heard from one of my business clients. He got a loan with minimum paperwork. May we speak with the loan agent he recommended, Randy Meyers?"

"Mr. Meyers is no longer with Bank by the Sea." She

scowled at me. "I believe I know the loan you're referencing, and while I can't go into details for confidentiality reasons, we have stricter procedures now than we had in previous years. We made significant policy changes. As a result, we have an advantage over most banks in the Coastal Empire today."

"We understand," Quig said, rising, "though we'd hoped for a simplified process. Thank you for the information, and we'll consider using your bank's services."

Quig and I exited the building and got in his Hummer. I caught his eye. "Good teamwork in there. Thought we'd head to Randy Meyers' home next."

"Works for me."

As Quig drove, I noted, "Ms. Clay at the bank seemed pragmatic about the failed loan. In fact, she considered the experience as a net positive for their business."

"Lemonade," Quig said. "Admin types do that. They put a certain spin on past events to present them in the best light."

Lemonade? I thought about the sourness of lemons for a minute and got it. "If her attitude is the norm there, a banker wouldn't have taken out Jerry Meldrim with an arrow to the heart."

Quig snorted. "She didn't strike me as the serial killer type. Not only that, but she isn't strong enough to move Jerry's body to your grandparents' grave."

"She could've had help."

"Possibly, but the more people who know a secret, the less likely it is to be contained. My gut says she isn't who we're looking for."

I didn't want this lead to die. I had to find someone else who might be the guilty party. "Might be Randy then. He could easily shoot down US Route 80 from Whitemarsh Island to Savannah in no time flat." I pronounced the island's name in the manner of locals, ignoring the "e" so that it came out wit-marsh.

We kept our thoughts to ourselves for the rest of the drive

to the island, which had tidal creeks on three sides. Not even the crowded Berry Good corner gas station along the way received a comment from either of us. The affluent neighborhood consisted of well-groomed yards and a blend of home styles, everything from soaring concrete and glass contemporaries to squatty brick ranchers. Randy Meyers' older no-frills two-story boxy home was off the main drag on Whitemarsh Island.

His driveway ended at a wooden privacy fence. Since Quig's Hummer sat high, I stood on the running board to peek over the fence before I stepped down. My gaze landed on a stack of hay bales with a paper target full of holes.

I tapped on the roof of the vehicle. "Quig! I see a target practice set-up back there."

He stepped on his running board and peered over the fence. "Someone's been shooting."

"It looks just like the archery target set-up we had in my class."

"Could be. I suppose he wouldn't be shooting a pistol out here. Too populated."

"This could be the break we need."

A stern voice from behind me asked, "Who are you people, and what are you doing on my property?"

Chapter Twenty-Two

Busted! Heat flushed up my neck to my face, and dang if my palms didn't turn into watering pots. A mockingbird chided me from a nearby tree. Investigating wasn't for sissies.

I stepped down from the running board and offered my hand to the lean stranger. It was ignored. "Mr. Meyers, hello. Pardon our intrusion. I'm Tabby Winslow, a local businessperson, and this is my boyfriend, Dr. Quigsly, the Chatham County Medical Examiner. We came to speak with you about Bank by the Sea."

The man blinked and turned to Quig, who'd rounded the vehicle to stand by me. "I recognize your name, Dr. Quigsly, and so I'll grant you a minute to convince me why I shouldn't call the police."

"Thank you, Mr. Meyers," Quig said. "We're seeking information about Jerry Meldrim. Given that you knew him, we hoped to speak with you regarding your dealings with him."

"My connection to Jerry was as his loan officer. I'm no longer associated with the bank, and I remain bound by client confidentiality even though I'm not an active employee."

"Since you popped out here so quickly, I believe Ms. Clay

Tallowed Ground

called you as soon as we left her office," Quig said.

Randy Meyers' foggy aura pulsed. I had to look away from it, or I'd surely mention how troubled he seemed. I radiated calming energy to go with the bright sunshine warming our shoulders.

"Though our questions are about Jerry Meldrim's loan, perhaps you can speak to us in generalities to avoid a conflict," I said.

He brushed away my suggestion. "I can't speak about bank business."

"Even so, there must be a way you could help us," I said. "We wouldn't be here if it wasn't important."

"My retirement account is administered through the bank. I won't jeopardize that."

I started to speak again, but his face clouded as if he wanted to say something but was working through it. Curious, I waited. Would he cough up the break I needed?

"Bank by the Sea follows the guidelines for our industry, always has, and always will, is the company line," Randy said. "Before the bank enacted stricter procedures early this year, some loan seekers might have taken advantage of social connections during their application process. I can't say more than that."

I tried to suss out what he hadn't said. Jerry and Joe got their loan under the old system. "So those loans had more trust and less verification involved?"

"I can't say." Randy chewed his lip and then shrugged. "You want to know who got screwed by that deal? Jerry Meldrim. He lost his job, home, and family. I felt sorry for the guy."

Not what I expected, but at least this guy was talking now. "Do you blame him for losing your job?"

"Heck no. I wasn't fired. I got an early retirement at sixty-two with benefits. Can't beat that."

"I see." My thoughts jumbled as I realized the top guns in

the bank were more likely to have been upset with Jerry Meldrim for defaulting on the loan. After all, one of them had greased the application. "Did anyone at the bank want to harm Jerry for damaging the bank's reputation?"

Randy Meyers pressed his lips together. Silence prickled on the back of my neck.

I recognized a conversational dead end. Worse, the answers I sought weren't here. Oh, but I had one more question. Would he answer it?

"Did many of these preapproved loans fail?" I asked.

Quig froze at the question, focusing his attention on the man before us.

Randy didn't answer at first. As the silence lengthened, I worried he wouldn't respond. His aura flared again, flashing with negativity. Instinctively, I soothed it until he breathed easier.

"All of them," he whispered. His eyes looked bleak.

Another surprise. Dang. This sounded like financial misconduct. And it might be relevant, or it might have nothing to do with the murders. It was hard to make any assumption.

"Couldn't help but notice there's a shooting range in your yard," Quig said, doing a complete one-eighty in topic. "I thought noise ordinances out here would prohibit gunfire."

Ah. Quig was fishing. Good for him. Would Randy take the bait?

"It isn't for guns," Randy said. "My grandson got a bow and arrow set for Christmas. Took him a while to get the hang of it, but he's improving little by little."

Ack. I wanted to wail out my frustration. This guy had a pat answer for everything, not that his responses hinted at guilt or innocence. On the drive out here, I wanted him to be Jerry's killer. But there was no proof and certainly no strong emotion, not unless Randy was lying about that loan. Unfortunately I didn't know him well enough to make a call about his truthfulness.

Randy crossed his arms. "I've said more than enough. Time for you to leave."

"Thank you for your time," I said, handing him a business card from my shop. "If you think of anything else you'd like to share, here's my number."

"Why are you doing the job of a police officer? You're not a cop." He glanced at the card. "You're a candlemaker."

"I'm trying to find the real killer, same as the cops are. Trouble is the cops think I had something to do with it. But I didn't."

Randy looked thoughtful, but he didn't say anything else.

Quig and I hopped in the Hummer and split. At the stop sign, I glanced over at him. "We never even made it out of Randy's driveway. Worse, he didn't tell us anything new."

"Sounded to me like he couldn't talk, even if he wanted to," Quig said. "He must've signed a non-disclosure agreement, though he was not a top dog there. We were lucky he said as much as he did."

"You believe him about Jerry's loan being a done-deal and the grandkid archer?"

"No reason to doubt him. He didn't seem to have an axe to grind against his employer, but I'm not the investigator in this car."

"Maybe, but I have confidence in your many talents."

"I've talked to plenty of people over the course of my career as a Medical Examiner. Perhaps that skill is an asset for investigation. You asked good questions. You're the hired gun of our team."

"How odd that you use a weapon to describe my interview style."

He regarded me steadily after he stopped the Hummer at the stop sign. "I noticed that he visibly relaxed, twice."

Ruh-roh. Quig saw what happened when I sweetened the energy around us. I offered a possible explanation. "I often have that effect on people."

"Be that as it may, we tag-teamed him effectively. If not for the warning call from his former coworker, he wouldn't have seen us coming."

Thank goodness he'd dropped the conversation thread about Randy visibly relaxing. "That call reminded him to keep his mouth shut."

"He followed her advice. We didn't get much out of him."

"Do the cops know about his archery target? I could call Detective Belfor."

"No point in that. They'd fuss about you meddling in their case, and they might *invite* you to the station again. I've got way better ideas for the rest of the day, and they start and end at home with you."

Though I'd been looking forward to researching the board members for Bank by the Sea, I appreciated Quig helping me and driving me around today. We must be on the right track now. It felt right in any event. "I approve of your investigation-and-reward reaction chain. Count me in on that idea."

Chapter Twenty-Three

You up for a sister night? Sage sent on our twin-link hours later. Her message came across tense and a little cross-sounding. *The black clothes spying kind of night?*

From the comfort of Quig's arms, I tensed automatically, worry dampening my happiness. Had something happened to my sister? *Yes. I want to see you as well. Everything all right in Sage-and-Brindle land?*

We're great. Why do you ask? Do you know something I don't?

Hmm. Maybe nothing was wrong. Maybe my hearing made something out of nothing. *Relax. No cause for alarm. It's just...you rarely date any guy this long. Add in Auntie O staying there, and your place is a pressure cooker.*

Sage didn't respond right away. At first, I felt guilty for alarming her, but then confidence in my judgment asserted itself. My assumptions were valid based on thirty years of knowing my sister. Her behavior had changed. I waited for her to continue, hoping my honesty hadn't been too much for her to handle right now. Then she spoke in my head again.

I suppose you're right about me and the crowded apartment, but here's the thing. I don't feel trapped with Brindle. He's supportive and values my time and opinions, something I can't claim for former boyfriends. He dampens the part of me that spoils for fights. I don't feel restless. I feel…content, for the most part. Our B&E sideline fills my need for excitement, so I want to go a-sleuthing tonight, to take the edge off, so I don't do something stupid and push Brindle away for no good reason.

Ah. Our sleuthing filled an important void for her as a pressure release valve. That made sense. What I'd interpreted as tension in her twin-link voice instead was her need to color outside the lines. She craved an adrenaline rush much like our wintery beach days. Some families went to the gym together. Ours preferred skirting the edge of danger.

Or at least Sage did. I wasn't so sure where I fit on the spectrum of risky business, given my tension and stress level. I'd rather not break the law, but our eyes-on approach helped in every investigation we'd undertaken. I could set aside any misgivings temporarily because we weren't stealing anything. All we did was look around.

Aware that I needed to answer, I shot her a quick message. *Happy to learn that. Meet you in the alley at seven?*

See you there.

~*~

Quig left for the gym before I joined Sage in the alley. Good thing he wasn't here because he might've noticed my different clothing and realized we were up to no good. I don't know what he thought we sisters did on my nights with Sage, but he never begrudged the time I spent with my twin, even if we weren't being straight arrows.

Even so, I added a tote of the clothes I'd worn earlier today. I could change in the car on the way home and leave my dark clothes in Sage's car.

"Good news about my plant farm," Sage said when I joined her in her compact sedan. She'd been lucky with this used car purchase in that the interior looked new, and the car ran like a dream. "Brindle signed a lease yesterday on property not too far out of town. He insisted on making the purchase since I won't let him kick in for rent. Anyway, water and power are on the lot, so I have few start-up expenses. I'm selling this car and getting a pickup, which would be better for hauling plants in and out of the city."

"That sounds wonderful. Having a nursery grow-space is something you've dreamed of for a long time. I can see why you need different transportation. Probably couldn't fit many plants in this car. Congratulations, no wonder you're beaming. Everything is falling into place for you."

"Thanks. I'm psyched about it. Back to this car. It runs well and isn't a lemon. Are you interested in purchasing it from me? If not, Auntie O is interested, but you have first dibs."

I'd been proud of my car-free life this past six months, but it was darned inconvenient having to arrange rides for everything. Though my orbit revolved around downtown Savannah, it was a pain to schlep groceries home in a taxi or go to and from doctor appointments. I'd been toying with the idea of buying a used car but figuring out which one had been daunting. Sage's proposal appealed to me.

I looked around the ten-year old Honda Civic with an assessing eye. Pros: didn't smell like cigarette smoke, ran forever on a tank of gas, no maintenance issues with it during the two months Sage owned it, and the interior was in good shape. Cons: car payments, car tag, auto insurance, routine maintenance fees, and parking fees. Could I afford it?

"I'm tired of hitching rides and borrowing cars," I said. "How much are you selling it for? This car would be a godsend for local driving, but I need to crunch the numbers. I should talk it over with Quig too."

She told me her price along with her insurance and tag costs. It was a better price point than what I'd had before so I could cover the full cost with savings. "You sure you don't want to trade it in toward the truck?" I asked.

"Nope. Brindle knows someone who needs to sell their dad's old truck. It's been garaged for a few years but otherwise is in great shape. Staying out of a car dealership keeps the prices lower for me and you."

"How'd you finance this car originally? I'm wondering about the red tape of the sale."

"Borrowed from myself, and I've been paying my savings back each month as if the debt was a car payment. I have the title in my lock box. A sale is as simple as you writing a check and me signing the car over to you."

Ah. I wouldn't have thought to use my savings and pay myself back. I swelled with sisterly pride at Sage's sharpness about financial matters. "I'll let you know tomorrow." I noticed she hadn't pulled out of the lot yet. "Where are we headed?"

"Thought we'd hit Joe Block's apartment on Pennsylvania Avenue first and Jerry Meldrim's place in Garden City next."

"You have the addresses?"

"Turns out it pays to date a lawyer. Brindle looked up their business license for that bankrupt yogurt shop. Both home addresses were listed on the application. That was odd as it would've been likely that they formed a corporation and used a post office box for their mailing address. However, nothing about that yogurt shop is straightforward. I drove by Jerry's place an hour ago and saw other people moving in. Got the distinct sense we are too late to get in there. Let's start with Joe Block."

As we rode over there, Sage's rock and roll station pounded the airwaves. I did my best to virtually stick my fingers in my ears so I could think. The home addresses for both men weren't in prime locations, which likely meant they couldn't afford the price tag that came with most rentals in the historic district. The value of these assets wasn't much, assuming they owned the places where they lived. How the heck did they get a loan?

The facts did not add up. Did the bankers use Meldrim and Block somehow? I wondered if the other two victims took out loans from Bank by the Sea. The bank had three branch locations in Savannah. It was possible the bank had been convenient to all three victims, but was it probable?

All too soon we were in East Savannah. I wasn't keen on walking around in a redeveloped neighborhood, even one with security cameras but where I knew no one. Good thing I could make us invisible, if needed. Sage found a parking spot not far from the apartment complex. Some young people stood on a corner between us and the building. We watched as a runner approached the group, spoke with a lanky man, shook hands with the guy, and jogged on his merry way.

Did that just happen? Looked a bit like a slick drug handoff. Sage said.

Maybe though I think the people who live here are teachers, cops, and others with low-paying or entry level salaries and are good people on the whole. Since we're planning to do something illegal, we're in no position to judge what happened on the street corner. Can you see Joe Block's apartment from here? Is it dark?

It is. Also, there isn't a car in his assigned parking spot.

For our own safety, let's go invisible now. But move fast. Cloaking is exhausting. If I can't pull from shadow energy, we only have fifteen minutes or so before I run out of juice.

Understood, Sage said. *Let's go.*

We hoofed it past the corner people, keeping in the shadows to minimize my energy burn. Sage made quick work of the lock, and we found ourselves in a small one-bedroom place where the air smelled stale and cold. Both of us pulled gloves from our pockets and began searching. The jumble of furniture in the living room looked like thrift shop decor, but nothing appeared out of place here.

I tiptoed over to the stack of mail on the kitchen counter, moved the stack to the floor to use my light, and carefully shone my penlight on the envelopes. Everything was addressed to Joseph Block. This was his residence for sure, but the place felt abandoned. His wall calendar showed a few appointments for a security company, a cardiologist, and an oncologist.

Oncologist meant cancer doctor. If the guy had cancer or heart trouble, either issue might explain his absence.

Stacks of dirty dishes filled the bone-dry sink. Since there wasn't a curtain on the kitchen window, I didn't dare open the refrigerator where the interior light could give us away, but the appliance was running.

Well-worn polo shirts, black pants, jackets, and ball caps imprinted with the name of a high-volume car dealership filled his closet. On impulse, I picked up a pair of his shoes. Holes in the soles. Definitely used. This man didn't have new anything.

Dirty clothes were mounded in one corner of the room, adding a pungent aroma of dried sweat to the air.

Sample-sized toiletries and a dingy towel looked lonely in the narrow rectangle of a bathroom. I looked in the john and wished I hadn't. The tub needed power washing and five-gallons of bleach. How long did it take to get that many layers of funk on every surface?

Sage caught my eye and nodded toward the front door. I understood. We'd pushed our luck enough already. It would mess up everything if we were caught snooping.

We returned as swiftly as we'd arrived, skulking through the shadows and sneaking to Sage's sedan. She cranked the car and sped out of the area.

"Whew!" I said once we were west of the Harry Truman Parkway and I could draw a deep breath. "That was intense."

"Speak for yourself. I thought it was a rush. If we lose everything, we could have a second career as burglars. With our complimentary skill sets, we'd soon be rich."

"No thanks. I don't get a rush from our snooping. For me, it's more of a pit in my stomach reaction, and it burns until we're free and clear."

"How's your energy after taking us invisible twice?" Sage

asked as she tooled up the ramp to the highway. Cars roared past as we came up to speed. "Take some of mine now if you need it."

I blinked. Sage never volunteered to share her energy. Ever. "Thanks, I'm okay for now, but I have to ask. What's gotten into you?"

Sage changed lanes before she replied. "All my life, I've fought the world every step of the way. Now that we have experience running the shop, Brindle and I are steady-eddy, and my plant business is almost a sure thing, I have a life-is-good mentality. I quit trying to swim against the current. Everything is much easier. I'm easier."

I gripped the armrest to keep from getting slung around in the seat by Sage's aggressive driving. She preferred going fast, of course. "It's good that you seem more content. All that irritation and anger you used to carry on your shoulders can't be easy to live with. I'm happy for you, but I'm also concerned about this murder charge that's bearing down on me like a rogue wave. What was your impression of Joe Block's place?"

"His apartment had an empty, even abandoned, feeling to it. He's missing, is my best guess. He's poor, that's a certainty from his lifestyle and possessions. I saw no sign of a female in that place. Only guy clothes and guy funk."

"I agree. His mail wasn't opened. Perhaps someone collected his mail for him, or he never opens it. I tend to believe someone is collecting it because the dirty dishes in the sink looked dry. Like you said, his place felt vacant. The energy of the space felt depleted and dreary. Maybe illness does that. I haven't been in the home of anyone who's been sick enough to die so I have no basis of comparison."

"Block might be on the lam. Maybe we could get a lead on his present location by calling that car dealership tomorrow and asking to speak with him."

"Sounds good. Also, I could ask Quig to check the morgue records. He can still access the computer system there because he has a journal article to finish, even though he's on administrative leave."

As Sage processed my comments, she swerved over the fog line on the road's edge and back into our lane, narrowly missing debris in the road. "The morgue? You think Joe's dead?"

"Saw appointments on his calendar for an oncologist and a cardiologist." I related the info to her. "Joe could be in a hospital, nursing home, or morgue if his cancer is aggressive."

She beamed approval at me. "Slick. I missed the calendar. Did you take a picture of it?"

"Nope. Herbert R. Ellis said not to write anything down about this case, and he extended the precaution to cell phones and photos. I didn't write anything in my phone about our investigation, nor have I taken any case-related photos. I can't chance my observations being used against me."

Sage zipped around a slow-moving car. "A few weeks ago, Tabs, I would've said he was ridiculous to be so paranoid, but intense police scrutiny is awful. When they came after me in your last case, I couldn't sleep for days."

I reached up to stroke my locket, momentarily forgetting it wasn't there. My hands clenched in frustration. "I'm at the same breaking point. I hope we come out of this unscathed, same as last time, but the right-now part is hard. Remember how I broke the chain on Quig's locket? It vanished. Either I'm losing my marbles, or Quig did something with it. Since our relationship changed from platonic friendship to lovers, there's a little voice inside my head that I can't silence. It makes me doubt that my situation is real. Why can't I trust in the good part and silence the nagging voice?"

"Whoa, Sis. I didn't know you had doubts. Trust me, what you have is the real deal. Fear is clouding your judgment. No fair doing a role reversal on me. I'm the twin who dives off the deep end into paranoia. You're the calm and collected Winslow."

"Not anymore. I'm on edge these days. I don't feel like myself."

"Relax. Quig is crazy about you. Everyone can see it. You know it in your heart too. Believe in what's real and ignore those doubting voices."

Sage charged her words with energy. Guess she wanted to make sure I got the message. "I hear what you're saying. I need to wind down and quit second guessing what he thinks of me. That's easier said than done."

"Did you ask him about necklace?"

My fingernails dug into my palms. "I meant to ask him the morning I lost it, but his career imploded the same day. I couldn't work the necklace into a conversation that day or any day since."

Sage poked me with her finger. "First off, stop obsessing about the necklace. If you don't have it, he does. Your place is as secure as Fort Knox. Second, Quig is deeply in love with you. He wouldn't dump you over this. Third, if I'm wrong about him and he breaks your heart, I'll make him pay. That's a promise."

Her comment alarmed me. I dashed the moisture from my face. "Don't hurt him. Ever. I couldn't bear it. I'm so gone on him it's pathetic."

"You're in love with him. It's natural to have strong, protective feelings."

"Natural?" I snorted. "I've never felt so out of sorts and anxious in my life."

"Welcome to my world, Sis. Hormones, drama, and anxiety destabilize my energy currents all the time."

"I wouldn't recommend feeling like a walking thunderstorm to anyone, but not having Quig in my life would be much worse."

Sage squeezed my hand. "It'll work out, or it won't. Either way, I'm right here."

"Thanks."

A few turns later we were in Garden City. Sage pointed out Jerry Meldrim's apartment, still ablaze with lights. From the street, I saw two female silhouettes inside the space. "That's not Jerry's place anymore. We should have done this days ago."

Sage whipped the car around and headed home to Bristol Street. "Maybe not. We believe Jerry and Joe wouldn't have been successful loan candidates at any other bank. Joe has a serious medical issue, and Jerry's drinking problem has been years in the making. The bank must be the key."

I found myself nodding in the relative darkness of the car. "We should dig into the bank more. But another thing is bothering me. Why did Joe Block have an appointment with a security company on his calendar? From the looks of his rental, he was barely getting by. Why would he make that investment in a property he didn't own? Wait a sec. The security company. Quig and I noticed security cameras all over the lobby of the bank we visited, which I expected, but none were visible near the loan officers' desks. There were two different levels of security in the bank."

"Security cameras absent in some areas. Hmm. This is a big reach but what if someone from a security company extorting a bank director into making bad loans and then seizing the loan collateral at bargain prices? Brilliant but wicked set-up."

If Sage guessed right, that would be chilling indeed. Even so, it was a guess. The cops had me trained to think in terms of needing hard evidence, even if we started out with guesses. "That line of reasoning is a stretch for me, and how would we prove it? Besides, I don't want to focus entirely on the bank until we know more."

"Did the other victims have accounts at Bank by the Sea?"

I chewed on that for a moment then frowned. "We don't have the resources to vet the bank or the security company. The other possible connections between victims are the accountant, The Oaks, and alcoholism."

"There was no indication from their homes that Jenae Pendley or Butter Rawlins drank too much," Sage said. "No empty liquor bottles in the trash or open bottles anywhere in the living space."

My attention was drawn to groups of people enjoying this mild winter evening illuminated by the cozy spills of light from the pole-mounted lanterns. I was ready to go home, to be thinking about anything other than the case. In spite of myself, I responded. "Perhaps, but high functioning alcoholics are deceptive. They act like teetotalers, but in reality they must keep drinking daily to maintain equanimity."

"You've given this a lot of thought."

I reached for my tote of extra clothes. "Just remembering Mom's friend Hazel who always smelled faintly of booze at any time of day but was sharp as a tack. I'm just trying to figure the case out but I'm stumped. Worse, time is running out. Every night I close my eyes, I see Detective Nowry's face and enormous handcuffs."

Sage grimaced as she parked the car. "Not good."

Chapter Twenty-Four

After two days of leisure time, I looked forward to making candles in my stillroom. However, to achieve the level of Zen required for crafting aromatherapy candles, I needed to be stress-free. The victims, their stories, and the elusive killer intruded on my thoughts.

I drifted out to The Book and Candle Shop, talked with Gerard, our store clerk, and dusted everything in sight. I chatted up customers. I added more St. Patrick's Day decorations. I hugged the cats.

Herbert R. Ellis dropped by, and I sighed with relief. "You have news?" I asked.

"Nice vibe in here." He drew in a lungful of air and radiated serenity as he exhaled, as if he'd imbibed the very spirit of the earth. "I have lots of news. Be more specific."

"Are the cops moving on to another suspect?" I wished I could ask my attorney for his recipe for attaining bliss. I could use some right now. "Because that would make my day."

"I doubt it. Sharmilla gave me a tip to be here because it will expedite matters. They're coming this morning."

Ugh. Another cop visit. Not on my agenda today, but perhaps the tide was turning. The female detective appeared sympathetic. "You're dating Detective Belfor again?" Oops. I hoped he didn't think I wanted to date him. A few months ago he'd said he'd date me in a heartbeat, but his romantic focus was on Belfor. They were good together.

"Yes. Why are you tightly wound today?"

Thank goodness he wasn't alarmed by my personal question. I'd always liked Herbert's demeanor. He had an innate ability to get the cops to back down. "Coupla things. Step into my work area."

I escorted him to my stillroom. "So here is my list of possible associations between victims. The connection might be alcoholism, the club, the bank, the security company,…or even Old Savannah families, which just occurred as I spoke. Moneyed people with hidden connections abound in this case."

He whistled. "You're paranoid as hell."

"Is that a problem?"

"Nope." He strolled over to the hanging ferns by the window and sniffed appreciatively. "Your edgy thoughts give me options to propose to the cops. I love setting Nowry back on his heels."

"Just a heads-up. I don't allow cops back here. This is a private, creative area, a space free of toxic energy, especially the kind the cops carry around."

Herbert sipped in another breath nice and slow, as if my stillroom wore the finest perfume. "Your shop feels cozy and welcoming, but this area is something very special. You're wise to protect it. Sanctified isn't the right term, but I can't quite describe the vibe. It's an after-the-rain smell blended with freshly turned earth and the pungent notes of evergreens. You'd make a fortune if you bottled this atmosphere."

"We don't sell air, but I imbue our soaps and candles with this energy."

"I want two of everything you make. Seriously, Sharmilla

loves the products here, but she can't come by too often because she and Nowry spend almost every waking moment together. As I'm discovering from dating her, detectives are work all hours of the day and night."

"The cops are responsible for my edginess. My gut is telling me I'm out of time. I'd planned to make candles today, but it feels like a strong storm system offshore is heading my way."

"Nowry is no prize in the personality department but he's honest. Sharmilla Belfor is honest too, but I mostly notice her other aspects."

"Why is it always them? Savannah has other detectives," I said. "Surely the cops rotate shifts and crimes."

"There's a rotation, but anything related to an ongoing investigation defaults to the detectives of record, regardless of the hour."

The implications of his statement pelted me like a hailstorm. I groaned aloud. "So I'm doomed to be *handled* by them because they have familiarity with me?"

"Not quite."

"They were the detectives for two unrelated cases prior to this one, in which my clerk was suspected of a homicide, but the cops were wrong. In my opinion, they build circumstantial cases, and I'm wondering now how many innocents are in jail."

"Not our problem."

"Not *your* problem. They aren't after you."

He waved off my concern. "Neither of us is in the business of saving the world. No profit in it."

"Right." A nervous laugh welled up from my belly. "About my other issue. With the DNA. Any progress there?"

"My specialist assures me it is gone."

I heaved out a sigh of relief, glad to hear that news.

"Tabby!" Gerard called. "Your cops are here."

"Not my cops," I mumbled under my breath as I hurried

to the shop, Herbert hard on my heels. Both cats skidded through the back door and bolted up the stairs. Cowards.

From his trembling voice, my clerk sounded like he could use a break. These cops put him through the wringer a few months back. "Take an early lunch, Gerard. I'm not sure how long they want to talk to me."

His face lit up. "Ordinarily I wouldn't abandon you to face trouble, but you've got back-up. We're in a customer lull, so I'll be at Southern Tea. Text me when the coast is clear."

With that, he exited the rear door and the cops entered through the front. I sidled behind the counter, and Herbert followed. "What can I do for you, detectives?"

Belfor was sniffing the air like a hound. No, like Herbert. Maybe she was like him. I hoped she'd give me the benefit of the doubt.

"We need to talk privately," Nowry said.

"One sec." I zipped around them to lock the front door and change the sign to "back in twenty minutes." For some reason, people would wait twenty minutes but not thirty. I eased around Herbert to stand behind the counter again. "This is as private as it gets."

"This is off the record," Nowry said. "As in not an official interview and what we say is confidential. The feds are still leading the investigation. This is us talking."

"What do you want to discuss?" Herbert asked.

"The case, what else?" Belfor said, her face flushing. "The captain is pushing for an arrest, but we want to get it right. Level with us, Ms. Winslow. What do you know?"

Herbert edged a shoulder in front of me. "My client is looking for something that links the three victims. She believes there are possible connections between the victims. Perhaps alcoholism, The Oaks Club, the bank, the security company, and even Old Savannah."

"How so?" Belfor asked, earning a dark look from Nowry. She glared at her partner before facing me. "Please share an example of your reasoning."

I hadn't discussed that level of detail with Herbert. Might as well chime in this time myself. "I started with Jerry Meldrim. He had a drinking problem. The Oaks is a bar, which loops in Jenae Pendley, who worked there. Bands play at bars, which possibly ties in Butter Rawlins and Southern Nites. Thus all three spent evenings in bars. It's feasible they knew each other."

"Weak," Nowry muttered, "unless you can prove they interacted."

His scathing tone made me shrink inside, but my ideas were just that, ideas. "I can't, but Belfor asked what I'd figured out."

"So I did, and you've turned up a new lead. What's this about a security company?" Belfor asked. "We don't have one on our radar."

This "friendly face" of the cops could be the real deal, or they were fishing differently today. Hedging my bets, I whispered my answer to my lawyer. He smiled. "My client suggests all three used the same security company."

"Which company?" Nowry asked, his brows arching at our newest information.

"King Tide Security," Herbert said.

"We will check out King Tide. It's fairly new, only a year or so old, but the buyer merged several existing security companies to create King Tide," Belfor said with an easy nod. She made a circular motion with one hand. "Keep going. What about Old Savannah?"

I wasn't ready to move on. To be sure I had Nowry's attention, I cleared my throat before speaking. "While you're checking my *ideas*, find out who owns that security business. Looks like a bunch of dummy corporations own it. That's a red flag to me. Why conceal your identity?"

He nodded and repeated his question about Old Savannah.

On a deeper level I felt besieged by the cops' negative energy. The longer they were here, the more negativity took root, and I had to fight the fatigue that it caused. I squared my shoulders. "Jenae worked for a business that catered to Old Savannah. If you come from new money, you can't get a reservation at The Oaks. They turn you away at the door. Next, the Southern Nites Band that Butter Rawlins played in performed at many private events there. Butter wasn't Old Savannah, but he met many of them at his accounting job. It follows that due to his being a familiar entity, his band was invited to perform in their clubs. Jerry knew Old Savannah. He'd known them since childhood."

"I follow your logic." Belfor flashed a big smile Herbert's way. "But along those lines, The Oaks could be a problem. We investigated Pendley, but we didn't do more at the club than interview several employees about her."

I didn't want to go down the rabbit hole of investigating The Oaks. "Jenae Pendley's job put her on the front line for the club," I offered into the sudden silence. "If she had strict orders on who to admit and who to reject, a person rejected might resent her."

"Belfor talked to the kitchen staff and I interviewed the bartender," Nowry said grudgingly. "They weren't fearful. They spoke openly, without a lawyer. They had no complaints about Pendley."

"I'm no expert," I began slowly, deciding alpine spruce scent would lift my spirits and leaning toward that display, "but a serial killer would hide in plain sight."

Nowry glared at me.

Belfor chuckled. "You're not the expert. We value your ideas though. If we keep playing our 'Tabby Winslow' card, the captain won't invite other law enforcement agencies in to close our high profile cases."

My blood burned, then flashed icy cold. "Y'all are dogging me night and day because of your pride? What about my peace of mind? I'd rather be making candles."

"We hate others butting into our cases, even if they're invited," Belfor explained.

Then they must be tired of me solving their cases, but at least I didn't hog the limelight. Far from it. They could keep the extra attention. I wanted to focus on the shop and put this behind me.

"Is that everything?" Nowry asked. "You're not holding onto information to give the feds, are you?"

I kept my mouth shut, and my lawyer took over. "My client has been forthcoming with you, despite the harassment and persecution of your persistent scrutiny."

"The evidence points to Ms. Winslow," Nowry said, as if that explained everything.

"I like coming here," Belfor said, as if that justified their frequent visits.

"You might consider *why* the evidence points at her," Herbert said in a wry tone. "Someone knows she's solving your cases. Not only is this guy hiding in plain sight, he's also privvy to city undercurrents."

Herbert's analysis struck me as profound. I echoed his refrain. "Putting me away would weaken our shop's position and likely cause it to fail. Without my help, my twin couldn't run the shop by herself. She'd have to sell. The fallout would domino and crush straightshooter Quig, if he survives the witch hunt for his Medical Examiner job. And that's probably just the edge of the storm. The killer is smart. His kills seem organized. He's crafty too."

"Deep," Belfor said, "and I'm trying not to be offended that your lawyer thinks we can't solve homicides without you, Ms. Winslow. We're professional investigators with years on the force. That's decades of solving crimes and murders."

I exhaled slowly, glad I wasn't under arrest.

"Don't shoot the messenger," Herbert said. "I call 'em as I

see 'em. Ms. Winslow's fresh and untutored approach gets results. She discovered a loan problem at one of our top banks. She found a security lead you missed. Both leads point to area businesses that have been repackaged. Look at other emerging businesses that follow the pattern, such as that gas station guy with ads on every Savannah radio station. Tabby's insights are a threat to the killer."

Nowry let loose a string of profanity. I mentally shot air darts of good energy at those cuss words. Neither Herbert nor Belfor paid his posturing any attention, so I focused on our tapered candle display. The riot of happy colors failed to move me today. My fingernails dug into my palms. This off-the-record talk could go very badly for me, or maybe, just maybe, I had grudgingly earned the respect of Detective Belfor by leveling with them.

Belfor turned to me. "All right, Madam Investigator, who is this brilliant mastermind? You must have an idea by now."

Wow. Belfor believed me. I'd never looked at my investigations as any kind of approach. They just *were*.

Time to jump on the glory train, to go big or go home. "I don't know yet. My intuition tells me we'll soon discover the killer's identity. He's been toying with us, so he's aware of progress in our separate investigations."

"No way. How could he follow both of us?" Nowry grumbled. "He'd have to be in two places at once. No one can do that."

"He could have a partner in crime," I said, thinking aloud. "Or if he focused on your end, he'd get a big dose of me as our paths converge often."

"You believe he knows the details of our investigation?" Nowry shook his head. "There are no moles in our department."

I tried to quell his angry tone by showering the cop with good energy. "I don't have all the answers, but here's a guess—"

"We don't use guesses," Nowry growled. "We need facts lawyers can use in a court of law."

Belfor elbowed her partner. "Let her finish, grumpy."

I took a deep breath. "Someone who owns a security company could watch any number of places covertly."

"Police investigations don't work like this," Nowry said. "We answer to a higher authority. They's why we don't jump to conclusions and then try to prove them. We follow the evidence."

"You followed the planted evidence to a dead end, same as I did," I said. "The killer has been three steps ahead of us this whole time, setting us up to fail."

"Excuse me. I need to make a call." Belfor stepped outside. A minute later, she returned, a lightness to her step that hadn't been there earlier. "I verified that The Oaks uses King Tide Security outside the club and in their entryway. This idea has legs."

For once I appreciated being fact-checked. "There you go."

"I asked Officer Willis to discover what connections our victims had with King Tide. In some cases, it might be that a neighbor had a system." She paled. "I use that company at my place."

"You might consider another firm if this one has gone rogue," Herbert said.

They stared at each other while Nowry and I pretended not to notice. I spent the time studying my cuticles, wondering when I'd last shaped them. From their ragged edges, it'd been a while.

Belfor glanced at her detective partner. "We have a full day's work ahead of us."

Nowry's gaunt smile looked macabre. "Anything to wipe the stain off our reputations."

They left, and I realized smooth jazz had been playing on the sound system in the background. Funny how my ears tuned that out when the cops were here. "Thank you for facilitating our meeting of the minds. It went well, considering," I said. "And thanks for passing along that tip about Dr. Chang to Quig."

"My pleasure. Cases involving you two are always interesting. Your attraction could be for the greater good. I now have a similar problem with Sharmilla Belfor."

I grinned. "I sense you're no longer pining away for me. She must have won you over."

"She loves me," Herbert said. "Why can't she admit it?"

I understood his frustration and uncertainty with his love life. My desire to be with Quig had intensified the attack on him from all quarters. Far as I could tell, love wasn't easy to understand. It just was.

With the cops gone, my spirit lightened. Another thought occurred to me. "Herbert, she's trying to keep her job. But given how deep this trouble runs, your relationship could take a hit. The killer expects me to take the fall for him. What if the powers-that-be pressured Detective Belfor to keep you off-balance and me in the guilty seat?"

"Could be. But I won't go quietly into the night. I'm fighting for Sharmilla Belfor."

"That's how I feel about Quig too. This person or these people, whoever they are, messed up by coming after me. This attack from every compass direction makes me dig my toes in the sand and fight. They can't scare me off like this. Quig either."

Herbert patted my back. "You're good people, Tabby. My buddy Quig needs you now more than ever."

"He has me, unless the cops get me first."

Chapter Twenty-Five

A little before four, I took Quig's call in the stillroom.

"I took a shower at the gym, and now I'm headed to Herbert's office," Quig said. "He's got a new strategy for these hostile meetings and scathing accusations."

I winced at the tightness of his voice. Why would people destroy a good man's career? "I'm sorry this case became so personal for you. This is unfair. Worse, I feel responsible because of the feathers I ruffled."

"We are innocent of wrongdoing. This is about greed, plain and simple. Critters always show their true stripes."

He sounded exhausted, and who wouldn't be after enduring days of long meetings followed by a suspension? Time to inject hope. "As long as Herbert works his magic, we'll get through this."

Silence pulsed through the line, as virulent as static. My skin prickled. "Quig? You still there?"

"I'm here," he said slowly. "You know about Herbert?"

"He's very good at his job." I began slowly. "He keeps getting me out of scrapes, and I'm thankful he's good at what he does."

Quig drew in several deep breaths. "Yes, he is, and I need

him to double down on my behalf immediately. Don't hold dinner for me. I'll be very late."

I hated that his dream job had become his worst nightmare. "Dinner will be waiting for you at our place. Count on that. Count on me."

"Thanks."

After hanging up, a dark thought intruded. Was he trying to see if I'd say something about the necklace? For that matter, if he took it from my dresser, why hadn't he mentioned it?

Where had that come from? Guilt, I guessed. Maybe like Sage I tended to sabotage my relationships. I had no past live-in relationships for comparison. I needed to shed these fears, to stop thinking the worst of people.

I should do a special dinner for Quig tonight. I envisioned us sharing a cozy late night meal. I'd treat Quig to the night of his life. He deserved it after the month he'd had.

First, I needed to arrange our carry-out meal.

I placed the delivery order at a top restaurant. As the afternoon progressed, candle shop staff and family left for errands. So it transpired I worked the last half hour of the shop day alone. I never minded that, in fact sometimes it was easier to close for the night by myself.

With only a few minutes before closing, I picked up my phone to call our sculptor consigner to bring more product, but a potential approaching customer made me hesitate. I set my phone aside when a familiar face peered through the shop window. As the doorbell chimed I tried to figure out how I knew this man, but it wasn't until he spoke that I recognized his voice. It was the radio spokesperson for Berry Good gas.

"Glad I made it before you closed." The forty-something man marched straight to the sales counter where I stood.

His July suntan looked downright oramge in the middle of February. Either he'd visited the tropics, or he was on a first-name basis with a tanning booth. "Mr. Berry Good," I said, using his nickname from those radio spots and billboards. "Welcome to The Book and Candle Shop. I'm Tabby Winslow, one of the shop owners. What can I do for you today?"

He panned the room with a critical eye. "Quaint place. Super location too. Easy access to downtown shops and most historic-area restaurants from here. It's a wonder developers haven't hounded you out of this honey hole."

The words "they tried" vaulted to my tongue, but I felt wary. His snide tone and the cloying feel of his energy pushed me into high alert. I slipped into my other vision and gasped out loud at the scary darkness pulsing in his aura.

Ebony threads knotted and snarled in the midnight and crimson energy field pulsing erratically around his body. This man was trouble in a big way, despite all those affable commercials he made about his gas station chain.

I was thankful for the physical barrier of the sales counter between us. I created an egg-shaped energy shield around my body, not trusting this guy one iota.

My pulse thundered in my ears. Whatever happened would be bad. How could I warn my family? If only I had one of those under-counter buzzers to summon cops like bank tellers used. If I survived this encounter, I'd see how much those cost.

I opted not to respond to him and shot Sage a message via our twin-link. *Sage, you there? I'm in trouble in the shop. The gas station guy named Mr. Berry Good is here. His aura is seriously jacked up, and my skin is crawling. I'm concerned about his intentions, worried he might be the serial killer. If you can hear me, call the cops.*

Sage didn't reply.

Rats! She must be too far away.

"This place reeks of happiness and joy," he said. "How can you stand it?"

Strange and stranger. "I love this shop. The vibe is perfect for me and our customers."

"I know about you." He leaned over the counter, crowding into my personal space. "Your kind are a pestilence on the city, and your interference won't be tolerated."

He stopped at the edge of my energy shield. That gave me hope my protection was working. Now to get him away from me. "Leave this shop. You aren't welcome here, Berry Tibbit Moody. If you don't go immediately, I'll call the cops."

The man gave a nasty chuckle. "Oh, I'm leaving right away. So are you."

"No."

He tapped my forehead with a finger as if I didn't have an energy-repelling field in place. I yelled silently. No matter what I said, no sound emerged. I tried to move. Couldn't. *What the heck?* Panic loomed like a tidal wave.

I'm gonna die. That thought thrummed through my mind, until I managed to regain control of my rampaging thoughts. Dwelling on the negative didn't help. What could I do?

I could breathe.

I could think.

That was it.

I quaked with fear on the inside. My brain hit the panic button again. Then he spoke, slicing through my paralysis. "You will come with me, and you will do *exactly* as I say."

~*~

Where am I?

My mind felt foggy, my limbs heavy. I opened my eyes, but utter darkness terrified me. Intuitively, I switched to my other vision, but it didn't matter.

There was no horizon, no landmarks.

Was I up or down?

What happened to me?

Why can't I remember how I got here? I knew my name, where I lived, and how old I was, so my entire memory wasn't gone. Just some of it. The short-term memory.

A musty scent wafted in my nose, that of a closed-up

space, of dank air that smelled like muddy feet. I strained to listen, but the only sound was the ever-constant ringing in my ears, a mild tinnitus I'd had most of my life. I tried to lift a finger. If I could feel where I was, I could figure this out.

Nothing happened. Not even a twitch of a pinkie finger.

I shot another twin-link message to Sage. *I'm in real trouble, Sis. I need your help immediately. I can't move, can't figure out where I am. I'm afraid. Please find me.*

I waited.

And waited.

No response from Sage.

Not good, not good at all.

Something blocked my energy, but what?

I felt drugged. Out of sync with my body. My thoughts bent and lunged at odd angles. Nothing connected as I expected. Had I used my invisibility talent too much? Whatever happened, the energy burn felt huge. What could cause this level of sensory deprivation? Why couldn't I remember?

Cold. I felt cold.

And now that I pondered the air again, it smelled earthy. I tried pushing energy out in a barrier. If that was successful, at least I'd know how big this space was. But that failed.

Panic struck again, and I mentally thrashed.

I couldn't catch my breath.

Okay, okay. I had to calm down, or I would hyperventilate and die. *Think, Tabby.* Earthy smell plus a dank, fetid smell. Chilly air and coolness under my back. Unrelenting darkness. What was so dark that had absolutely no light?

Dire thoughts spun in my head. Few basements or caves in Savannah. Our water table was too high for that. I could be in an interior room somewhere. Or in a crypt or coffin.

Oh, dear Gussie. Had I been buried alive?

My breath came hard and speedboat fast again.

I wrestled it back to normal.

Panicking wouldn't help.

I tried to connect the facts. This place felt unfamiliar to me. Someone must've dumped me here. That made sense. But who? Why did they do this?

Who was my enemy?

Save yourself, Tabby, I said to myself.

I strained to hear sounds, but all I heard was my heartbeat, my breathing, and that faint ringing in my ears. Seconds and minutes ballooned into eternities.

Time passed, and I may have dozed. Awareness snapped my thoughts into critical mode again. My body felt whole. My thoughts were jagged. I couldn't move, but I wasn't in pain. Muddled thoughts, short-term memory loss, and full-body paralysis were my symptoms.

My stomach rumbled. The urge to relieve myself came and went. I shivered, dozed, and startled awake. Adrenaline shot through my veins.

Still pitch black.

Still alone in a cold chamber.

Then my right index finger twitched. A toe wiggled. I focused on moving my fingers and toes. After a few minutes, I could wiggle all of them, plus bend my knees. Progress.

I couldn't give up. I had to escape.

A man's face flitted through my thoughts as I struggled to bend my elbows. I knew him, or at least, I recognized him, but who was he?

I kept working on different joints and muscle groups, willing them to respond. Using my aura vision, I scanned the space around me again. Every living thing had an aura, but according to this assessment and the ones prior, I was the only thing alive in this space.

Another thought grabbed me.

Am I dead?

To check, I inched my hand toward my mouth. The breath upon my fingers felt warm and moist. I was alive. I reached straight up to make sure there was enough space to sit, if I wished. Yes, I did want to sit. So I rolled on my side and worked my way into a sitting position.

The space was taller than a casket. With some scooting around on my bottom, I realized I might be in a small crypt or similar style of monument. Given the lack of city noises and the extreme silence, I assumed I could be in a cemetery.

Fear mounted.

How would my family find me?

Was I entombed alive?

Stop! If you give in to despair, you lose hope, I said to myself.

Trust you'll get out of here.

Know your family is looking for you.

Keep working the solution.

I closed my eyes to gain breath control.

My hand strayed to my comforting locket, only it wasn't there.

I gripped a handful of hair instead.

I hoped like anything whoever stashed me here wanted me alive.

That likely meant they planned to return.

I needed my wits about me.

Then I heard a faint noise.

I strained to listen until I identified the sound.

A rasp of metal on metal.

Someone was coming.

Chapter Twenty-Six

Hinges creaked.

Frigid air, starlight, and dark energy whispered into my tiny prison, filling me with dread. I stared wide-eyed toward the shadowed opening, the urge to hide throbbing in my veins. I tried to go invisible, but I couldn't fade out.

"Come out, my pretty," he said.

It didn't take a psychic to know that was a bad idea. Since I couldn't see him with my regular vision, I switched to my other vision. His aura took on menacing hues as it seethed in the narrow opening. Dark upon dark, throbbing and pulsing from thin vapor to a twisted snarl of nightmare currents. I shrank into the space, not wanting the tainted energy to touch me, fearing it could enslave me again.

Without warning, the man grabbed for me several times. I tucked into a fetal position, but he caught my ponytail and used it to drag me out. Power jolted through me, as his tainted currents shocked every nerve in my body. The pain of his touch added to the blinding headache from being dragged by my hair.

Don't be a victim, I told myself. *Fight back.*

I tried shooting him with an energy spear.

Nothing happened.

I willed energy into my aura, intending to fry his senses and escape.

No dice.

Tears rolled down my face in the midnight air. I shivered uncontrollably.

"You're powerless against me, Winslow."

His bold claim fueled my desire to fight. I struggled against him. Pain intensified. He held me down and cackled in my face. "Go ahead. Wear yourself out fighting me. Makes my job easier."

I stilled at this ugly truth. Death beckoned in his aura. I foresaw my demise and knew he'd likely tormented his other victims too. He got off on their fear. No, he craved it.

If only I had my phone, I could tape him bragging, and it would be the physical evidence the cops needed. But my phone wasn't here. All I had was my scattered wits. How could I escape?

Think, Tabby.
It's nighttime.
No one is around.
Rescue yourself.

I glanced at my surroundings. Starlight and a sliver of moon yielded a faint twilight that revealed pale shapes on the ground. Not shapes. Familiar tombstones. I was in Bonaventure Cemetery.

Clarity returned in a blinding flash. This was the serial killer's stomping ground. I couldn't access my power. I had to outwit him, or I'd be his next victim. "Why kill Jenae Pendley?"

"Why should I tell you anything?" he countered, yanking me to my feet. "Walk. You're on my turf. We're playing by my rules."

Sharp pain slammed into me again, but I braced my legs, wobbling until the agony subsided. I couldn't take many aura strikes like that. Not if I wanted to survive.

Was his arrogance a way into his head? I had nothing to lose by stroking his ego. "You are a smart guy, but the feds will eventually catch you. Don't you want someone to know your story? I'm a good listener."

I waited, slowing my already slow steps, hoping he'd respond. I tried Sage again on the twin-link. *Sage, are you there?*

No response.

I was truly alone.

Tears blurred my vision.

I urgently needed to wake up from this nightmare, but it was real.

Keep being positive, keep believing in the future you want. An opportunity will present itself.

I had to believe that.

Had to believe I had a chance.

With each breath I felt more like myself, with the exception of my flatlined extra senses. I could do this. All I needed was time to regroup.

Time to try another tactic. "By all accounts, Jenae Pendley was a nice person who never hurt anyone. You killed an innocent woman."

"Pendley refused to admit me to The Oaks. The club rules were that as a member's guest she had to admit me, but she denied me. That woman had to die. Same as you."

Hearing his intention unleashed an army of fear. I had to fight him some way; somehow, I had to beat him. Jenae didn't know Savannah had a serial killer when he went after her. Did she see him coming? I sure didn't.

Berry jabbed me in the ribs with an icy fist. "That way."

I stepped over a slab as we cut across a plot. I apologized silently to the departed whose graves I trampled. I tried my question again. "Why kill Jenae for doing her job? That wasn't justified."

"She gloated over my humiliation. To even the score, I dug into her life and discovered her shoplifting secret. I told her I knew her obsession. When she slammed the door on me, she signed her death warrant."

He liked telling his story. I could work with that. "How so?"

"Those with secrets pay to live. Jenae wouldn't pay the extortion so she died. That's the rule."

Lots of secrets in Savannah. He must be a rich guy by now. Something about his voice sounded familiar, but I couldn't place it. *Yet.* If only I could see more than his back. He was shorter than me with a shiny bald head. Possibly Caucasian, but that was a guess from the sound of his voice. His skin seemed dark. Who was he?

I tried to keep the conversation going. "Did Butter Rawlins have secrets? He was an accountant who spent much of his time home alone."

"Rawlins did creative financing for the in-crowd. Once I learned of his dirty sideline, I used the secret for leverage to get him to do my books. He passed. Said he had *standards.*" My kidnapper paused as if to gather himself. "Standards. Can you believe that, coming from a crook? One night I drove to his place and demanded he pay me to live. He laughed. Said he was protected by the movers and shakers. I showed him how protected he was. Smacked him with his own frying pan. Twice. He deserved to die."

Holy cow. This guy had a razor-thin sliver of patience. Surely my senses would revive soon, and I could defend myself. "I see how those people upset you, but Jerry Meldrim could not have been a threat."

"Jerry Meldrim. Caustic person, as you know. He needed cash, I needed trouble at certain service businesses and their shops. I employed him for a most of a year. He made the rounds, creating mayhem, and skipping out before the cops arrived. One cop pitied him and forgave several public disturbance scrapes. Once I acquired all the businesses I wanted and discontinued his services, Jerry tried to shake me down. Can you believe his gall? Said he'd rat me out to the cops. He paid for trying to extort me. His betrayal wounded my heart, so I pierced his heart with an arrow."

An argument sprang from my mouth not fully formed. "If you killed the three of them because they crossed you, why me? You and I are strangers."

"I realized what you were last year when you solved two murder cases in a row. Savannah doesn't need another strong energetic in the brew. This is my town. I leaned on the right people, whispered in the ears of others, and still you weren't arrested for the murders. That's how you crossed me. You were supposed to take the fall."

I nearly blurted out there were other energetics around town, but I had to protect my family. Especially if he had the power to take us out. From everything I'd seen tonight, his talents were off-the-chart strong. "I didn't kill anyone."

"Prison is full of innocents. Ask any ex-con." He laughed, the maniacal sound echoing through the tree-canopied space. "But you could've killed. It's easy for energetics. Don't tell me you haven't thought of it."

Aha! Recognition flared. I knew that voice. Gas station commercials. Berry Good gas. Berry Tibbit Moody to be precise. A memory surfaced. He'd come in the book and candle shop recently. Made comments about it being a prime location. "My death will seal your fate. The cops are onto you."

"They're mired in the false trails I laid, the trails that lead straight to you. Your death will close their investigation."

"No way. I'll be investigated."

"In their minds, you're a villain. Your death will get a cursory investigation at best."

He was wrong. My family and shop friends would demand a full investigation. This guy wasn't thinking straight. I had to get away.

Our footsteps and voices made the only sounds in the eerily silent graveyard. Other creatures of the night hid in the face of this deadly predator. "My family will demand results and an autopsy."

"Dr. Chang will do exactly as I tell him. He's been very open to bribes so far. Can't imagine him developing a conscience."

Chang. My hatred for what he'd done to Quig churned in my gut. I'd deal with Chang later. Right now his handler wanted to kill me. "They know about your associates at Bank by the Sea and King Tide Security."

He stopped for a second. Then he made a dismissive motion with his hand and began walking again. "You're guessing. I'm disappointed in you, Winslow. Thought you were the brains of the local police operation."

I tried another twin-link SOS to Sage. *If you're out there, Sis, I'm in Bonaventure Cemetery with the serial killer. I need your help. Now!*

No reply.

I had no way of knowing if the telepathic message went anywhere.

Did this man's energy field dampen my mine?

Why couldn't I call Sage for help?

Calls. When I didn't have enough signal for my cell, often a crude sketch of an image would go through when all else failed. I should send an image telepathically, but which one?

Would Sage respond to a random image?

Quig responded to images I sent him, though he didn't realize I'd sent them. Thought it was his intuition, and he'd proven he was a receiver. Not the same as a high-powered energetic, but he had several minor talents, from what I'd observed.

Quig was my best hope, but I'd send it to Sage too, just in case.

I sent them an outline of my grandparent's headstone. No words, just the outline. I thought harder and harder about pushing the image through a barrier, sending the message over and over in hopes one image slipped through Berry Moody's dampening energy field.

While I was distracted, Berry grabbed my hands and cinched them tight in front of me with a zip tie. Then he shoved me to the ground. Uh-oh. I should've been paying closer attention. Would he shoot me now?

I needed the cover of darkness to slip away from him. I tried with all my might to short out the few distant floodlights in the parking area. The lights didn't so much as flicker.

"Not so high and mighty now, are you, Winslow? You're mine now. You will do as I say until I steal your last breath. Get up and walk, or I'll drag you by your hair again."

My legs failed as I tried to stand. I took several headers into the ground. "I can't get up," I said. "Why'd you push me down?"

Berry laughed at my flailing around. "To show that I own you."

A sudden chill overcame me. Cripes! The ghost dog was here. I'd had enough encounters with him over the years to know his energy felt masculine. But maybe I could benefit from his attraction to me. In desperation, I tried to draw energy from him. Something buzzed in my head. I tried again. There! A faint influx of energy. *Thank you,* I thought to the ghost dog, unaware if he heard me. His energy iced me from the inside out and then he moved on. *Come back,* I cried silently, my fingers digging into the grass-covered sand. The energy influx wasn't enough power to make a difference. I needed more. Much more.

Berry nudged me with his foot. "All that nonsense about equality of the sexes and yet you're the weaker gender. Admit it."

Irritation soared into outrage instantly. Control. I had to

stay in control. Even so, I couldn't rein the strong emotion in all the way. "That has nothing to do with this. I was imprisoned against my will and not allowed to move for hours. You bound my hands. You did this to me."

"Yes, I did, and it's delicious." His teasing voice went stone cold. "If you don't get up, I'll drag you across the cemetery, which will be worse for you."

Son of a gun. I swore silently, determined to use this darkness from the ghost energy to stand. I didn't want him to touch me. Not now. Not ever.

I scooched to the nearest tombstone and braced against the ground with my bound wrists, willing my wobbly knees to work. Took me a few tries before I managed to walk my back up the stone while crab-walking my feet underneath me, and him laughing hysterically at my every attempt.

If only someone would hear him.

Would he kill me outright if I screamed?

The cemetery was locked now. This late at night the likelihood of anyone being within earshot and having good intentions was zero. Screaming wouldn't help me, and it could accelerate my death, as impulsive as he was.

"Why Bonaventure?" I asked.

He nodded toward a tall monument. "It's where *they* repose."

His hand prodded me in the back, his touch prickly as sleet. "Go," he commanded.

My feet stumbled forward and then moved of their own accord. I tried to stop them but couldn't. Chills arced from where he touched me, as if that numbed tissue were dead. I couldn't survive if he kept doing that. My only option was gathering information.

"They who?" I asked with more confidence than I felt.

"The ones who made the rules," he said. "The ones who controlled the city throughout time. I intend to destroy their descendants one at a time."

"I'm not one of them. Trust me, the Winslows have never been Old Savannah."

"And yet your family survived despite them. You're nothing in their eyes, same as me."

I prayed he kept talking. "You must own a dozen prime location gas stations by now. I've heard you on the radio."

"Thought you recognized me."

His smug tone grated on my nerves. I allowed myself to daydream of his end. He should be punished in retribution for his crimes. Buried alive, perhaps. Then, after he suffered for days, I'd zap his heart with an energy spear. It would be justified. After all, he'd already killed three people, maybe more. "Your face is on billboards all over town. Your voice is on every radio station."

"So what? The hallowed doors I want to enter still slam in my face. Savannah is a small town at its core."

I frantically sought another question when he didn't continue. "Why kill me? I'm trying to make a living same as you."

"Because you know things you shouldn't know. And because of who you are."

My blood iced another few degrees. He knew about my paranormal talents? "I haven't done anything to you."

"Your family's been a thorn in my side from the very beginning. I planned to go after your interfering aunt first but killing you will make her suffer for her past deeds. Then I'll stalk her and kill her next."

He could've knocked me over with a magnolia leaf. "My sweet aunt? What's your beef with her?"

"A lot." His scrutiny burned on my skin.

"You don't know about her do you?" he asked.

I shook my head mutely. Whatever he said next wouldn't be good. "She's a big gun in the paranormal world. Losing an elite assassin like Oralee Colvin will hurt Savannah's paranormal community, but I don't care."

He was talking gibberish. Had to be. My aunt was no more an assassin than the man in the moon. But if he killed me, I couldn't protect her. I kept my thoughts to myself. This man wasn't thinking right.

My silence had no effect on Berry Moody. He continued eagerly. "The city will pay attention to the pattern of kills. I can get to anyone any time. I've got a bead on Savannah now."

Certainty welled inside me like a thunderhead. "You're not just tied to the security company. You own King Tide Security."

His death-head grin sent fresh chills down my spine. Not only that, but he was also more than marching to his own drumbeat. He was flat-out crazy.

"It's mine all right, and a useful tool it's been. The bank president belongs to me as do several chumps in city and county government. I'll destroy Old Savannah one block at a time and erect hideous buildings on their precious squares. The founders' hallowed history will be erased because a new era dawns. Between the bank, the security company, and my gas stations, I'm the new sheriff in town. I make the rules now."

I balked internally at blindly following him, but I couldn't stop. He controlled my walking feet. If I didn't act soon, I would surely wake up dead. But how? I couldn't run away. I didn't control my body.

How could I stop him? My thoughts were all I had, and they hopped about like summertime feet on a hot sand dune. "This is nuts," I mouthed silently, wishing I could think of something, of anything.

"Stop at that tree."

My feet obeyed him, much to my horror. Was he a mesmerist? What power gave him authority over my body?

More importantly, could I block it?

In a fluid motion, he looped a rope through my secured

hands, cinching my hands high overhead to a dangling rope. It happened so fast. I could beat this guy if I could figure out how he sped time up to his advantage and how he controlled me.

Behind me I heard the sharp crackle of a plastic tub opening. Then a telltale beefy aroma wafted into my nostrils. The sound and the telltale scent brought to mind that tub of Auntie O's I'd found in the supply closet.

Oh no.

Dread oozed from every pore.

Then pure white terror.

I darted to the end of my tether and swung back three times, pain blasting through my taut shoulders. I stumbled until I found my footing. The only thing I learned from all that flailing was that I now controlled my feet.

A small gain but a victory, nonetheless.

"Stop and be still," he commanded.

Once again. I couldn't move a muscle. *He's been toying with me, getting off on my fear. I had to save myself, but how can I control my fear?*

My mind screamed silently as his icy fingers worked tallow into my hair.

Chapter Twenty-Seven

I'm gonna die. I'm gonna die. I'm gonna die.

The thought cycled in my head like hurricane winds as his creepy fingernails raked my scalp. The beefy fragrance of tallow nauseated me, and the gloppy substance felt colder than the arctic. I couldn't stop shivering.

Somehow, despite the terror gripping my heart, I remained alert, hoping against hope that this guy would make a mistake. I needed to conserve energy until then so that my actions would count.

Then he tried to work more tallow into my saturated hair. Chunks of it slid down inside my shirt. I wanted to bolt like a wild animal. My feet seemed free. Could this be what he wanted? For me to fight him?

Think, Tabby. Don't let fear rule you. He gets you scared, and then he acts.

I blinked. Could that be how he controlled me? He fed on the energy of my fear?

While I tried to process my thoughts, I heard the snip of scissors. "What are you doing?"

"Taking a sample."

More likely a souvenir. That was often a serial killer trait.

He would add my hair to his collection from his victims. If his plans succeeded tonight, he'd leave this cemetery alive, and I would not. I would spend my afterlife haunting the sandy lanes of this hallowed ground with the ghost dog who was once again pressing against my leg. He'd brought another dog ghost who leaned against the other leg. Greedily, I latently absorbed their energy donations.

A thought rose out of the blubbering dreck in my mind. If I could pull it together, I could defend myself thanks to the energy influxes. I couldn't accept that my talent wouldn't recover. I practiced optimism and envisioned it recovering. Energy was energy. And I'd had more than a ten percent boost, albeit from atypical energy sources.

Energy was energy, I repeated to myself. Stay calm. If I lost it and got scared again, that would give him power.

Staying calm was a good strategy. It helped me while it hurt him. Perhaps this was how I'd beat him. Because he couldn't be allowed to kill off Savannah citizens. Three deaths was three too many. He wouldn't add me to his collection. Not if I had anything to do about it.

First, I needed to block his terrorizing actions from my thoughts. I envisioned Quig and how much I cared for him, of the future we could have if my vision for the night prevailed. I imagined smooth jazz playing in my head. I let the syncopated rhythm of bluesy notes flow over, around, and through me. I imagined breathing in my favorite aromatherapy blended scent of coconut and salty air. Immediately, I became aware of a centeredness I hadn't felt in hours.

Good. I worked on my breathing next. Slow and even. Drawing air in and out.

I felt stronger and yet... he kept sliding his fingers through my hair as if it soothed him. This was my chance. I used every ounce of concentration to siphon energy from him. It trickled in slowly at first, but the infusion did me a world of good. The more I took, the tighter the bond between us became. I upped the ante and slurped dark current through each of his fingertips. They functioned as conduits, and his energy surged into me like a tidal wave.

"What are you doing?" Berry yelped. "Stop that."

I pulled harder, the streaming energy conduit keeping his fingers rooted in place. My internal energy field saturated, so I bolstered my aura and engulfed him with my power. I couldn't form an energy spear, yet, but I electrified my aura enough to hurt him.

He tore free and howled in pain. "What did you do to me?" he said. "You'll pay for that. You're a dead woman. And you don't even know it."

I couldn't break free of my bonds, so I marshalled my inner strength for the fight of my life. Timing was everything.

Meanwhile, he stepped off exactly ten paces, turned, and waved a corded strap at me. "I'm the shepherd boy who felled a giant with the tool of his trade, a sling just like this one, except mine is made of paracord. I've been practicing, and while I'm not a crack shot with this, that will add to the fun for me. You're a proxy for the titans of Old Savannah, and I'll kill you with a stone. All I have to do is embed the stone in your forehead. Just in case there's a misfire or two, I have a whole pocketful of stones." From his pocket he withdrew a small object. A smooth stone.

I stared at the sling and the stone. This couldn't be happening. It shouldn't be happening. Everything in me wanted to scream for help. But he got off on fear. If I screamed he'd have more energy to hurl that stone at me. I didn't want any stones hurled at me.

Now or never, I said to myself, focusing my newfound energy and my reserves into a deadly laser spear. I aimed for his heart and fired without remorse.

Kill or be killed.

Berry didn't collapse to the ground. He pushed back with

his mesmerizing voice. "Stop. I command you to stop what you're doing."

With such a rush of power flowing through me, I blocked his attempt at hypnosis and kept my attacking energy beam tightly focused. I trusted my abilities. I would prevail.

Car doors slammed. Footsteps raced my way.

"Help! Over here," I cried.

"Drop your weapon," Sage yelled. "I have a gun."

"Leave her alone," Quig shouted.

Berry ignored them.

He tried to rev his talent, but he was no longer at full power.

We were locked in mortal combat. He tried to control me with his voice. I sent wave after wave of tightly focused energy into his heart. That organ kept pumping and pumping. I needed an easier target, one that wasn't so invincible. I shifted my beam to his lung and willed it to collapse to prompt a breathing crisis.

I wanted to speak to Quig and Sage, but I couldn't stop what I was doing. Berry was too powerful in his current state. I intensified my efforts.

"No!" Berry screamed. "It can't end this way!"

Quig launched himself at Berry and flattened the man. Berry's mental attack stopped abruptly. I wanted to punish my tormentor with another energy spear, but emotion overcame me. Ugly sobs came out of my throat. I cried for nearly dying. I cried because I was alive. I cried because I couldn't stop.

"Get off me," Berry muttered before falling silent.

My knees gave, and I once more hung by my arms. Pain exploded like winter thunder in my shoulders. I'd never expended so much energy in my life, and even then I hadn't killed him. His mesmerizing talent must've given him partial immunity to my energy attack.

Sage cut me down, and I sagged to the ground, sobbing

and trembling.

"Bring the rope, Sage," Quig said, urgent and commanding. "Now. I need to hold Tabby, but I'll secure him first. He seems to be out cold, but I don't trust him for a second."

I tried to gather myself, but I couldn't stop my thoughts from racing. *I was safe. The killer was beaten. I nearly died. But I made it. I held out 'til reinforcements came.*

Cold. I am so cold.

When Quig wrapped me in a bear hug, I melted into warmth and safety.

Sage shot me a twin-link message. *Why didn't you twin-link me?*

I tried many times. Berry blocked the messages. He's a psychopath and a rogue energetic, with several talents.

Quig got your message, and so did I. He told me he saw the family headstone, that the image zapped him repeatedly. I was on the verge of coming to Bonaventure anyway, since it's the killer's dumping ground. We jumped in the Hummer and barreled over here. He plowed right through the locked gate.

Cops?

Called them. They're on the way.

"Talk to me, Tabby," Quig urged. "Did he hurt you?"

My shoulders still ached, and my body brimmed with tainted energy. Who knew how this would fall-out in regard to my health. "Scared me. Bad. He got off on my fear. But no. I'm not hurt. I'm tired and sore. It was horrible — his mind attacked me. He's a hypnotist. He planned to kill me with a sling and a stone, like David killed Goliath in the Bible. That's the strap he had in his hand when Nowry cuffed him. Said he'd throw the stone so hard it would crush my forehead. My hair…" I broke off on another ugly sob. All I wanted was to shower and sleep for three days.

"Easy, babe," Quig murmured in my ear. "I'll wash away the tallow when we get home."

I'd lost track of my sister. There. Over by Berry. She towered over him with a murderous look on her face, most likely draining him dry. Good for her.

I turned my attention to Quig, calmer and clearer than a few minutes ago. "He admitted killing the others. Said he wanted Old Savannah to know he was coming for them. Because they excluded him."

"Bull," Quig said. "He hit soft targets because the movers and shakers were protected."

Sirens wailed in the distance, a blessing and a curse. I dreaded being grilled by the cops, and if I never saw Mr. Berry Moody again it would be too soon.

"What was so important he'd kill for it?" Sage asked.

"Here's my guess. One of the oldest reasons in the book. Envy. He wanted what someone else had," Quig said. "I thought this case was about greed, but Berry Tibbit Moody has scads of money. He craved the status of being Old Savannah. The way I see it, the harder he tried to attain it, the farther he distanced himself from that reality."

Talking helped me gather myself, gave me an outlet to let off the tension still roiling inside. "The social gap between in-crowd and everyone else may be true in every community. You can't buy or earn your way into Old Savannah. Berry never stood a chance of reaching his goal."

Quig held me at arm's length. "You sympathize with his killer tendencies?"

"No way, no how. There's no excuse for homicide, but I understand his wanting to belong. I've been excluded by others for years. I'll never be a banker, lawyer, or doctor. I'm a candlemaker born a hundred years too late."

Quig kissed my cheek. "You were born just in time for me."

"Thank you. And thanks for rescuing me."

"Looked like you stopped him before we got here."

It was a lot closer than I would've liked. "I wish. I couldn't have survived without your help. I'm running on adrenaline and I can't stand this crap in my hair."

"We'll wash it out, love. You're safe now."

A familiar sedan pulled up in the adjacent lane. Blue lights splashed over the graveyard, adding to the otherworldly sensation. Detectives Nowry and Belfor charged over to us. "What happened?"

I pointed to the bound man on the ground near my twin. "Berry Tibbit Moody is your serial killer. He kidnapped me this afternoon and stashed me in a Bonaventure crypt with the intent of killing me. Given the serial killer's habit of leaving bodies in or near this cemetery, Sage and Quig acted on a hunch and drove here tonight. They arrived in time to stop him."

I blinked the moisture from my eyes. All in all, I gave a coherent rendering of the facts, considering how much I had to omit.

Nowry roused Berry when he traded the rope ties for handcuffs. "I'm innocent," Berry said. "She set me up."

"You'll get a chance to tell your side of the story," Nowry said as he marched Berry to his car, stuffed him inside, and stood guard outside the vehicle.

Belfor listened to and taped my statement. Then she asked me to write it down, while it was still fresh. I tried to write, but my hands wouldn't cooperate. *I'd nearly died.* If Berry had prevailed, I would be dead right now, felled by a stone to the head, David-and-Goliath style.

I handed the blank form to Belfor. "I can't do it. Too much adrenaline. Can't you transcribe from the recording you made?"

"I'll run the tape through a voice to tape program and you can review it tomorrow and sign it." Belfor pursed her lips. "Why did you follow him? You should've stayed in your shop."

"I had no choice. He's a strong hypnotist." I shuddered,

twice. "When I awakened in that tomb, I feared I'd been buried alive. Claustrophobia scared the bejeebers out of me. I didn't want to be a victim, but he hypnotized me, same as the others. When I tried to resist him a little while ago, he strung me up to that tree and bragged that he would kill me with a rock and sling. I realized fear increased my susceptibility to his hypnotic voice. So I tried to stay mentally strong until help arrived. He bragged about his other kills."

"I see." Belfor jotted a few notes on her pad. She must not completely trust electronics either. "What happened next?"

"The tallow." My breaths came too fast, like storm-driven ocean waves. I consciously slowed my breathing before I continued. "He's into fear. I swear he snapped the top off the tallow bucket in slow motion to terrify me. He took great pleasure in massaging it into my hair. It was awful."

"He completed the tallow ritual, then he got into position to kill you with a sling and a stone?"

"Yes. He walked about ten paces like this was a gunfighter battle. Fortunately, Sage and Quig arrived, and Quig tackled him. They saved me."

"You were lucky."

I made my own luck, but I couldn't reveal that part. I couldn't admit how I'd stolen energy from ghost dogs and Berry, or how I'd used Berry's energy against him until my rescuers arrived. I couldn't share how Sage would've drained him of life as punishment for coming after me. And I definitely couldn't explain how I telepathically summoned Quig and Sage to Bonaventure. None of that could go into any written record, form, or database.

Though I brimmed with stolen energy and felt like my aura needed a thorough scrubbing, I yawned, very much needing to be far away from this place. "Can I go home now? I'm exhausted, and I desperately need to shower."

"Not yet," Belfor stated. "We will collect evidence from your body and your clothing. A female officer will accompany you home to collect the samples we need and your clothing. This is a special one-time privilege we're extending to you. You'll fully comply, or we'll finish at the station. Understand?"

Belfor was breaking procedure for me, and that was a huge deal for her. But I desperately wanted to go home, and I'd get there any way I could.

I was alive and that was everything.

From somewhere I managed to summon the energy to say, "I'm all yours, Detective."

Chapter Twenty-Eight

A repeated horn sound rent the air. Five short blasts. For boats, that indicated trouble on the water. Not sure what that meant for cops on land. But if it was trouble... My body jolted into a full-on red alert. I huddled closer to Quig and Sage. It couldn't be what I was thinking, could it?

Quig's arms wrapped around me and my sister. Sage made no comment about how gross I smelled or looked as we huddled together.

Detective Belfor's gun came out. She spoke crisply to the officer standing nearby. "Stay here."

She stalked over to the feds' car, which had just sounded the alarm. Both feds peeled out of their vehicle, weapons drawn. The flashing blue lights no longer seemed weird. It felt like I'd awakened in an alternate reality where strange was normal.

Over the nearby officer's radio I heard the terse call for an ambulance, followed by "Officer down. Repeat, officer down." I feared the worst, but I didn't want to believe it.

Then another message went out. "All units. Be advised the suspect escaped. Radio in any sighting of Berry Tibbit Moody. Approach with extreme caution. Secure the area. No one is allowed to leave."

It took me a few fumbling moments to process the words. Berry had escaped. He could come after me again. My knees gave out. The sudden change in my posture caught the others unaware, and we fell to the ground in what seemed like slow motion. Quig rolled under me to cushion me.

The fall forced air into my lungs, and my head cleared. Fat chance of anyone catching Berry, not in an area of a hundred and sixty acres. Not with Berry's hypnotism talent.

It wasn't over.

Berry had escaped.

I wasn't safe. None of us were.

"Are you injured?" the officer asked. He stood beside us now, his gaze prowling the dark cemetery.

"I'm shaky, but okay," I said.

"I want to take Tabby home," Quig said. "She's been through hell tonight."

The officer spared us a glance. "No one is going anywhere. You're safest here for now."

The tension radiating from him struck me like a hammer. I burrowed into Quig, quaking from head to toe. Oh, how I wanted to wake up from this nightmare.

It's gonna be okay, Tabs. Berry will pay for what he did to you. Don't worry about that.

I cringed at Sage's continued mental barrage of profanity and insults to Berry's parentage. She railed against him with the hatred I felt toward him. Her vitriol flowed over and around me, as if I was in a slipstream. Berry's attack on me had tripped Sage's ground wire. From past experience I feared she was on the verge of lashing out.

Somehow I drew the strength to talk her down. *Let the cops chase him. I can't go after Berry tonight. I've got nothing left. I'm running on fumes, and if you go off the deep end on me, I can't help you. Not tonight. Let's fight him another day. Please.*

I thought I'd drained him enough that you'd be safe. I would've taken him out completely, but the cops arrived too soon.

I'm scared. I already stared death in the eye tonight. I can't do it again. I just can't.

Sobs overwhelmed me. I lost it. Totally lost it, but I didn't feel alone. Sage stayed glued to our friendly dogpile, and Quig's arms reaffirmed the promises he was making verbally, that I'd be all right.

Minutes passed and the quaking stopped. Though I pushed out of the pile, I could do no more than sit up. Quig and Sage sat up on each side of me. I realized Sage was sharing her energy, and though I wasn't back to feeling like myself, I no longer felt like a swag of Spanish moss caught in a gale.

"Are you...okay?" Quig asked.

After the ordeal of this night, I grew teary-eyed with gratitude. Berry's escape troubled me, but the cops would beat the bushes for him since he'd attacked a cop. "Yes. Thank you for coming. You and Sage saved my life. I wouldn't be here if not for you two."

"You're welcome," Sage said, a smile in her voice.

"Sorry about dinner tonight," I said, sniffling. "I had something special planned."

"Don't give that another thought," Quig said. "As soon as we get clearance, we're going home."

Overcome by emotion again, I nodded and hugged the two cornerstones of my life.

~*~

Berry was gone. Long gone some of the cops said, but I knew better. Savannah meant something to him. His assault on Savannah wasn't over, not by a long shot.

Detective Belfor approached. "These two female officers will escort you home. One will drive Dr. Quigsly's vehicle and the other will follow in a patrol car. Tabby will be processed in her home, and that will be all for tonight. Questioning will continue tomorrow."

"Is Nowry okay?" Quig asked.

"I'm fine," Nowry groused as he walked over to join us, an EMT following him. "Just a bump on the noggin. I was guarding him in the car when I suddenly walked over, let him out, and unlocked his cuffs. I didn't want to do it, but I couldn't stop myself. I couldn't call for help either."

"Berry Moody is a hypnotist," I said. "That's why you couldn't stop. He hypnotized me. That's how I ended up here. He's also a monster and a serial killer."

Nowry nodded. "He was talking the whole time he was in my custody. Made me think he wasn't right in the head. Instead he was getting into my head. Even so, this is a minor setback. We'll get him. He left a witness this time."

A dire realization dawned, and tears ran down my face. "I'm a loose end. He'll come for me and kill me. I'm not safe, and neither is anyone who helped me."

"We'll get him," Belfor echoed. "You'll have officers guarding your door tonight, and regular patrols down your alley. If Moody's still at large in the morning, we'll move your family to a safe house."

"The feds are issuing the BOLO as we speak and coordinating roadblocks through the area," Nowry said. "We'll use a large team to bring him into custody. No way can he use that mind mumbo-jumbo on so many at once."

"Tabby's been through a horrific ordeal, and I need to take her home now. Can you make that happen?" Quig asked. "Let's make tomorrow easy for her too. Why don't you two come for breakfast at nine? Bring the FBI team if you like, I'll make enough for everyone."

"We need to process her first, but I think we can make an exception this time. But only if Ms. Winslow agrees to a female officer accompanying her and processing her at home. As for the other, I'll need to get special approval."

"I agree," I said. "I want to go home. I'm exhausted."

"We understand. Wait while we run your request past

Captain Haynes," Belfor stated.

~*~

"Rise and shine." Quig strolled into our bedroom with a mug of coffee and the newspaper. "Also, you made front page news, above the fold no less."

"I'll read the paper later." I nestled deeper into the covers. "I wish I didn't have to see anyone today. I wanna spend the whole day in bed."

"Fat chance of that. The cops are coming here for breakfast in half an hour."

Ugh. I felt hungover from the emotional rollercoaster of last night and not up to the task of talking to cops, much less feeding them. Luckily their meal didn't hinge on me. Quig was a fine cook, and it smelled like he had something delicious baking in the oven.

Even so I reached for the coffee and the paper. "Thanks for this."

"Your protest is noted, but if you remember, they are continuing the process of recording your statement. You could be at the police station still debriefing from your kidnapping, still have that tallow in your hair. Instead you got a shower and slept. The cops need answers. That's how law enforcement works."

My lower lip jutted out. "I don't have more answers. They have my statement already."

"I know, love, but like it or not, you're police business, and they are interviewing you here, instead of at the station. You can do this. You're strong, plus, I brought you coffee in bed."

"So you did. Thank you again for that kindness. I could get used to you being home all the time."

"Be careful what you wish for." He gazed out the sunny window, his expression pensive. "It's unlikely I'll get my job back anytime soon. At least they're still paying my salary."

I set down the mug and caught his hand in mine. "What if you're not the Medical Examiner?"

"I'll be okay. Medical examiners are in demand to review autopsy reports for trials."

"Being M.E. here is your dream job, though. How can you be so blasé about losing it?"

He sat beside me on the bed. "Jobs come and go, but you're the love of my life. I nearly lost you yesterday."

I drew him close for a kiss. "How long until they arrive?"

He pulled back. "Very soon, I'm sorry to say. Plus, Herbert is joining us as well."

~*~

When the cops arrived fifteen minutes later, I was caffeinated, dressed, and coherent, for the most part. Couldn't dredge up a smile, though nobody commented on my lack of cheer.

Before we'd seated Detectives Nowry and Belfor, along with Agent Kimora Easton, at the extended kitchen table, Herbert R. Ellis arrived. He gave me a big hug. "We nearly lost you, gal. That was too close for comfort."

"Thanks. I'm glad to be alive."

"Still. We can't have serial killers hauling you off like that. It's bad for all of us."

I turned to Detective Nowry. "Did you catch him yet?"

"Not yet," he said.

"My one rule is no case talk until after everyone has eaten," Quig said, herding us to the kitchen table. He served our plates from the stove and made sure everyone had coffee.

The food tasted amazing. I wolfed down my portion and would've gone for seconds, but I needed to be fully alert during questioning. Later I'd show Quig how much I appreciated him and his cooking.

To my surprise, Nowry, Belfor, Easton, and my attorney tucked into the all-in-one egg casserole like they hadn't eaten in weeks. Nowry ate seconds before he pushed back from the table. "Captain Haynes wants the Tallowed Killer in custody," Nowry said. "There's a huge fugitive hunt going on for him in a two-hundred mile perimeter. Agent Easton is here for our Savannah PD interview, but the feds want Ms. Winslow in the Federal Building later today."

Two interviews in one day sounded awful. "Why? You'll have all the information from this interview."

"When questions are asked a different way, new information often comes to light," Agent Easton said. "We're ensuring we know everything you know."

My graveyard experience was etched in my brain, and the killer's creepy touch in my hair would haunt me all of my days. Berry Tibbit Moody must be eliminated. Otherwise, he'd kill again.

I glanced at Herbert and back to Nowry. "I'll follow the lead of my attorney in the FBI interview and this one."

"I hope you can keep this interview informal and minimize the stress," Quig said. He stopped busing the empty plates to the kitchen and stood behind my chair, his hands resting on my shoulders. His presence and his touch meant so much. I drew comfort from his caring nature.

"Tabby will be treated fairly during the interview," Herbert said. "That's a promise."

He looked at ease today, and so did Sharmilla Belfor.

Nowry cleared his throat. "Speaking of the case, is there anything new you've remembered about last night? If not, start at the beginning and don't leave anything out."

I hated having to relive the experience again, but as the words tumbled out, I rose from the table. Fight or flight instinct kicked in. My gut said to run. My grit said to stand my ground and fight.

To ease the telling, I stared over the tops of their heads and out the sunny window. "Nothing new. I remember being paralyzed in a pitch-black space. The cold from the hard floor seeped into my bones. I didn't know where I was. It was so quiet. I had no way to call my family. I thought I'd gone blind. I couldn't see anything, not even a shadow."

My voice broke, and I took a moment to collect myself.

"Worse, I couldn't remember how I got there. Not-knowing terrified me. I thought I would die in there, and no one would ever find me."

A strand of hair tickled my nose. I swept it back and noticed my hands were shaking. The longer I looked at them the more they shook. Then my knees started to feel like gelatin. I tried to steady myself on the chair, but my hand missed.

Quig caught me before I fell. "This was supposed to be easier for you." He picked me up and carried me over to the hulking grey sofa, it's squatty appearance reminding me of a thick fog bank.

I could do this. I could wade through the worst night of my life and be done with this. Courage. I needed more courage. I wished Sage and Auntie O were here, but my aunt was in the wind and Sage was over at her place.

"It's all right," he murmured in my ear. "You're safe now. I've got ya, just like when we were kids."

I clung to him until the trembles stopped. His nurturing support was a miracle. No wonder Sage had tried at love so many times. A bond like this was what she'd sought.

The cops, federal agent, and my lawyer followed us to the seating area in the adjacent living room. Belfor went back for kitchen chairs for her and Nowry. Easton chose to stand, while Herbert flanked me on the sofa.

"I'm sorry we didn't figure out where you were sooner," Belfor said in her chipper, good-cop voice. "Your ordeal sounds horrid. At what point did you know your captor was Berry Tibbit Moody?"

"When I woke in the crypt, I couldn't remember my abduction. After he opened the tomb and talked for a bit, it started coming back to me. There was enough starlight in the cemetery to make out his general features, though he kept to the shadows and walked behind me most of the time. His voice was recognizable from his Berry Good radio ads."

"Did he boast about his previous kills?"

I scrunched up my face as I dove into that memory. "Only the three that were in the paper. He said he controls the president of Bank by the Sea as well as powerful county and city officials. Oh, and he claims to own Dr. Chang. He also said he owns King Tide Security."

"That explains so much," Nowry said in a grudging tone.

"Jerry Meldrim's wife has a King Tide Security system," Belfor said. "The Oaks Club and Bank by the Sea also use King Tide Security. Tabby's hunch that security systems linked the victims proved to be correct. It appears that Moody invaded his customers' privacy by using their monitoring equipment to discover secrets about them. Then he extorted everyone for favors. Both the club and the bank confirmed this information."

It felt weird that she was sharing so much information. I guess now that I was a victim, they felt they could be open with me? Funny how I distrusted this flow of information, except I'd already sorted most of it out already.

"Tabby's brilliant," Quig said, pride ringing in his voice.

The questions kept coming, until finally Nowry, Belfor, Easton, and Ellis concluded the session. Easton told me the time for my appointment with the feds. It would be at the federal building. I crawled back into bed and didn't give it another thought.

~*~

A few hours later, I sat inside the federal building with my lawyer waiting for the next go-round. This interview would be recorded via audio and video with Special Agents Lewis Oxley and Kimora Easton directing the questions. My fingernails dug into my palms. I wished I was anywhere but here.

Quig, Auntie O, Sage, and Brindle had been invited inside the federal building, but they were sequestered elsewhere in the building. I hated how my kidnapping and near death had forced such a drastic shift in our lives. Herbert R. Ellis stuck to me like beach sand. He was my lifeline, my prized Monopoly get-out-of jail-free card, not that jail was in my future. The entire world knew Berry was the serial killer. The cops made sure of that.

Detectives Nowry and Belfor watched from an adjacent room, so it was four of us in the interview room instead of six.

"Take us through what happened from start to finish," Oxley said, clearing his throat.

So I recited the story, same as in the morning.

"Interesting," Easton said, though she'd listened to everything this morning. "As it happens, we've had Mr. Moody on our radar for another matter for months. He went from nothing to top dog in South Carolina recently. His company acquired gas stations seemingly overnight, and then people started dying."

It may be *interesting* to her. To me it was horrifying. "Berry Moody used those surveillance tapes as his personal playground. He invaded his client's privacy easily once he offered cloud storage of videos for a small fee." I blinked in shock as virtual wires crossed in my head. "This isn't his first go-around as a serial killer?"

Easton nodded. "We believe that's the case, though we didn't have a Tabby Winslow helping us in the other case. We have agents sifting through his finances and his personal contacts in both locations."

"I hope you put him away for a very long time."

Special Agent Oxley bristled with energy. "Moody thought he outsmarted us by operating in two states, but that tripped him up. Now he's wanted for arrest for your attempted murder and the murder of three other Georgia residents. We will untangle the briar patch he used to hide in plain sight."

Berry was an evil man. He sought to avoid detection in the cemetery murders by varying his means of death. "Did he have a criminal record?"

Easton gave a soft chuckle. "A person of interest in two west coast states. One agent was certain this guy did it, but he couldn't prove it."

The news kept getting worse and worse. "He's done this before?"

"Guys like him are slippery, ma'am," Oxley said. "You've been a few steps ahead of us in the Tallowed Killer investigation, so our hat's off to you. When did you figure it out?"

"The same time you did — when he grabbed me. Thinking back, his overnight success struck me as suspicious. His gas stations were everywhere, and he was on the radio every day touting those stations. He came by The Book and Candle Shop before he kidnapped me, looking our business over with an appraising eye, and my gut intuition kicked in."

"How so?" Easton asked.

"I told you. Instinct made me wary of him. The first time we met, he was unpleasant, but that was as far as it went. I didn't consider him a killer until he kidnapped me. He passed for normal, but he isn't normal."

"He fooled everyone, but we'll capture him again. You are our ace in the hole because you're the only victim who got away. Interestingly, Moody told Nowry on the way to the car that you killed Pendley, Rawlins, and Meldrim. He insisted you're a...vampire, of all things."

Aack. Outwardly I froze. Inwardly, my thoughts churned. *Better shut down that line of thought fast,* even though Berry was technically right. Everyone in my family could steal energy from others. To divert the feds from this topic, I pointed to my canine teeth. "See. Regular-sized teeth. Not a blood-sucking vampire. Moody will say anything to avoid paying for his crimes."

Eason nodded as if in agreement. "Don't worry. Before this interview we confirmed his version of events doesn't jive with the trail cam footage from Bonaventure."

"Video recordings?" My mouth went dry at the notion that cops surveilled mourners in the graveyard. Talk about invading someone's privacy.

"With the cemetery's permission, we mounted temporary motion-sensitive cameras after the third murder. Moody is clearly your captor in every frame of footage we have."

Outwardly I nodded, but inwardly I sighed with relief. Thank goodness my invisibility talent didn't work last night. No way could I have explained that to anyone's satisfaction. "I'm glad you believe me, and your evidence corroborates my account."

"Trust but verify," Oxley said. "Start over telling that story, beginning with waking up in the tomb. We don't want this guy to walk on a technicality."

Chapter Twenty-Nine

"Perception won't fly in court," Oxley stated after I'd finished going through what happened at the cemetery. "Your insights on Moody are worthless."

"Come now, there's no need to be dismissive of my client's statement," Herbert R. Ellis said, rising to his feet as his chair scraped over the tile floor.

The feds interrupted me multiple times during their interrogation to ask unnecessary questions, much to my irritation. From Herbert's outburst, I got the sense my lawyer was irritated as well. Perhaps beyond irritated. I believed he could've given my statement by now.

Herbert glared at the male agent. "You can't tell me FBI agents don't rely on intuition, or they don't get a certain feeling about people."

Oxley rose to match my lawyer's cold stare, two fierce word-slingers at the ready. "Oh, they do consider insights, but not as evidence. Rather, they employ those aids to evaluate behaviors."

From the posturing in this interview room, my senses insisted Oxley didn't care how long this took. He seemed content to waste the entire afternoon with an eddy of never-ending questions. I felt certain Herbert didn't think much of Oxley. The tension in the room rose even higher.

Herbert's chest pushed out, and he glowered. "No way in hell did Jerry Meldrim circulate in the elite world that Berry Tibbit Moody aspired to occupy."

"Our understanding about Meldrim's role in this is evolving. By all accounts, his behavior was characterized by impatience, a sharp tongue, and bullying. Some suggest Jerry's unpredictable ramblings around town put him in the wrong place at the wrong time. Others suggest Meldrim and Moody were acquainted. The combination of Meldrim's caustic personality and Moody's killer instincts didn't go well for Meldrim."

No kidding. Moody killed Jerry Meldrim. What else did they need from me? This interview felt like a waste of everyone's time. I'd shared everything I remembered the first two times around. Three times around the horn felt excessive.

"Let's tone this down, boys," Easton said, asserting her authority as the senior agent. "We closely observed Meldrim's funeral. From his daughter Fawn's remarks, she was estranged from her father." Easton exchanged a glance with her partner before locking eyes with me. "We also discovered that you and Fawn have a *close* relationship."

What were they implying? My nails bit into my palms as I swallowed the emotional response his inuendo deserved. "She's a frequent patron at my shop. We're acquaintances, that's all."

"The agent who questioned Fawn after the funeral said Fawn revealed her father was arrested in your shop in her presence."

Herbert waved a hand. "Hold on a minute. That is an unrelated event. The daughter and her friends often came to the shop several times a week. Either Meldrim knew her pattern and consciously followed her inside or his presence was coincidental. Heck, for all we know, Moody and Meldrim were associates back then, and Meldrim put him up to the whole thing."

"Your *theory* is weak. Do either of you deny Meldrim was humiliated in front of his daughter?"

"More likely *she* was humiliated, given his scathing threats and his out-of-control behavior," I countered. "He was unrepentant, disruptive, and verbally abusive the whole time he was there."

Herbert fired me a pointed look as if to say he had this. I clamped my teeth shut. These agents were slick. Herbert was a pro, and I should let Herbert drive this conversation.

"It follows that others knew of the incident—it was all over social media, after all—and Moody used it in key groups through an anonymous account to portray your shop as a dangerous place, Ms. Winslow. We checked that angle since it was his M.O. in South Carolina," Oxley said. "I'm certain you weren't meant to survive the midnight rendezvous with Mr. Moody, and yet here you are, unscathed. What's your secret? How did you extricate yourself without injury?"

I glared at Oxley, heat steaming up my collar and searing my face. Words churned in my throat and shot out my mouth. "I will have nightmares for the rest of my life. If I relax my guard for a second, my hands and knees tremble. That man hates me with a purple passion. He doesn't even know me, and he *hates* me. I didn't come out of this unharmed. Not by a longshot. You are completely off-base with your assessment."

"My client has no further comment," Herbert said. "I suggest you discuss your conjecture with Moody when you find him."

"Hard to do that," Oxley drawled softly, "when he is certainly long gone by now."

While he bemoaned at length the need to capture and question Berry Tibbit Moody, I leaned over to whisper to Herbert. "Remind them about the mesmerist angle."

"About that, Special Agents," Herbert said, "my client

believes her kidnapper is a strong mesmerist. Special precautions should be taken once he is in your custody."

"We read her statement and plan to take appropriate precautions, considering Detective Nowry was hypnotized, allowing Moody to escape," Easton said. "We will question Moody's business associates until we have the opportunity to talk with him in person. Meanwhile, agents are combing his place."

A memory surfaced, and I brightened. "Did you find his collection?"

Easton leaned in. "Moody took souvenirs?"

"Yes!" I repeated the part about him snipping a lock of my tallowed hair.

"I'll contact the team and bring them up to speed," Oxley said.

Despite the fact that I was being grilled to a crisp, I had the sense they believed me. Moody would probably try to spin them a story when they caught him, but then he didn't know about the cameras. He was in for a rude awakening.

The shop camera would've caught him entering the shop and us leaving together. But he hadn't tied my hands until after I'd been in the crypt for hours. It would've looked like I accompanied him by choice. That might look suspicious.

My gut ached because I knew the truth about this killer. He wouldn't change his ways once he accomplished his goals. He enjoyed killing people. And because he'd confided in me as he tried to kill me, I was in his way. Time to remind the feds of that. "Moody will keep coming after me."

"That's why your entire family is headed to a safe house."

Chapter Thirty

Two days later, Auntie O had baked her third batch of cookies since we'd landed in the safe house. Sage and Brindle acted like randy teenagers and kept to their assigned room. Quig and I read magazines, entertained the cats, ate Auntie O's cooking, and stared endlessly at the heavily curtained windows of our three-bedroom FBI lodging. We'd had to surrender our phones, computers, and tablets in case Moody could track them.

When this started two days ago, Sage and I considered asking Gerard and Eve to keep the shop open in our absence, but we decided that would put them in danger. Instead, we asked the FBI to place a closed-for-repairs sign in the window and tell our clerks that they were on paid leave this week.

My initial paralyzing fear for our lives was still there, but I felt safe in this place. Moody hadn't been spotted since his escape. His radio ads were off the air. People were outraged and boycotted his gas stations. TV news stations touted the fugitive hunt for a prominent Savannah gas station tycoon, and then they flashed Berry Tibbit Moody's name and picture on the screen.

Savannah cops didn't know our location because no one

trusted Berry Moody not to hypnotize one of them. The feds were keeping us a deep dark secret. Quig selected a novel off the shelves and wandered back to our room to read. I drifted to the kitchen and helped Auntie O wash the dishes.

"Will he find us, Auntie O?" I asked as the afternoon shadows stretched across the yard.

"He will."

I did a double take. That wasn't the assurance I longed to hear. "How will we stop him?"

"We'll defeat him."

"How can you be certain? This guy is super-talented. And powerful."

With an eye around the room at possible hidden cameras and monitoring devices, Auntie O mouthed these words, "So are we."

"With everything that's happened, the cops and feds still refuse to credit his mesmerism skills as a killing aid. But he hypnotized Nowry to escape, same as he did to me. It was so creepy. I didn't want to comply with his commands, but I couldn't stop obeying them. I've never felt so powerless in my life."

"I understand," Auntie O said, empathy welling in her eyes. Her aura looked perfectly healthy now. None of those black threads remained.

Her clipped responses suggested I should stop talking about the case. But I needed to talk about that very thing.

Inspiration struck, thanks to the years of my mom watching our bird feeder across the alley. "Would you like to visit the backyard with me? Birds will visit the feeder as sunset approaches."

Neither of us spent time birdwatching, so she should catch on to my ruse right away.

Auntie O's face lit up, and she turned off the pot of soup she'd been simmering. "Let me find a sweater and my binoculars."

I grabbed the portable phone that came with the house and carried it outside.

Soon we sat in the backyard a short distance from the house. A tall privacy fence gave this thinly lit space a secluded, hideaway feeling. "Cameras back here?"

Auntie O covered her mouth as if she were going to cough. "Not that I can tell. There are a few mounted on the exterior of the house."

I followed her lead of casual yard-scanning while faking a yawn. "Feels like we're the ones behind bars. How long will they confine us here?"

"Long as it takes to find Moody, I reckon."

She hadn't concealed that answer. I got the message. Stay on guard. No case talk. "Tell me about my dad."

Auntie O scowled like she caught a stingray on her fishing line. "Why bring him up?"

"He's been on my mind since I became aware of Fawn's father issues. I have that in common with her."

"Adam Winslow's been gone so long, I rarely think of him anymore."

Her comment irritated me. "My memories of him have faded. I remember him reading to me and hugging me, but that's it."

"Not everyone who comes into our lives stays put. Some have wanderlust, some need more personal freedom than a relationship allows, and some can't handle the fiscal, physical, and emotional demands of a family."

I stared at her point-blank. "Did my dad fit in one of those categories?"

She didn't respond. Instead she brought the binoculars up to her eyes and stared at treetops. If I hadn't been watching her intently, I'd have missed the slight head nod. She didn't feel free to speak plainly here.

The last thing I wanted was for the FBI to take an interest in my missing father. I had enough interest for everyone.

Sage strolled outside and stretched under the darkening sky, accompanied by our cats, Harley and Luna. My twin looked relaxed and not nearly as edgy as I felt, which annoyed me. Didn't she believe the danger was real?

My hand strayed to Quig's locket, a prized possession I also wore for comfort and self-soothing. When I realized it wasn't there and I still didn't know where it was, I let down my guard. Immediately, my sense of doom and gloom intensified. I scanned the area seeking the source of the dark emotions, but I saw nothing out of the ordinary. Was my fear urgent because I'd witnessed Moody's powers firsthand? Or was something else currently putting me on edge?

There was nothing and nobody else here. Feds were watching the house out front. We were safe.

But still, I knew better than dismiss what my senses were telling me. If I sensed danger, it was here.

"Maybe we should go inside," I said as Sage joined us.

"Nonsense," Auntie O said. "We're right where we need to be."

I glanced around in trepidation, unsure of the threat's direction. Once again, all seemed as it should be. Rats. I must be losing it. Could it still be residual irritation from taking Berry Moody's dark energy? On the other hand, I hadn't slept at home for two nights and that alone could account for feeling jittery. But my mind immediately circled back to the serial killer.

Ohhh. The cameras. Did the FBI use his security services? Surely not. But I started feeling more certain of our vulnerability.

Had Berry found us? His presence would account for my skin-crawling sensation. I didn't know all of his abilities, but he claimed to have eyes everywhere. He had at least two extrasensory talents that I knew about. During that awful night at Bonaventure, he'd implied he was an energetic. Like my family.

A locked house under guard wouldn't stop him. He would find a way inside. After all, he'd hypnotized Nowry to escape earlier. He could do the same thing to our guards.

Further, whatever problem I'd caused to his lung two days ago likely was a nonissue by now due to an energetic's swift healing ability. Having multiple talents and an unstable personality could explain his off-the-wall thinking. No way would that man hide out until the furor to find him died down.

His blood would burn for revenge.

My blood iced at that truth. I glanced around, sure that my perceptions were on point. He had to be nearby.

In reality, our safe house doubled as a gilded bird cage with us as bait to lure him in.

"Whatcha thinking about?" Sage asked. "Everyone's so serious out here."

"I'm searching for birds," Auntie O said. "The uh, electronic kind." This last she said coughing into her hands.

Their light-hearted bantering added to my agitation. Didn't my sister and aunt sense trouble pulsing around us? Couldn't they tell we were sitting ducks out here in the open?

Sage laughed and darted over. "I want to see."

"Be my guest. I had no luck," Auntie O said. She slowly lifted her hand and tapped her temple with a finger.

I tamped down my resentment and irritation, appreciating the covertness of Auntie O's suggestion. With haste, I composed a message to my twin and pushed it out via the telepathic twin-link. *Sage, my seriousness is due to all my senses hitting a treasure trove full of warnings. Something indefinable changed in the last few minutes. He's coming for me right now. Auntie O can hear us, remember? Because of the mental link she shared with Mom.*

Sage sobered as she digested my message. *I remember. And I'm ready to stomp on this joker and get my life back on track. These last two days felt like we were on a low budget vacation without the margaritas, sunshine, or surfboards.*

Berry is an expert in hiding in plain sight. Shadows are his element. I've felt antsy all day. He knows where we are, and he'll be here by full dark if not sooner.

Her words made me uncomfortable, since shadows helped me hide as well. I didn't want to have anything in common with Berry Tibbit Moody. Best to ignore that shadow remark. *Could be. Look at the cats. Both of them are focused on that corner of the fence. I'll walk over and check it out.*

Be careful. This guy is a deadly trickster.

The house phone rang, and I answered the wireless extension sitting in my lap. "Hello?"

"Your cover is blown," Agent Easton said. "Get out of there. Run!"

Chapter Thirty-One

Auntie O wouldn't budge, and if I could've snatched her up from her chair, I would've. "We have to leave. He is coming." My voice sounded sharp.

"Don't worry." Auntie O said, "I won't let him use me against you. This is the only way for you to be safe. He won't stop, you see. I've encountered his type before."

"Be reasonable," I pleaded aloud, envisioning him overpowering her. I had to save Auntie O, even if Berry Moody had called her an assassin during my ordeal. "This man forces people to obey him, but hopefully if there are a group of strong-minded individuals, surely we can defeat him. We're stronger together."

"Absolutely not. He can't hurt me." Auntie O's knuckles whitened on the chair arms. "Not anymore."

"What are you talking about?" Sage demanded. "You aren't safe in the backyard. Come away with us."

Auntie O gripped the arms of her chair, as if she thought Sage and I could force her to leave. "I should've done this long ago. Berry is someone from my past. A relative by marriage who had a troubled youth."

"This man is dangerous. A coldblooded killer. Please,

come with us," I begged.

She made a dismissive motion with her hand. "Run along, dear heart. This is my responsibility I'll take care of it."

Prudence warred with danger and lost. I planted my feet. "I'm not leaving if you aren't."

Auntie O shook her head and spoke whisper-soft. "Quig and Brindle can't see the confrontation or how I stop him, and I'd rather the Feds didn't see it either. Far as I can tell there are a few cameras back here. I'll fix this. It's my duty to end this since I couldn't bring myself to do it thirty years ago. He was a boy then. Trust me."

Her answers baffled, intrigued, and irritated me, all at once. "You can't drop something like that on us and expect us to leave you alone to face a dangerous predator."

"Your mother will hound me for all eternity if Berry harms either of you. I'll tell you the sorry tale later. Much later. I have to do this. Get out of here. Let me clean up my mess."

Alarm bells rang in my head. She was no match for a powerful mesmerist. "I can't leave you."

"Save your fellows. They won't go if you won't. You know us energetics have to keep a low profile. Nobody else can know what happens here. You two are the future of our family. If something happens to you, Marjoram will never let me hear the end of it, even if she is dead. Please, go. Before it's too late."

She asked for the impossible. We twins should protect her, not the other way around. We were young and agile. She wasn't as quick or flexible as we were. If Auntie O died, Sage and I would have no other living family members. I wanted to guard her.

Sage tugged my arm. "Come on, Tabs. Time to leave. If you don't come voluntarily, I'll tell Quig to carry you." To our aunt she said, "We won't go far. Cry out if you need us."

My how the tide had turned. Sage was now the compliant, agreeable twin. I was the one who balked at directions. Why had Sage agreed to Auntie O's hairbrained plan? I did not, but I didn't have time to change her mind without putting Quig and everyone else at risk. I bleakly accepted her plan. We bent to gather the cats.

Auntie stirred to clap her hands, and the cats skirted away from us to guard her chair. "Leave them. Harley and Luna can help me chase trouble away."

I hugged her, catching her by surprise. "Don't be a martyr. Whoever he once was to you, he isn't that person anymore. He's ruthless killer and mentally unhinged. He's strong too. Make sure there's no doubt he died by his own hand. We need you."

"We'll see, child. Go on now. I used my talent to disable all the cameras and listening devices nearby. The one across the street will prove all of you left."

When we ran inside and shouted for the guys to follow us. Quig and Brindle joined us as we raced out the front door. "What's going on?" Quig asked.

"Feds called. Our cover is blown. We're running away."

"But where's Oralee?" Brindle asked, matching Sage stride for stride.

"She isn't coming," I said, breathlessly. "Hurry. We aren't going far."

~*~

We halted two doors down and hid behind a neighbor's garage. I needed to monitor Auntie O. I fired up the twin-link. *I have to go back, Sage, This isn't Auntie O's mess, despite whatever she hinted at in the past. Since I brought Berry into our lives, I should be the one to remove him. Permanently.*

Not smart, Sage replied.

Perhaps, but it's the right thing to do. Buy me a minute or two. Make up something to keep the guys from coming back immediately.

With fear sending my heart into overdrive, I darted to the safe house and went invisible right before I burst into the backyard.

Auntie O sat in the same chair she'd been in when I left five minutes ago. Berry Tibbit Moody stood about ten paces away from her. It looked like their minds were dueling, each trying to overpower the other. I noted my aunt's thin and pale aura and Berry's wildly fluctuating dark one. Auntie O did not appear to be winning.

Still invisible in the twilight, I moved to stand behind her chair, resting my hands on her shoulders. It felt like a lopsided tornado of energy swirled between Auntie O and Berry. I added my energy to Auntie O's and tipped the battle in our favor. Less than thirty seconds later, Berry wrenched away from the energy duel, the swirling wind sensation ended and Berry raced toward the back fence.

Needing maximum power, I became visible and stopping feeding Auntie O energy. I joined her in pushing energy and fear at him. Then I realized the impact of hitting the tall wooden stockade fence that hard could knock him out or worse. I dialed back my energy, not wanting to kill him.

To my amazement he still hit it at full speed. The resounding crack was hard enough to break every bone in his body. Then he dropped like a stone and didn't move.

I loped to the fence, checked for a pulse, and found none. I hurried back to Auntie O, kneeling beside her chair. Footsteps sounded at the gate, and I called out, "Come here. I need your help."

Sage, Quig, and Brindle ran to us. I took my aunt's hand and shunted energy her way. She'd been near the end of her reserves and needed an energy transfer. Sage followed my lead on the other side of the chair. Quig held onto my shoulder; Brindle held onto Sage's. How did they know to do that? I hesitated to accept their energy.

I arched an eyebrow at Sage. *Do it,* she shot back on the twin-link. *They want to help too.*

How do they know?

Who cares? Save Auntie O.

The cats came over and leaned against us, and that's how the cops found us. One big energy-sharing tangle of people and cats.

"Everyone all right?" Oxley yelled as he blazed past us to reach Moody.

"Yes," Sage said. "We're fine. Just lending moral support to our aunt."

At first, Auntie O barely responded to our energy transfer. Her body remained cold to the touch. I placed my other hand on her thigh and doubled my energy flowing her way. I could sense the energy transfer reviving her.

Special Agent Easton trotted in view. "What happened?"

"We left the property on foot as soon as you called," I said. "Auntie O didn't come with us because she insisted she had to confront him. When we heard her cry out, we feared for her life and returned. Berry seemed to be hurting her with his mind then he bolted. I can't explain what happened next. He ran into the fence at full speed. I thought he'd merely knocked himself out, but I checked and couldn't find a pulse."

"I checked as well. He's dead." Oxley tapped his phone and made a note of the conversation, people, date, and time. Then he studied my aunt who'd finally stirred somewhat. "Take me through what happened, ma'am."

Auntie O stirred and spoke, though her voice sounded frail. "He kept shouting at me, 'where is Tabby?' Then the kids returned, and he balked. I'm shocked that he hit the fence like that. I thought he would leap over it. How did he forget it was there? He climbed the fence to get in here. He wasn't right in the head."

"How so, ma'am?"

"Berry muttered to himself the whole time he was here. Then he stole some of my thoughts." She met my eyes with sadness. "He plucked a mental picture of you all running to safety from my mind. I was afraid for all of us. That man freaked me out. His pupils…"

"What about them?" the agent asked.

"They were weird. His eyes looked all black. I know that's impossible, but that's how they appeared to me."

I drew in a quick breath. Was she talking about a demon? Had Berry been possessed? If so, I hope the spirit was long gone. I shielded myself, Quig, and Auntie O because we were touching.

"Were his pupils dilated?" I asked.

"I don't remember. It was hard to see clearly in the waning light." Auntie O's voice trembled. "I was so scared that I don't trust what I saw."

Oxley's expression softened. "I called an ambulance for you."

"No." Auntie O's chin quivered. "I won't go to a hospital. They poke and prod you all the time. All I need is a good night's rest."

"You're in shock, Ms. Colvin. They'll evaluate you in the hospital and make sure you get the care you need."

"Don't need the hospital. I'll be fine. The girls will take care of me."

"I would be negligent if I didn't have the squad check your health, ma'am."

"Stop ma'aming me, young man," Auntie O snarled. "What if I reminded you of your age every time I opened my mouth? You wouldn't like it."

"No, ma—" he grinned. "See? I didn't do it that time. Let's compromise. The squad will take your vital signs, and you can refuse transport. Sadly, people do that all the time."

Auntie O sniffed dismissively. "Thank you for understanding."

Chapter Thirty-Two

A few days later, Sage and I drove to the shore. The wind swept across Tybee Beach and whipped my hair about my face. It was a challenge to speak without eating mouthfuls of sand and hair.

Even so, the powerful natural energy here tickled all my senses in the best way. I couldn't physically draw energy from nature, but the net effect felt like immersing yourself into an electrical field might. Adrenaline and excitement sluiced through my veins.

My spirits soared. "I can't believe it's over."

Sage spun in tight ballet circles, exulting in the crisp winter day and the empty shoreline. "Freedom! Thanks to Berry's death, we can be who we want to be."

"You and I still have the shop," I cautioned. "We can't run off to live a sparkly life on the Riviera."

"Yes, but the shop no longer defines us. Don't you see? Through Berry's death, we gained a precious gift."

I didn't share her epiphany, but I took a stab at it. "We're in stable relationships. Is that what you mean?"

"Yes. I'm happy. You're happy. The guys are happy. It's strange to have so much happiness around Winslows."

"Speak for yourself. I haven't felt this good in, well, forever. I wish Auntie O had stayed in town. At the cemetery the other night Berry claimed our aunt was an assassin for the energetic community. I didn't believe him at the time. But right before we got word from the feds to run, our aunt mentioned she should have taken care of him thirty years ago." I waited a moment for Sage to make the connection. When she didn't, I added, "Berry was right about Auntie O, and I can't quite wrap my head around the news."

The color drained from my twin's face. "Wait. You've been holding out on me. I didn't know about their mutual history."

"Nope. Our sweet aunt, the woman who nurtured and fed us, the woman who helped teach us right from wrong is an enforcer in the paranormal community. Years ago, Berry was marked for death by the local paranormal council because of the people he'd already killed. Auntie O got the job, but she couldn't bring herself to kill a teen, much less a relative. Instead, she set him up with a new life elsewhere."

"Oh." Sage's voice trailed off.

"What?" I demanded.

"Though I'm trying to grasp this new reality about Auntie O, I see how it transpired. Both of us could be assassins if we chose. We have the ability to drain a person's energy dry."

I skittered backward. "No way. Too much bad karma." Another thought occurred to me. Auntie O's aura had been jacked up with black threads when she came home, but it normalized with the good vibes of Bristol Street.

Auntie O's boyfriend Frankie's wan face surfaced in my memories. He looked ill at the cemetery. I didn't believe Auntie O would harm him. Surely she didn't.

Sage shook my arm. "What? You figured something out. You got that aha look on your face. And then emotional distress radiated from your body."

"I can't... What if I'm wrong, and I give it power by saying it?"

"What if you're right? Shouldn't I know?"

"Oh, Sage. This is so dark. If Auntie O needs to live on Bristol Street the same as we do for recharges, how does she recharge when she lives elsewhere? She must've been recharging another way. Being an enforcer could be how she survives energy-wise."

"I'm not sure I follow this. You think there's an Orlando hive of energetics, she joined them, and then got tasked to kill for them? I'm not buying it."

I fumed. I shouldn't have said anything. Now my twin thought I'd landed in paranoia world. Time to toss the ball her way. "All right then. How do you think she recharged in Orlando? You spent a summer in Europe."

"That was a horrible time. I never found a recharging location. I stole energy from people multiple times during the day. It was never enough. I came home exhausted. Auntie O came home with a bounce in her step."

I waited for her to realize there was no other answer.

"Auntie O can't be a killer," Sage said. "She's too nice."

"I've heard that refrain before. Family members and neighbors never believe their loved one killed someone."

"What you're suggesting is terrible. I love Auntie O."

"So do I, but I've had time to think this through. You don't have to make up your mind today, and I'm open to other explanations. I just don't think there are any."

"I don't want to accept it. You've made your point clear, but even if it's the truth I can pretend it isn't. I wish you hadn't told me."

"I wish that was it, but there's more. Remember at the cemetery on Valentine's Day how Frankie's color was off? He looked ill, but we both know energetics don't get sick like regular people. Perhaps Auntie O used him as her rechargeable battery. Further, since he didn't return with her, he might be dead. It's possible she killed him."

"You are giving me the worst headache ever. I can't take

this in." Sage broke off to watch three gulls soar and skim just above the breaking waves. "She might kill rogue energetics to protect her family or the community, but she loves Frankie. She wouldn't kill him."

"Consider another gap in our family history. Two men in our family, Dad and Oralee's husband, Edgar Colvin, are no longer in the picture. We don't know what happened to Dad, but Uncle Edgar died six months after their divorce. Heart failure, Auntie O told me."

"She never told me squat about her husband," Sage said. "I always thought they weren't a good fit, and he moved on."

"Did you ask her?"

"No. Now my brain is cooking up bizarre ideas."

"Mine too. When Auntie O and I were pushing Berry away, I saw the privacy fence looming in front of him and quit pushing. Auntie O's energy surged. She smashed him into that fence. On purpose. She killed him. What if Auntie O is a Black Widow Killer? As in men in her orbit die?"

"I can't accept that reality, but for argument's sake I'll assume this is someone else's family we're talking about." Suddenly Sage's eyes darkened. "Or the men were *disposed of* after heirs were born, or in Edgar's case, after no heirs were conceived."

Heaviness settled on my shoulders and chest. Could our wild suppositions be true? Were Quig and Brindle safe from Auntie O? I wouldn't let her kill Quig. Sage could watch over Brindle. Or at least I hoped it would play out that way.

Something else clicked. "It makes sense now why Mom didn't want us connecting with other energetics. She didn't want anyone to inadvertently reveal to us that Auntie O was an enforcer."

Sage winced. "Or maybe Mom feared we'd learn she was one as well. Since they were sisters, their talents might have been similar."

I knelt in the sand, overwhelmed by the direction Sage had

taken the conversation. The fire in my brain flared out of control. There was another dot to connect. I gazed into Sage's eyes. "If Mom and Oralee were assassins...what about us?"

"I could do it, and heaven knows I've been angry enough to kill before," Sage said as she sank down beside me, "but you're too soft."

I meant to concur with her claim. Instead, I said, "I'd kill in self-defense or if someone tried to murder a member of our family, but that's it."

We sat there in horrified silence until Sage spoke. "We might be a family of assassins. What the heck? When I woke up today, I had no idea this revelation was coming. I was still shaken by nearly losing you in Bonaventure."

"I agree with you on everything but the family of assassins idea. It'll take years for that Bonaventure near-death experience to fade. I thought I was going to die. First I thought I'd been buried alive. Then, afterward when Barry came and I couldn't control my body, I died a thousand deaths. I hated being strung up and having tallow mashed into my hair."

"You never stopped fighting, Tabs. You skirted his psychic block and reached me and Quig. I'm proud of you."

I sniffed back tears. "I tried to kill him with energy spears, but his heart wouldn't stop."

"I tried to drain him after Quig tied him up, but he was too strong."

Her confession made me snort. "In his own way, Berry protected us by surviving our attacks. We aren't killers."

"Not yet."

"We're both in steady relationships," I said, deliberately changing the subject and then I winced internally. Were Quig and Brindle in danger from the women of our family? I snuffed out that thought immediately. "Is this the happily ever after part of our lives? Is this what a fairy tale feels like?"

"Time will tell, but I'm not wasting another moment of beach time thinking about bad news or the possibility of even worse news." Sage rose and darted to the surf line. Ocean water surged around the soles of her knee high rain boots and she shrieked excitedly. She called over her shoulder, "So, is the case closed?"

Though I followed her to the intertidal zone, the cold Atlantic Ocean water chilled my booted feet to the bone, despite the upper fifty-degree air temperature. I edged to the high water mark and willed sensation back in my toes. "Far as I know. Fawn said Jerry Meldrim knew Berry, though he called him Tibby. As Jerry's life unraveled in alcoholism, Tibby's professional star ascended, but his mental state was another kettle of fish."

Sage's expression turned stormy. "I researched serial killer profiles again, and these people often exhibit early behavioral cues that predict their leanings. Again, I couldn't find anything online or in the papers about Berry's childhood, so several theories are possible. Either he didn't get caught in his teens, his family pulled strings to keep his record clean, or he changed identities. We'll never know what shaped him. Only that his path intersected with our aunt's three decades ago."

I nodded. "Until Berry, I assumed Auntie O's heart was soft. She told us Mom did most of that coercion the times they solved trouble in the community."

"Possibly, but a softie wouldn't drive Berry Moody into a fence and cause his death. Auntie O has grit. Has to be that way if she's an assassin."

Waves rose and fell. Gulls and terns screeched from the high beach. My family history was rewriting itself. Mom and Auntie O were badasses. Sage and I were pretty badass ourselves.

"Regardless, Berry needed to die," I said. "He wouldn't have stopped coming for me, and he could've hypnotized his way out of anywhere. Now we have a Berry-free future."

"Thank you, world," Sage said, extending her arms and throwing back her head.

"Let's keep our speculations to ourselves. We don't want the cops to learn our aunt is a vigilante."

"I won't mention it. Family secrets need to stay family secrets."

Sage watched the waves until I spoke again. "Auntie O took off, allegedly to visit her new Orlando friends, but perhaps she needs time to make peace with killing a monster. I've had nightmares about Berry, and I'm sure I'll have more."

It felt good standing together. We were united in our devotion to family, even though there were no promises in life. My twin and I would stay together through thick and thin because we loved each other and needed each other.

"I just had a bizarre thought." Sage's voice quivered with dread.

I wasn't sure if I could handle a bizarre thought on top of our other theories and realizations. "I don't want to know."

My twin laughed. "My turn to blow your mind. Okay, here goes. It takes a killer to catch a killer."

I considered that for about the two seconds it deserved. "Let's make a pact to never kill Auntie O or each other."

"Done."

~*~

Captain Kenzo Haynes marched into The Book and Candle shop the next day in full uniform. Funny how I'd never noticed how shiny the two gold bars on his collar were. His stocky build and aura crackled with energy. He was a man on a mission. Whatever he wanted, he intended to get.

"Don't take this the wrong way," I said as I edged onto the stool behind the counter, "but seeing cops in my shop is never a good thing. Besides, the serial killer case is closed."

"Everything tied up nicely," Haynes said. "The feds are happy. I've just come from an interagency meeting. My boss, Captain Jefferson, is thrilled this case closed so fast."

"Why is that?"

"Guys like Moody don't stop. We received a gift from the

universe. He won't bother Savannah again. Is your aunt around? I want to thank her personally for her bravery."

On my side farthest away from the cops, I crossed my fingers. "She left town again. Said she needed peace and quiet."

"Sorry I missed her," Haynes said, "but I need to speak to you on a related matter. I want to add you as a police consultant. You closed three cases faster than most detectives can close one."

There it was. A job offer I did not want. I came off the stool and planted my hands on the counter. "No, no, no. I'm a candlemaker. This is my world."

"A successful one, too, from the looks of things," Haynes continued. "But you have a knack for solving crimes. Your eye for detail and your creative approach get results. You're a catalyst that speeds our investigations along."

Part of me bristled with pride at his remarks. "Thank you for the compliments. I was highly motivated to look into those cases as they involved friends and family. I'm hoping my future has no crime investigation in it. No, thank you to a consultant position. I am content here."

"I hope you'll reconsider. Nowry and Belfor would be your primary liaisons. Our case closure rate would skyrocket. The three of you make a great team."

Since most of my case observations resulted from Sage and I sneaking into other people's homes and looking for items that didn't fit the pattern, the combination of me plus the detectives would never work.

"It won't work. I investigate my own way. I rely heavily on intuition to direct my inquiry, which is a no-no for cops. Also, you'd be tying my hands by putting me on your payroll."

His eyes lit up. "You'll do it for free?"

"I won't do it at all."

"The offer is open-ended. Think about it."

Chapter Thirty-Three

On Saturday, Sage and I closed the shop at three-thirty so we, along with Quig and Brindle, could visit Bonaventure Cemetery before it closed at five. Our destination was Grandmother and Grandfather's grave in the Wayfare plot. Sage carried Mom's ashes with us.

As I expected, the ghost dog mugged me before I made it ten steps into the hallowed grounds. I said hello, and he bounded along in his happy-go-lucky way.

My gaze strayed to the small crypt where I'd been entombed and nearly died. A sharp flashback reminded me of the terror I'd felt. *Never, ever, wanted to do that again.* I came to my senses and realized I'd stopped walking.

"You okay?" Quig rested his hand on my shoulder, concern in his tone.

Sage shot me a quick *Tabby?* on our twin-link.

"I'm okay. I thought it wouldn't bother me to come to Bonaventure, but it will be a while before I can visit here without reliving my brush with death. I'm thankful to Quig and Sage for rescuing me."

"You're welcome but know this: you're a Winslow," Sage said. "Mom would say to toughen up, but I say take your time processing everything. It would be weird if being here didn't trigger stress. I'm available anytime if you want to vent."

"I'm here for you, always," Quig said.

I smiled at them in turn and squared my shoulders. "Thanks. I appreciate your caring and concern. I can do this."

We arrived at the Wayfare plot and began our visit-opening ritual, only this time my twin lit a sheaf of sage leaves and set them in a dish she'd brought. Then she placed Mom's ashes on the double headstone.

Together Sage and I recited the ancestral prayer. "In the name of the heavens and earth and all the directions, we share our love for Rosemary and Dwayne and Marjoram. May their ways of spreading peace and joy be reflected in us as we make our spiritual journeys. Grant them a sacred rest, peace, and radiance until the new day dawns. So be it."

When we finished, Sage waved the smoldering leaves around to smudge the air, then we poured the water in each compass direction around the double tombstone, followed by joining our energy and sealing the prayer into the ground.

Immediately, a heavy weight lifted off my chest. During this investigation, I'd had vengeful and selfish thoughts. I was no longer a Pollyanna-ish creature of light. In opening myself to my abilities, darkness had entered my soul.

My family needed the spiritual cleansing, both the living and the dead. Sage and I would be fine, and our living family had grown to include Brindle and Quig. We weren't alone.

As I meditated, I wished Auntie O well, wherever she was. I missed her, but now that I believed she used her energy to kill Berry Tibbit Moody, I realized no one was all light or all dark. We were blends of yin and yang of cosmic energy but also of good and evil.

That was sobering. I couldn't deny that I'd felt dark thoughts, that I'd wanted to kill Berry for what he'd done to me and as punishment for his killing spree. But I lived in a civilized society. The correct thing was to trust in our justice system, not that it would've been effective against Berry. He would've found a way to walk.

I understood what Auntie O had done to him. I even knew why she did it. But more importantly I had a startling insight into my actions. I wasn't a killer merely because I wanted to kill him. I chose to pull back. My choice defined me as the person I'd been for years, the woman who spread healing energy and sunshine.

Though the darkness was inside me, I didn't have to let it out.

I nodded to myself and glanced at Quig. He offered us a hand up. Sage and I each took a hand, and he lifted us effortlessly. I ended up in his arms. Sage melted into Brindle's embrace.

"I have something for you," Quig said softly. "I picked it up this morning and meant to give it to you before we left home."

He withdrew a jewelry box from his pocket and gave it to me. My heart thudded as I cracked the box open. My locket! I pulled him in for an effusive hug. "Thank you. I meant to talk with you about this days ago, but everything happened so fast with this case and your career. The time never seemed right to mention it. I thought I'd misplaced this when I couldn't find it on my dresser. Then I realized you must have it."

"Sorry if I caused any anxiety. I, too, was distracted by the events of our lives. When I noticed the defective chain, I returned it to the jeweler because it was under warranty. He offered to replace it, except he didn't have another one in stock. Took a bit for the order to arrive with so many packages shipping during the holidays. Your chain is brand new."

Quig reached for the locket. "May I?" At my nod, he tenderly affixed the necklace around my neck.

I fingered the white gold locket. "I am relieved to have this again. Although I only received it in December, I quickly realized I never want to be without it. This represents us and how much we care for each other."

Quig frowned, and I wondered if I'd upset him. "What's wrong?"

"I meant to propose to you on Valentine's Day, but everyone and their brother were proposing. I didn't want the most important question of our lives to be remembered that way."

"Stop right there," Sage said, leveling her index finger like a gun barrel at him. "You are not proposing to my sister in a cemetery. That is absolutely maudlin."

"Go away, Sis," I said. "I'm fine with it."

Quig ignored the interruption. "I love you, Tabby. I have from the first moment I saw you. It took you twenty-four years, three months, and seventeen days to see me as more than a friend, and I'm glad you did." He dropped to one knee. "Tabby Winslow, will you do me the honor of becoming my wife?"

"Yes!" I drew him to his feet and hugged him again, followed by an inspired kiss.

Sage tapped my fiancé on the back. "There's supposed to be a ring, Romeo."

"I forgot to bring it," Quig said, with a sheepish smile. "But I have her engagement ring at home. I hope Tabby likes it."

I beamed my approval. "I will love it, as I love you. Honestly, if you didn't propose today, I would have proposed tonight. You're the one I want to spend my life with, Quig. You're the man I love."

Congratulations went all the way around, along with Brindle giving back thumps to Quig.

"I take it back," Sage said. "Your cemetery proposal was lovely, and it's a fitting tribute to share the special occasion with our mom and grandparents."

"I hadn't considered that," I said, "but I'm glad they're part of our lives."

Sage nodded, staring at the headstone. "It also occurs to me that the Wayfares ultimately had their revenge on our family. The very words they objected to on the Waltz headstone, 'felled by an assassin,' attracted a serial killer and almost got you killed, Tabs. But enough about the past. We purified the grave. Our work here is done."

As we walked to the Hummer, I had another realization. No matter who or what we were, my family would survive. I shared another goofy grin with Quig at the thought of having children. To heck with just surviving, we'd thrive. So what if darkness tried to taint our happiness? From deep inside, I felt the universal truth inscribed on my heart.

Love is the ultimate light in the darkness.

About the Author

Valona Jones is a pen name for Southern author Maggie Toussaint. She writes mystery, suspense, and dystopian fiction. Her work won three Silver Falchion Awards, the Readers' Choice Award, and the EPIC Award. She's published twenty-seven novels as well as several short stories and novellas. The first two books in the A Magic Candle Shop Mystery series, *Snuffed Out* and *In the Wick of Time*, released in 2023. Maggie is a member of Mystery Writers of America—Southeast Chapter, and the Sisters in Crime Guppy Chapter. Maggie and her husband live in coastal Georgia where live oaks and heritage cast long shadows. Visit her at https://maggietoussaint.com

Author's Note

Thank you for coming along on this wonderful journey with me. I hope you've enjoyed this fictional visit to Savannah, GA. As a native Georgian who grew up near Savannah, I have long been in love with the city's historic buildings, parks, and waterfront. In writing the A Magic Candle Shop Mysteries, it has been my honor to show you the city through my eyes and senses via my sleuth, Tabby Winslow. Speaking of Tabby and her twin sister Sage, I have long been fascinated with twins. We have a set of twins in my father's line: his grandfather was a twin. As far as I know, twins didn't follow down through "our" twin's descendants.

It was hard to write the scene where Tabby was in a "tight spot" (no spoilers here), and I was as relieved as she was when things started improving tremendously in her favor.

There are two more books to come in this series. The next one, *Candle with Care*, is scheduled to release in February 2025. Follow along with the series to find out what happens to the twins and…Savannah.

Remember, you can always help authors out by leaving online reviews about our books. No need for anything lengthy or in-depth. Honest reviews are what we seek, and they truly make a difference to the author and to other readers.

More Books by Maggie Toussaint

Thanks for reading *Tallowed Ground*. A list of my works of fiction follows.

A Magic Candle Shop Mystery Series, paranormal cozy mysteries
Snuffed Out (writing as Valona Jones)
In the Wick of Time (writing as Valona Jones)
Tallowed Ground (writing as Valona Jones)

Seafood Caper Mystery series, culinary cozies
Seas the Day
Spawning Suspicion
Shrimply Dead

Dreamwalker Mystery series, paranormal mysteries
Gone and Done It
Bubba Done It

Doggone It
Dadgummit
Confound It
Dreamed It
All Done with It

Lindsey & Ike Romantic Mystery Novella series, cozy mysteries
"Really, Truly Dead"
"Turtle Tribbles"
"Dead Men Tell No Tales"

Cleopatra Jones Mystery series
In for a Penny
On the Nickel
Dime If I Know
"No Quarter" (novella)

Single Title Mysteries
Death, Island Style
Murder in the Buff

Mossy Bog Romantic Suspense series
Muddy Waters
Hot Water
Rough Waters

Single Title Romantic Suspense
House of Lies
No Second Chance
Seeing Red

The Guardian of Earth Futuristic Mystery series
G-1 (writing as Rigel Carson)
G-2 (writing as Rigel Carson)
G-3 (writing as Rigel Carson)

Short Stories
"High Noon at Dollar Central" (A Dreamwalker story)
"Sand Dollar Secrets" (A Cleopatra Jones story)
"The Trouble with Horses" (A Seafood Caper story)

Made in the USA
Columbia, SC
01 October 2024